CHILD *of* PROMISE

BRIDES OF CULDEE CREEK • BOOK FOUR

KATHLEEN MORGAN

Revell

Grand Rapids, Michigan

Published by Fleming H. Revell
a division of Baker Publishing Group
P.O. Box 6287, Grand Rapids, MI 49516-6287

New paperback edition published 2007

Printed in the United States of America

Library of Congress Cataloging-in-Publication Data
Morgan, Kathleen, 1950–
    Child of promise / Kathleen Morgan.
        p.   cm. – (Brides of Culdee Creek ; bk. 4)
    ISBN 10: 0-8007-5761-0
    ISBN 978-0-8007-5761-8
    1. Women physicians–Fiction. 2. Colorado–Fiction. 3. Widow-
ers–Fiction. 4. Clergy–Fiction. I. Title.
PS3563.08647 C48 2002
813'.54–dc21   2001048927

Scripture is taken from the King James Version of the Bible.

The Scripture found on the first page of chapter 22 is from the HOLY BIBLE, NEW INTERNATIONAL VERSION®. NIV®. Copyright © 1973, 1978, 1984 by International Bible Society. Used by permission of Zondervan. All rights reserved.

For Jennifer Leep, my editor

In one way or another, you've been with me through this whole series. Thank you for keeping me on the straight and narrow. Thank you for being such a delight to work with. And thank you for all your patience and hard work in helping make these books the best they could be.

ELIZABETH
"God's Promise"

Ye have need of patience, that, after ye have done the will of God, ye might receive the promise.

Hebrews 10:36

Prologue

The plains east of Colorado Springs, Colorado December 1903

Hope deferred maketh the heart sick: but when the desire cometh, it is a tree of life.

Proverbs 13:12

Today was the worst day of her life.

Today the world, as seventeen-year-old Beth MacKay had known it and had expected it to be, had turned upside down and inside out. Today her heart would surely break, her romantic dreams would be permanently crushed, and her love would shrivel and die.

Noah Starr was getting married.

Dear, sweet, magnificently handsome Noah would wed another woman. Another woman would carry his name, bear his children, and be his lover and lifelong helpmate.

With a sigh, Beth turned over in bed and buried her face in her pillow. How in the world was she going to

9

live through this miserable, heart-wrenching day? How was she to attend the wedding, pretend to a happiness she didn't feel, and offer her congratulations to the married couple?

It was too much to expect of anyone. She'd just have to plead a sick headache and beg off going.

Abby would understand. Beth's stepmother knew of her love for Noah, a love that had begun three years ago when Noah had rescued her from a rattler at a church picnic. As he had held her in his arms to comfort her after he had killed the snake, Beth had fallen in love.

Not that she had been the only female in Grand View to have lost her heart to the young, blond, and eligible pastor of the town's Episcopal church. Since that day seven years ago when he had first arrived from back East to assist his ailing uncle with his priestly duties, Noah Starr had been the source of much feminine speculation and maternal matchmaking.

But in Beth's mind, Noah had always been meant for her. Why else had he waited so many years after coming to Grand View to take a wife, if the good Lord hadn't intended him for her? And why, oh why, couldn't he have waited just another six months until she finished high school? Surely Pa would've allowed Noah to begin courting her then, even if she wouldn't have been eighteen for another two months. For all practical purposes, she would've been considered a woman, free to make her own decisions, go off to college, or marry.

Beth sat up and tossed her pillow across the room, striking the door. Then with a groan she climbed from bed. After a quick ablution in a washbasin of icy water, she dressed, brushed her hair, scrubbed her teeth, then headed downstairs to the kitchen.

As always on a cold winter's morn, Old Bess, the everfaithful, if temperamental, cast-iron cookstove, warmed the room. Abby, her chestnut brown hair pulled up in a neat, high bun, her cheeks flushed from the heat rising from the stove as she expertly flipped flapjacks, turned and grinned.

"Good morning," she said cheerily. "Could you finish up the rest of the flapjacks while I see to your sister? Besides buttoning her dress, I've still got her hair to brush and her shoes to put on, and Sean's too busy chasing her around the parlor to be of much help."

Beth forced a bright smile onto her face. "Sure. Sorry I took so long to come down. I was just . . . well, never mind. It doesn't matter much anymore."

Abby paused in her journey toward the hallway separating the kitchen from the parlor. "I know this will be a hard day for you to get through, Beth." She glanced over her shoulder with an understanding look. "Just remember you've always got your family to love and support you."

And what a family it is, Beth thought, comforted by the realization. Besides her older half brother, Evan, who was married and the proud father of two children, there was six-year-old Sean and three-year-old Erin, the two children of her father, Conor, and his second wife, Abby. Having such a high-spirited half brother and half sister certainly made for a lively household.

Still, Beth reveled in the warm sense of close-knit, affectionate family that had grown from her father and Abby's love for each other. Even their home, Culdee Creek Ranch, had prospered and bloomed in the years since they had wed. In addition to Evan, his wife, Claire, her brother, Ian, and Evan and Claire's two children, there was also her cousin Devlin, his wife, Hannah, and their four children. And when one added in the ranch hands who lived in the nearby bunkhouses, Culdee Creek nearly qualified as a little community in itself.

"Yes, I've always got my family," Beth agreed softly, "and I'm ever so grateful for it, too. I just wish it were

11

me getting married today, instead of Alice Westerman. I wish *I* were the one who'd soon be Mrs. Noah Starr, rather than my teacher. How am I ever going to face her when she and Noah return from their honeymoon?"

"The Lord will provide the strength, just as He'll provide the right man in due time, Beth." Abby smiled. "You have to believe that."

"But who could be better than N-Noah?" In spite of her best efforts, Beth couldn't keep her voice from quavering.

"Not many men, that's for certain." Her stepmother turned and walked back to stand before her. "Nonetheless, there are a few good ones still left out there, I promise you. And there's no rush, is there? I thought you still planned on becoming a doctor. Has that changed all of a sudden, and I'm now the last to know?"

A doctor . . .

Beth had wanted to become a doctor for years, no matter what obstacles were thrown into her path, no matter how difficult it still was for a woman to be accepted in such a role. Even nowadays, lady doctors were suspected of being involved in feminist causes, dress reform, sex education, and other inappropriate activities. Many were even accused of wishing to be men, of being little more than emotionally stunted women incapable of striking up social relationships or matrimonial links.

But none of that had mattered to Beth, not since she had read about the first woman doctor in America, Dr. Elizabeth Blackwell, who had graduated from Geneva Medical College in New York in 1849. Dr. Blackwell's profound love of medicine and heroism against opposition had inspired Beth from an early age. She had dreamed of following in Dr. Blackwell's footsteps and enrolling in the very same medical college.

And it seemed now, after today, there was no reason not to pursue that dream. Noah had betrayed her, even if unknowingly, and she couldn't conceive of ever loving another man enough to sacrifice medical school. For Noah, and only Noah, she had been willing to compromise her dreams. But never for any other man, and never, ever again.

"No, Abby," Beth said, gritting out the words even as she sealed the bittersweet pain tightly within her heart, "my determination to become a doctor hasn't changed. More than anything, I want to go to medical school. Indeed, I suppose Noah's actually doing me a favor in marrying Alice. A husband and family would've been a stumbling block to my ambitions. Everyone knows," she added, turning her head to hide her tears, "a woman who intends to be a doctor must be willing to pay the price."

"And you think you'll be happy paying such a price, sacrificing the joys of a husband and family, a normal life?"

"Yes." Beth nodded her head with grim determination. "Now, more than ever, I most certainly do."

1

The plains east of Colorado Springs, Colorado August 1909

To every thing there is a season, and a time to every purpose under the heaven.

Ecclesiastes 3:1

As the Colorado and Southern Railroad Company locomotive, affectionately known as the "C & S" or "Crooked and Slow" for its sinuous course and many stops, drew near the town of Grand View, the engineer sounded the whistle. On such a clear, sunny day, the shrill cry echoed in every direction. A small herd of pronghorn antelope stampeded. Wings tucked tightly to their sides, a flock of spindly legged sandpipers hiding in the grass beside the railroad bed scrambled for safer cover.

15

Dr. Elizabeth MacKay glanced up from her book and smiled. It was good to know some things, even after five years' absence, hadn't changed. The pronghorn still grazed the rolling hills. The birds appeared to be as abundant as ever. And in the distance to the west, Pikes Peak remained the ever strong, majestic sentinel.

Still, five years were bound to have an effect on things. From Abby's letters, Beth knew Grand View's population had almost doubled in size, now numbering nearly four hundred. Gates's Mercantile had been sold to a John O'Brien and had been expanded until it was now a large L-shaped building. Several new businesses—including a bank—had come to town. And Doc Childress, in his late sixties with rheumatism so bad he could hardly hold a scalpel, much less make the fine stitches needed to suture wounds, needed help.

Beth sighed, shoved her book into a side pocket of her traveling bag, and looked back out the window. Doc Childress had wasted little time, once he had heard of the completion of her internship, in offering her a partnership in his Grand View medical office. "A chance to get your feet wet under the supervision of an experienced physician before taking over the entire practice," he had written in a letter.

But Beth had mixed feelings about accepting the job. True, she missed her home and family. She hadn't been home to Culdee Creek in all the years of her medical schooling, fearing anything that might weaken her resolve to stick it out no matter what. Indeed, after a time, she had almost gotten used to the grueling work, the lack of sleep, the gut-twisting loneliness.

Her mouth tightened. It was the taunts, the ridicule, the purposeful obstacles placed in her way that had been the hardest of all to endure. Because she was a woman. Because she was part Indian. Because she was young and attractive. Because she was a fighter and gave as good as she got.

And then there had been Matthew . . . and the baby.

She sighed again. All told, the past five years had been the hardest years she had ever endured. They had left their mark—that much Beth knew. But she hadn't given up. She had persevered; she had won. They hadn't beaten her, just as they hadn't beaten Elizabeth Blackwell all those years ago. But the cost . . . the cost had been far, far greater than Beth had ever imagined.

"Are you getting off at Grand View or traveling farther south?" A stout, gray-haired, motherly woman plopped down in the seat across from her. "I've been watching you ever since I boarded in Denver and have been itching to visit with you. But"—she motioned to the volume protruding from Beth's traveling bag—"you seemed so engrossed in your book, I hated to intrude."

Beth felt a fleeting moment of regret for putting aside her book—hiding behind it was a trick she had long ago discovered to encourage others to keep their distance—and forced a smile. "Yes, I'm getting off at Grand View, and yes, I do love to read. It helps pass the hours, doesn't it?"

"It does indeed." The woman leaned forward and extended her hand. "My name's Cora Bledsoe. My husband and I run the bakery in Grand View. Bledsoe's Quality Baked Goods, it's called."

"And I'm Elizabeth MacKay." Beth took Cora's outstretched hand, gave it a quick squeeze, then released it. "My father's Conor MacKay, the owner of—"

"Oh, I know who your father is," Cora said with a wave of her hand. "Everyone knows the owner of Culdee Creek Ranch." She cocked her head. "But I've never seen *you* before, and we've lived here all of five years now."

"I've been back East for a time, attending medical school."

17

The woman's silver brows lifted. "Medical school, you say? So you're the one who went off to become a doctor!"

Beth nodded, already beginning to weary of the conversation. "Yes, I am. I've come home to go into practice with Doc Childress."

"A lady doctor." Cora shook her head in apparent amazement. "Land sakes. Grand View's going to have a lady doctor."

"Yes, it is."

Beth gazed out the window. Blessedly, the town under discussion was coming into view. Situated on a vast, grassy plain of gently undulating hills, Grand View looked like some child's toy town picked up and set down in the middle of nowhere.

Wooden clapboard buildings made up most of the dwellings. The wide streets were still of dirt, and boardwalks lined the front of the businesses. As the C & S passed over the summer-shriveled Cottonwood Creek, the long white buildings of the grain elevator and creamery seemed to leap out like virtuous guardians on the right-hand side of the tracks. On the left slumped the weather-beaten train station warehouse.

The locomotive began to slow. Brakes ground against iron wheels. Steam hissed. Then with a bone-jarring lurch, the old Crooked and Slow came to a halt.

A crowd had gathered on the train platform, and for an instant the blindingly bright sunlight seemed to meld all the people into one colorful, churning mass. Then Beth blinked, and the faces took on familiar, beloved appearances.

Three dark-haired men towered above the rest—her father, her cousin, Devlin, and her big brother, Evan. Though the two older men's hair was more streaked with gray than Beth remembered, they both looked just as strong and leanly muscled as her brother. All three

18

were dressed the same as ever, too, in faded, work-worn Levis, scuffed boots, and long-sleeved cotton shirts rolled up above their elbows, their heads covered by dark Stetsons.

Beth's gaze soon found Abby. Her stepmother was just as beautiful as she remembered her, her chestnut hair covered by a wide straw hat, her figure trim and lithe. Beside her stood Hannah, Devlin's wife, her blond hair gleaming in the sun. Claire was with them, too. Evan's Scottish bride was only five years older than Beth, and Beth still recalled the happy times they had once spent as Claire tried to teach her how to play her little Scottish harp.

"Well, I'd best be getting my things together," Cora Bledsoe said. "Now that you're home to stay, we'll have plenty of time to get to know each other better. In fact, once you're all settled in, stop by the bakery. You can meet my husband, Walter, and sample some of our specialties. On the house, of course."

"I'll be sure to do that, Cora." Beth bent over, retrieved her traveling bag, and stood. "It was so nice to make your acquaintance."

"Oh, pshaw." The woman began to sidle down the aisle to the nearest door. "It was my pleasure. It's not every day we get a lady doctor come to town. No indeed."

Beth pretended some problem with her satchel until Cora Bledsoe had departed the car. Then she placed her broad straw hat, trimmed with blue and white ribbons, on her head, paused to straighten her navy-blue traveling suit, picked up her bag, and headed for the door.

She was back home at last, a doctor and a grown woman. It was time to begin her life anew and put the past behind her. She only hoped that she could.

"How's my big girl this afternoon?" Noah Starr leaned over the little wicker wheelchair and chucked the blond two-year-old under the chin.

With a gurgle of pleasure, the child lifted her head—which promptly fell to one side—and, with flailing arms, reached out to him. Drool trickled from the corner of her mouth, trailing down to dribble onto her pink-flowered calico gown.

Noah dug out a fresh handkerchief and wiped his daughter's mouth. "Are you hungry, sweetheart? I brought you a special treat from the bakery."

"Emily's just now finished her lunch," Millie Starr said. "I'm sure she'd love a sweet."

"Then I've come home just in time." Grand View's Episcopal pastor pulled over a kitchen chair and sat directly in front of the toddler. "How's a nice cinnamon bun sound?" he asked, pulling a small paper-wrapped parcel from his coat pocket.

His daughter's flapping arms increased their movement in speed and intensity. Noah glanced at his aunt.

"She seems more excitable today than usual. Do you think she's ill or in pain?"

Millie shook her head. "No. You've just been working such long hours the past few days, Emily hasn't seen you much. You haven't made it home for lunch the past week, and what with you leaving in the morning before she wakes and coming home after she's in bed . . ."

Noah sighed and dragged a hand through his dark blond hair. Hair, he noted wryly, in dire need of a trim. Yet another chore he must see to, just as soon as he could make the time.

"Well, I'm glad Emily's not ill. I'll try to make myself come home for lunch from here on out, and take an hour or so off whenever I can to visit with her in the evenings, too."

20

"You might just want to make that evening visit about suppertime," his aunt said, eyeing him up and down. "Folk are beginning to talk that maybe I've lost my touch when it comes to cooking, what with you getting a mite scrawny there."

He knew she spoke the truth. He wasn't eating all that well, mostly because he chose to bury himself in his work. He didn't spend much time at home anymore, save for the few hours he grabbed for sleep. And, worst of all, Noah knew that, deep down, he preferred it that way.

Even though it had been two years since Alice's death giving birth to Emily, home still reminded him of all he had lost. The rectory was permeated with his wife's presence, from the framed photographs over the parlor fireplace, to the Montgomery Ward Windsor upright piano, to her beloved four-volume set of the American Encyclopaedic Dictionary. And that was just what he encountered in one room of the house.

No, he didn't find much joy in coming home anymore. Though Noah loved his daughter, her terrible birth injuries had crippled her for life. She had a brain palsy, Doc Childress had informed him, most likely incurred from a prolonged lack of oxygen during Alice's complicated labor. It was so painful to see Emily, know the dismal prospects for her future, and realize that even the sacrifice of Alice's life hadn't been enough to spare their child.

Noah exhaled a long, slow breath. "Yes, I suppose I am getting a bit thin. I'm sorry. I'll try to do better by the both of you."

Millie laid a hand on his shoulder. "Now, don't go adding us to all the other burdens you carry. I didn't say that to make you feel any worse than you already do. But if you don't start taking care of yourself . . . well, soon enough you won't be any good to anyone."

21

Noah unwrapped the paper, pulled off a bit of the cinnamon bun, and offered it to Emily. "You're right, of course. And just as soon as we get the fund-raiser going for the repairs to the church roof and bell tower and finish up on the side annexes, I'm sure things will slow down. We've just needed that addition for so long, what with the growing community, and—"

"That's not the problem, and you know it." Millie's hand gripped his shoulder. "You've got to make peace with losing Alice and what's happened to Emily. You've got to put it all, once and for all, in the Lord's hands."

"And what makes you think I haven't given it all up to God?" Noah could feel his muscles bunching, tensing. He ripped off another chunk of the bun and fed it to his daughter. "Sometimes, just because you submit to the Lord's will, it doesn't mean He chooses to lift the pain. Sometimes the pain's a lesson in itself."

"Yes, you're right, of course." Millie released her hold on his shoulder and stepped away. "And sometimes the greater lesson is found in letting go of the pain and starting anew."

Noah slid back his chair, stood, and turned. "Here." He handed her the cinnamon bun. "There's a church-board meeting in five minutes. I really can't be late. Walter Bledsoe and Harlow Peterson are itching to up the roof and bell tower budget, not to mention making noises about importing some Italian marble altar. I've got to be there to put a rein on those two, or we'll all end up in the poorhouse."

"Seems like Harlow'd love nothing more than to finance the loan we'd need, wouldn't he?" Millie shook her head. "Sometimes I wonder about that man. Even if he is the town banker, he puts too much store on money."

"Harlow means well enough, I suppose. He just needs to realize borrowing money isn't the end-all answer to what ails this town."

In the distance, a train whistle echoed plaintively. Millie's head turned in the direction of the sound. She smiled.

"That'll be Beth MacKay's train. She's finally coming home, after all this time."

"It's only been five years. That's not all that long."

"Isn't it?" His aunt cocked her head. "Five years is a long time not to come home even once. Passing strange, I'd say."

"Well, Beth's back now, and it's a blessing she's a doctor. Doc Childress doesn't have many good doctoring years left in him. I can't think of a more perfect solution."

"And neither can I," Millie said. "I just think it's passing strange she's stayed away so long. Mark my words, Noah Starr. There's more to that than meets the eye."

"So, tell me everything. About your trip home, about your plans, and why you took Doc Childress up on his offer." As she talked, Abby lifted the roast out onto the serving platter Beth held. "I'm so happy to have you home. I know I'm blathering, but I just can't help it. I've missed you so!"

Beth smiled. It was good to be home. She had forgotten how warm, loving, and safe her house and family had always been. But then, she'd had to forget. Such blessed amnesia had been her only defense against homesickness. She wondered now, though, if coming home might not have been wiser—and ultimately less self-destructive—than had been her choice to stay away.

"Well," she said as she carried the succulently browned roast to the table and began slicing it, "the trip was uneventful, the train relatively comfortable. Of course, traveling in first class helped a lot."

Abby nodded from her spot at the cookstove where she was preparing the gravy. "Conor and I finally traveled first class last year, you know, when we attended my mother's funeral. It was wonderful. I especially liked the dining car. Why, they made me feel like a queen!"

"Speaking of fancy travel, have you heard about the new horseless carriage, the Model T? It was just offered to the public last year and costs eight hundred fifty dollars. Instead of electricity, it runs on gasoline."

Abby laughed. "Well, at that price, there won't be a lot of takers anytime soon. Especially not at Culdee Creek."

"A horse and buggy will do me just fine." Beth grinned. "I saw a lot of newfangled things in New York City, but sometimes it's best to stay with the tried and true."

"I agree." Abby paused to taste the gravy and add some salt and pepper, then resumed her stirring. "So, what are your plans? There's no rush in going to work with Doc Childress, is there? We've so much catching up to do, and a nice rest and some good food would do you good."

Beth glanced down at her trim figure. "Are you implying I'm too thin? I prefer to think of myself as fashionably svelte. A waspish waist is all the rage back East, you know."

Abby made a disgusted sound. "Well, you're out West now, and you'll do just fine without a corset crushing all your innards."

"Actually, I'm not wearing a corset. I gave that up several years ago."

Her stepmother's eyes widened in horror. "Then you most definitely need some good food." She turned back to the gravy. "What's been going on with you, Beth? Is something wrong?"

Beth sighed. Leave it to Abby to cut right to the heart of things. This was one time, however, when Beth wasn't about to confide in anyone. Life was different out here. Simpler, kinder, more honorable. They wouldn't–couldn't–understand.

"Nothing's wrong. I've just been so busy the past year, I haven't had much spare time to sleep, much less eat. But all that's going to change. Grand View's patient population is nothing like Johns Hopkins's patients. Even as large as Grand View has grown, this'll be a virtual holiday after that."

"Well, if you say so." Abby gestured to a gravy boat sitting on the table. "Would you hand that to me? The gravy's ready."

"And so's the roast." Beth passed over the gravy boat. "Anything else that needs doing?"

Abby glanced at the kitchen table. The big bowl of mashed potatoes was ready, as were the green beans and carrots. An apple spice cake, already iced, sat on a sideboard. She shook her head. "Nope. The big table in the dining room's set. Get your brother and sister in here to help carry out the food."

Beth made a move to head into the parlor.

"Just one thing more."

"Yes?" Beth turned. "What is it, Abby?"

"The house is full, but we've prepared the bunkhouse for you. You're more than welcome to stay on here, even after you start work in Grand View, if you want. It's only a fifteen minute ride to town, after all."

Beth hesitated. She wanted to see her family, spend time with them, especially with her younger brother and sister. But she also needed time alone to sort everything out. Time to decide how much she wanted to

25

share and how much she wanted to store away in some deep, dark corner and never face again.

Problem was, too many people at Culdee Creek knew her too well. Abby, her father, Evan, Claire, Devlin, and Hannah. Any one of them, at the right time and place, could break down her defenses, and then the truth would come pouring out.

Beth had worked too long and too hard to build those defenses; she wasn't about to risk them. Not now, freshly home and more vulnerable than she had been in a long while.

She managed what she hoped was a regretful smile. "Thanks so much for the offer. I'd like to stay in the bunkhouse for a few days at least, relax, visit, and eat my fill of your wonderful cooking. I'm thinking, though, that I need to be closer to Grand View and more accessible to Doc and the majority of my patients."

Abby bit her lip. "Are you sure, Beth? Your father was so looking forward to having the whole family back at Culdee Creek again."

"Yes, I'm sure. It's for the best. You'll see." She turned, striding out of the room. "And it's not as if I'll be all that far away at any rate. Besides, Pa'll understand. He always has before."

2

Why beholdest thou the mote that is in thy brother's eye,
but considerest not the beam that is in thine own eye?

Matthew 7:3

Three days later, Beth stood outside Doc Childress's office and stared in amazement at his shingle. "John Childress, M.D." the simple black-and-gold sign read. Beneath his name, however, was another name.

"Elizabeth MacKay, M.D."

Beth swallowed hard. Technically, she had been able to call herself a physician since her graduation from medical school. Patients had addressed her that way, too, during the year of her internship.

Today, though, gazing at that sign, Beth could see her dream finally coalesce into reality. Elizabeth MacKay, M.D. She was a doctor, and now everyone who really mattered knew.

Her hand tightened around the handle of her black medical bag. She blinked back a sudden swell of tears, squared her shoulders, and walked into Doc Childress's—*their*—medical clinic.

The little three-room office hadn't changed much over the years. She imagined the tiny living quarters upstairs were pretty much the same, too. The waiting area, empty of patients this early in the day, was pleasantly furnished with a blue-and-white flowered chintz sofa, four straight-back chairs, a few potted plants, and an assistant's desk. The walls looked freshly painted—utilitarian white as always—a colorful rag rug covered most of the floor, and a pretty set of blue-and-white calico curtains hung at the single window.

Helen Yates, as much a Grand View fixture as Doc Childress, glanced up from her desk in the opposite corner. "Well, well, well," she said, shoving her spectacles up from the tip of her nose. "If it isn't our Dr. MacKay."

Helen rose, came around the desk, and walked over to Beth. With hardly a break in stride, she enveloped Beth in a hearty, breath-stopping hug.

"What a blessing. Oh, what a blessing you are, my sweet girl!"

Beth could do nothing but stand there, grasping her bag. "It-it's nice to see you again, too, Mrs. Yates," she all but choked out.

The older woman released her and stepped back, studying her closely. "Call me Helen. Doc does, and you're now just as much my employer as he is." A thin gray brow rose. "Don't they know how to cook back East? Land sakes, but you're little more than skin and bones."

With only the greatest of effort, Beth controlled the impulse to roll her eyes. First Abby, now Helen Yates. Did she really look that much in need of mothering?

She managed a laugh. "Have no fear. Abby's already seeing to that problem. I expect in another week or two, I'll be pleasingly plump and popping out of all my fine new suits."

"Sooner than that, once Doc gets a look at you." Helen leaned close, a conspiratorial grin twisting one corner of her mouth. "Bledsoe's bakery is only two buildings down. At least three times a week, Doc springs for a few sweets for us to have with our morning coffee."

Beth chuckled and shook her head. "So is that where Doc's at? Or hasn't he come downstairs for the day yet?"

"Oh, yes, he's here." Helen pointed to the second of two doors leading off from the waiting room. "Doc's in there, doing an inventory of his supplies. I told him I could take over that job, but he insisted he likes doing it. Helps him get his head on straight for the new day, he says." She laughed. "And I'm not one to try to change a man after all these years."

"Well, I guess I'll just go say hello then." Beth set her bag on a nearby chair and began unbuttoning her suit jacket. "No time like the present to jump in and get started."

Helen held out her hand for Beth's jacket. "Yes, you do that, Dr. MacKay. I'll put your things away in the other examining room. Doc bought a desk for that room, so you can also use it as your private office. Later on, look it all over and tell me what else you think you might need."

"That'll be fine, Helen." Beth turned toward the door to Doc Childress's office, then hesitated. "I'm really looking forward to working with the both of you. It's a dream come true."

"For Doc, too." A pensive look flared in Helen's eyes. "It took a while for him to admit he needed help. Even now he fights the truth some days. Reckon it's hard for a man to start facing his limitations."

"Well, maybe with our help, he won't have to face as many or as soon." Beth smiled. "It's the least we can do, I'd say."

Helen bobbed her head in agreement. "The very least."

Beth turned then, took the several steps needed to cross the waiting room, and halted at Doc's door. She knocked lightly.

"Come in."

She pushed the door open. The office wasn't overly large, only about eight by twelve feet. In front of the window at the far end of the room was Doc's desk, strewn with papers, charts, and several open medical books. A long, narrow table stood against one wall. On it was a brass scale, a metal cylinder holding thermometers, test tubes in a stand, an open tray wherein lay sterilized needles and syringes, and a microscope. Next to the table was a tall cabinet with glass doors, filled with bandages, splints, plaster of paris, catheters, adhesives, an assortment of colored bottles filled with various liquids, another tray with scalpels and holders, and a box of sutures. An examination table and rolling stool completed the medical décor.

Doc Childress glanced up from a box of supplies he was sorting on the exam table. At sight of her, his lined, craggy face broke into a grin.

Hands outstretched, he walked to her. "Welcome, welcome, my dear. I heard of your arrival on Monday but certainly didn't expect your visit quite so soon. I assumed you'd wish a week or two to rest and spend time with your family."

"I'd like a few more days to visit, to be sure." Beth took his hands and gave them a squeeze. "But I also admit to being most eager to begin seeing patients and working with you. And now that I'm home I can take my leisure visiting Culdee Creek and my family."

"Visiting?" His voice echoed the surprise in his eyes. "But aren't you going to live at Culdee Creek and come into town each day?"

30

"No." It amused Beth that everyone had presumed such a thing without consulting her. "I haven't lived at home for five years now, and I confess to cherishing my privacy and independence. I think I'd prefer finding my own place here in Grand View."

"Well, then we'll just have to find you a nice place to stay in town." He released her hands and, his brow furrowing in thought, scratched his chin. "Hmmm, now where'd be a proper place for a very pretty, unmarried young woman to stay?"

Beth eyed Doc with affection. He had definitely aged in the past five years. His hair had thinned until it was little more than a tonsure encompassing a bald pate. His fine blue eyes, behind a pair of wire-rimmed spectacles, had faded and seemed shrouded by sagging lids. His shoulders were stooped, and his long, talented fingers were little more than swollen knobs and twisted digits.

Still, the man she had known and idolized only a step below her father was still comfortingly familiar. His gaze was as sharp and assessing as ever. His voice was strong, his step firm. There was still much—and time enough—for her to learn from him.

"A few families might be willing to take in a boarder," Doc offered after a moment of thought. "And there's always Mamie Oatman's boardinghouse. It's across the street and four buildings down from here. She might have a room available."

"Mamie's sounds like a fine idea. I'll give her a try."

He nodded. "Tell Mamie I sent you. She likes me."

Beth arched a dark brow. "Does she now? And are you finally of a mind to start some long overdue courting?"

Doc blushed, removed his spectacles, and commenced to clean them. "Oh, I wouldn't go so far as to say that." A small smile quirked the corner of his mouth. "I've several possibilities, you know, and a man has to

31

have a care not to leave a trail of broken hearts in his wake."

"Agreed." Beth nodded solemnly. "One has to have a care not to be breaking hearts."

"And what of you?" As he spoke, Doc slipped on his spectacles and indicated the chair pulled up beside his desk. "Leave any broken hearts behind when you left New York?" he asked, walking around to take his own seat behind the desk.

Only my own, she thought grimly. "I really didn't have much time for socializing, what with medical school and then the internship." Beth managed a lame smile. "Besides, I figured a long-distance courtship was pointless."

"Well, no matter. There are plenty of fine, eligible young men in these parts. And I must admit to a bit of selfishness. With marriage comes children, and then I'd be sure to lose you."

Beth's stomach clenched. "I've no plans to wed, either now or ever."

The old physician gave a disbelieving snort. "And that's the most addle-minded thing I think I've ever heard you say, Elizabeth MacKay! You can't just discard the idea of marriage out of hand."

She inhaled an exasperated breath. She knew Doc meant well, but it really wasn't any of his business, or anyone else's for that matter, what she chose to do with her life.

"Forgive me if I sound impertinent, but what does any of this have to do with my medical qualifications?" Beth folded her tension-damp hands in her lap. "If you're concerned I might up and wed some handsome cowboy in the next month or two, you needn't worry. Or is it, rather, you've problems with me working after I wed—if I ever *was* to wed?"

"No, no, no." Doc Childress held up his hands in a gesture of conciliation. "Neither do I care if you wed, nor have I problems with you continuing to work for me if you did. I was just trying to make pleasant conversation and put you at ease." He smiled ruefully. "Unfortunately, I seem to have failed miserably at both."

Beth wasn't so sure she believed him. Was Doc like all the rest of his gender? More comfortable when a woman remained in her traditional role and didn't presume to an equality that wasn't hers? After all, now that she was here, she presented a threat, fresh from medical school, up to date with all the latest discoveries and techniques.

"You don't have to put me at ease," Beth said. "All I want is to be accepted as your colleague. I value your years of experience. I want to learn from you. And though I may be a bit more current on some of the newest practices, that's nothing to the sheer volume of knowledge you possess."

"I'd be very interested in hearing about all the new-fangled treatments." Doc's eyes gleamed with barely suppressed excitement. "So would the physicians in Colorado Springs, I'm sure. Well," he amended, "most of them anyway. There are a few old fogies who still have trouble accepting a woman doctor. But not me. No, not me."

"I'm glad to hear that. Since you offered me a partnership, I assumed you were a progressive man. Still, after you began interrogating me about getting married . . ."

"Well, why don't we just put all that behind us? In the future, I won't tease you about your romances, if you promise not to tease me, either."

"Sounds like a fair trade." Beth grinned, feeling a bit better. They had overcome their first disagreement well enough, she supposed. Time would tell, though. If things didn't work out with Doc, it wasn't as if she *had* to stay in Grand View. Colorado Springs was close enough. Given some time, she could make contacts there, feel out fresh job opportunities. Even Denver was a possibility.

Doc shuffled some papers on his desk, then patted them into a stack. He flipped closed a chart, added that to the pile of papers, and finally glanced up.

"Has Helen shown you your new office yet? I had her stock it with all the supplies I thought you might need starting out, but if you find anything lacking—"

"Oh, I'm sure it'll all be more than adequate. Helen did mention that the other room was my office and examination room, but I haven't had a chance to see it yet. I wanted to talk with you first and decide when I could get started here."

"Well, you can begin working for me as soon as you're ready. I generally see six to twelve patients a day, plus make house calls on another three or four." He smiled wryly. "And that's when we're not in the midst of a diphtheria or influenza epidemic. There's a lot more I'd like to do, like health screenings at the school, classes on proper nutrition, antepartum and postpartum care . . ."

Beth could feel herself growing excited. "I love to teach. I'd be happy to take on the classes and the health screenings, in addition to seeing whatever patients you'd care to pass on to me."

"In time. In due time," Doc said with a laugh. "First, I'd like you to sit in for several days as I see patients, both in the clinic and in the home. Then as new patients come or some of my old ones ask for you, you can take on your own. And we can always consult on any that appear unusual or provide exposure to problems you've yet to encounter. Eventually, I'd like to cut down to maybe half a day, three or four days a week, and give you the main responsibility. How does that sound?"

"It sounds perfect. I can start tomorrow!"

Doc laughed again. "Not too eager, are you?" He shoved back his chair and rose, coming around to stand before her. "Well, why not find yourself a place to stay first, get settled in a bit, and show up for work this coming Monday?"

Beth grinned sheepishly. "I guess I do sound a little overanxious, don't I?"

"Oh, I'm not complaining. I like someone who's not afraid of a little work and loves doing it. It's just that following me around for a while also entails any night calls. It'll be a lot easier on you if you're already residing in town. Otherwise, every time I have to ring you up on that bothersome telephone, I'll be waking up the entire MacKay household at Culdee Creek."

"You find it bothersome, do you?" Beth chuckled. "My sister Erin absolutely adores it. If she's not ringing up one of her friends, she's listening in on someone's party line. Abby says she's warned Erin countless times that if she's not careful the earpiece is going to grow onto the side of her head."

Doc chuckled. "Now that'll make for an interesting new surgical technique, I'd say. A telephonectomy."

Beth rose from her chair. "I'll have to tell Erin. Might scare some sense into her." She shook her head. "Only nine, and already the child's as bullheaded and high-spirited as they come."

"Not at all like her older sister, is she?" Doc said, an impish glint in his eyes.

Beth grinned. "No, not anything like me at all."

"Sorry, honey. I think you'd be a nice fit here, but I'm full to the gills just now. I'd be glad, though, to put you on my waiting list."

Her frustration rising, Beth set down her cup of tea and stared back at Mamie Oatman. She had just spent the better part of an hour sitting in the woman's parlor being "interviewed" for suitability, only to learn Mamie had no vacancies.

"And how far down would I be on your waiting list?" Beth asked, trying to maintain a calm demeanor.

Mamie scrunched her forehead in thought. "Well, there's Joanna, a chambermaid who works at the hotel, and Ivan, an immigrant Russian man from the creamery, ahead of you. Ivan, though, hopes to bring his family over in the next six months or so. He'll have to find himself a house by then, so *he* shouldn't hold you up long. Joanna, on the other hand . . ."

Beth sighed. "Well, in the interim, can you recommend another reputable establishment or family who might be willing to take me in? I really need to be quickly available whenever Doc or a patient needs me."

Once more, Mamie's brows migrated out of sight. "Can't say as how I do." Then, as if in sudden remembrance, she snapped her fingers. "But I did once hear talk that Millie Starr had been thinking about taking in a boarder. They've a room with a private entrance off the back side of the rectory. And with the size of the meals Millie likes to cook, one more mouth wouldn't present any problem at all."

Millie Starr . . . the rectory. *Noah.* Though well aware she'd see Noah frequently, what with working and living in Grand View, Beth wasn't so sure she wanted to see him on the daily basis that living in the same house would entail.

"I'm afraid that wouldn't do." Beth pursed her lips. "I wouldn't want to intrude on their privacy, what with Father Starr being a priest and all."

Mamie shrugged. "Suit yourself, but I can't say as how it'd be such a hardship, knowing Millie like I do.

Besides, it'd only be a temporary situation anyway, until a room opened up here. Why, I'd bet Millie would be plumb tickled for another woman's company. And you could help her out whenever she had problems with little Emily, too."

Emily. Noah's daughter. In several of her letters, Abby had mentioned her and the tragic circumstances surrounding her disability. Beth could well imagine that Millie—and Noah, too—might welcome some help with the little girl.

But did *she* want to get involved with them and their lives, even if only for a short time? She wasn't some love-struck girl anymore; Beth felt certain she was past her schoolgirl crush on Noah. But Noah and Millie weren't the sort of people you could keep at arm's length. And Beth wasn't all that keen on investing her emotions with anyone just now.

She needed time to crawl off into some corner and lick her wounds. She needed to rebuild her reserves, to find some answers, and to get her life back on track. What she definitely *didn't* need were two good, godly, loving people and a crippled little girl. *Especially* not another little girl, especially not in the close, cozy haven of a home.

"Well, I'm not sure what I'll do in the meantime, but would you be so kind to add me to your waiting list?" Beth climbed to her feet. "Until I find other lodging, you can always contact me at Doc Childress's office."

"I'll do that, honey. Keep Millie in mind, though." Mamie paused to scan Beth from head to toe. "Yep, Millie's might be just the thing for the likes of you. If you don't mind me saying so, you could use a bit of fattening up."

This time, Beth couldn't help it. Her eyes rolled back in her head as she turned to the door. "I'll take that suggestion under careful advisement, Mrs. Oatman. Thank you."

As determined as she was to do just the opposite, a curious thing happened just as soon as Beth departed Mamie's boardinghouse. Almost as if her limbs had suddenly taken on a mind of their own, Beth found herself heading down the boardwalk, in the strangest direction. Heading down through Grand View, toward the Episcopal church and rectory at the far end of town.

3

If any man think that he knoweth anything, he knoweth nothing yet as he ought to know.

1 Corinthians 8:2

Beth drew up before the white picket fence enclosing the rectory. Now that she was here, all her fears assailed her once again. She just couldn't live with people like the Starrs. It was crazy. She shook her head and turned to leave. No sense asking for—

"Well, are my eyes playing tricks on me, or is that little Miss Beth MacKay, all grown up and become a doctor?"

At the sound of Millie's warm, welcoming voice, Beth knew she had failed to make her escape. Plastering a smile on her face, she turned back around.

"Yes. Yes, it is, Millie." She forced a semblance of enthusiasm into her voice. "I'm home and decided to pay a call on some old friends."

As Millie stepped from her house and hurried down the gravel path to the front gate, her white head of hair

39

gleamed in the sun. "Come on in," she said, unlatching the gate and swinging it open. "It's almost noon. I just took a loaf of fresh wheat bread from the oven, the coffee's hot, and we're having warmed-up beef stew from last night for lunch. There's plenty for an extra guest."

"We?" Beth's heartbeat faltered. "Oh, you mean you and Emily, don't you?"

"Yes." Millie nodded. "Noah might or might not show up. The poor lad gets so engrossed in all his projects that sometimes he plumb forgets what time it is. He's been trying harder of late, though, to come home for meals, if not for himself, then to spend some time with Emily."

With any luck, maybe this would be one of the days Noah forgot about lunch. Beth certainly hoped so. She wasn't sure she could handle seeing Millie's handsome nephew right now, although why that was, Beth didn't care to consider.

"It's really not necessary," Beth said, shaking her head. "Inviting me to lunch, I mean. I didn't realize how late it was getting, and I don't wish to impose on your meal. I can come back later."

"Nonsense." Before Beth could back away, Millie grabbed her hand. "I'd love to have you stay. What with all the care that Emily requires, I don't get out nearly as much as I used to. Another woman's presence at my table would be a blessing. Besides," she added with one of her face-filling grins, "I'm eager to hear about your medical schooling and trip home. Abby always shared your letters with me, but hearing it all in person is ever so much more fun."

There was no way to refuse logic like that. "In that case, of course I'll stay." Beth allowed herself to be pulled into the front yard, waited as Millie closed the gate, then followed her to the house. "I've been looking forward to visiting with you and finally meeting Emily. How old is she now?"

40

"She's two—just turned two last Friday, as a matter of fact—and is as bright as can be." Millie glanced at her. "Abby told you everything about what happened, didn't she?"

Beth knew enough about poor Alice's difficult labor, how Emily's head was too large to be delivered easily, and the terrible toll it had eventually taken on both mother and child.

"Yes, she did. I'm so very sorry."

Millie drew up at the front door. "It devastated Noah, losing Alice. But the damage done to Emily . . . well, I worry about him, that I do."

At the softly spoken revelation, all Beth's fears about seeing Noah dissipated. Nothing remained but concern for him.

She laid a hand on Millie's arm. "Whatever I can do to help, just let me know. Noah has shared of himself so unselfishly all these years. I'd like to give him some measure of assistance now in return."

"Be his friend then, honey. Just be his friend."

They entered the rectory. It was just as bright and welcoming as Beth had always remembered it, with colorful rugs on the hardwood floors, cheerful lace curtains fluttering at the windows, and all of it spotlessly clean and shining. The fragrant aroma of freshly baked bread, mingling with the mouthwatering scent of a savory beef stew, wafted to her. Her stomach gave a most unladylike growl. She grinned sheepishly at Millie.

"Guess my appetite's finally starting to return."

"The fine, high air of Colorado does that to a lot of people."

A wicker wheelchair sat beside the big kitchen window, facing out onto a backyard where sparrows and chickadees hopped about in the branches of a crabapple tree. The wheelchair began to shake, and Beth caught a fleeting glimpse of flailing arms.

41

"Bir—bir—bir!" a childish voice exclaimed. "Bir!"

"Yes, darling, there's birds." Millie came around to stand before the wheelchair. "And aren't they all so pretty and sweet?"

"Mih-mih!"

"I've a new friend for you to meet, darling." As she spoke, Millie wheeled Emily around to face Beth. "This is Dr. Beth. She's come to stay and help take care of us when we're sick."

Beth swallowed hard and pasted on a friendly smile. She could get through this, just like she had gotten through all those other times since the baby. A doctor planning on entering general practice couldn't turn away children. Besides, she had seen several children with palsy during her pediatric rotations. Emily's wild, uncontrolled motions, jerking head, and unfocused gaze were quite the norm.

And for all her unnatural mannerisms, the little girl was pretty as could be. She had her father's blond hair, although it was several shades lighter. Her eyes were a rich brown and framed by long, thick lashes. Her mouth was her mother's, full and delightfully curved, her pale skin smooth and flushed with health.

Beth walked over and knelt before her. "Hello, Emily. I've heard so much about you. It's wonderful finally to make your acquaintance."

The child stared solemnly down at her for such a long time that Beth began to wonder if she had frightened her. Then, with a gleeful chortle, Emily touched her face.

Well, more like a pat and rub of the face, Beth quickly amended, because of the uncontrolled motions of Emily's hands and arms. Nonetheless, the gesture was a sign of the toddler's acceptance. At the action, something within Beth relaxed, if only a little, its tight grip on her heart.

She smiled and grasped Emily's chubby little hand. Turning her face into it, she kissed the child's palm. It smelled of chocolate. In fact, now that Beth looked more closely, it was also smeared with chocolate.

"I'm only making a guess here," she said, glancing up at Millie before turning back to Emily, who was now tugging on her jacket sleeve, "but do I perhaps have some brown streaks on my face?"

To her surprise, instead of Millie offering a reply, a deep, masculine voice answered instead.

"Yes, as a matter of fact, your face is now quite charmingly decorated. Consider it Emily's mark of approval. She doesn't usually warm to strangers quite as quickly as she seems to have warmed to you."

Beth gasped, lost her balance in attempting to rise to her feet, and unceremoniously fell backward onto her bottom. Her cheeks flushed.

"You could've warned me Noah was here." She sent Millie a chagrined look.

"And if I'd known he'd come in, I assuredly would've, honey." The older woman hurried forward and offered Beth her hand. "Some men seem to possess a special talent for sneaking about, they do!"

Noah laughed. "If I've offended, I beg pardon. But I wasn't sneaking about. You two ladies were just so preoccupied with Emily, neither of you heard me come in."

By now Beth had regained her feet. She tugged down her jacket, smoothed her skirt, and brushed off whatever dust clung to her heretofore impeccably tailored suit.

"Well, maybe we *were* pretty engrossed with Emily. Still"—to hide her discomfiture, she forced a smile—"a little extra warning, a heavier tread or a clearing of the throat, would've been most appreciated."

Beth looked up then, her gaze careening straight into Noah's. He stared back, a stunned look on his face.

43

Then, as if it had a mind of its own, his glance moved from her face down her body and back up again.

Her eyes widened; her throat went dry. But if Noah perhaps seemed a little too blatant in his amazed perusal of her, she was equally surprised at the sight of him. He looked far older than she imagined he would, even considering it had been five years since she had last laid eyes on him.

Thanks to the regular sparring and boxing workouts he had first done at the YMCA while attending seminary, Noah had always been a fit, strongly built man. Now, however, he was so leanly muscled as to be almost on the thin side. Though a man in his prime, his temples were beginning to show silver among the dark gold strands. His face looked careworn, his eyes—his beautiful, green- and gold-flecked brown eyes—appeared drained of energy.

Compassion swelled in her. Compassion and a fierce resolve to help him rediscover joy in whatever way she could. Then Beth caught herself. Even with Noah—especially with Noah—she must keep a safe emotional distance. Help him the best she could, yes, and all the while hold high the shield before her heart.

"Does the chocolate look that bad?" Beth asked, realizing Noah was still staring at her.

Noah blinked, swallowed hard. "What? What did you say?"

"I said," Beth held out her hand to him as she repeated her question, "does the chocolate Emily has smeared on my face look all that bad?"

Noah's glance skittered from her to Millie, then back again. "No, not really. As I said before, it's quite charming." As if finally gathering his wits about him, Noah smiled, took her proffered hand, and clasped it between both of his. "I'm sorry if I seemed a bit distracted there for a minute, but I haven't seen you in all of five years, and you've grown into an absolutely stunning young woman." He turned to his aunt. "Hasn't she, Millie? Hasn't Beth turned into a beautiful woman?"

"Yes, of course Beth's beautiful. She's all grown up into a fine young woman."

Her face flooding with heat, Beth eyed them both. Though Millie's statement was calm and matter-of-fact, Noah seemed ill at ease. Whatever was wrong with him?

"Well," she said, gently tugging on the hand still clasped in his until he finally released it, "thank you very much for the compliment. It's nice to know all my growing up has been duly noted and appreciated."

She had meant the comment to lighten the increasingly strained atmosphere in the kitchen. Her little joke, however, seemed totally lost on Noah, who had turned his gaze to stare out the window, apparently deep in thought.

Beth looked to Millie. A smile tugging at the corner of her mouth, the older woman shrugged and motioned to the table.

"Time to eat, I'd say. Sit yourself down, honey, and I'll start serving up the stew. And you, young man"—she leaned over to poke Noah in the arm—"can set out some extra silverware for Beth, then slice up the bread."

With a jerk, Noah seemed to return to the present. He nodded, smiled brightly, and did as asked. In no time they were seated around the table. Noah said grace, Millie and Beth finished with "amens," and they all dug in.

The sharing of food eased the tension. Emily helped lighten the mood by chortling and mashing her food onto her bowl and face. Finally, Beth, who sat beside the little girl, began to feed her, and Emily's wild movements seemed to ease a bit. Beth caught Millie's approving glance and slight nod of her head. Encouraged, Beth worked even harder until Emily at last shook her head and clamped her mouth shut.

"She's full, Beth," Noah said. "That's her sign for it."

"Oh, yes. Of course." Beth laid down the spoon.

Millie leaned forward, sudden interest in her eyes. "So, what are your plans? When are you starting work with Doc? And where will you be staying? At Culdee Creek, or here in town?"

The question reminded Beth of her original reason for coming to the rectory today. She looked down. "I think it'd be best if I find a place in town. Problem is, Mamie Oatman's boardinghouse is full right now. I'm on the waiting list behind two other people."

"Yes, that's been a problem this summer. We've had an unexpected influx of immigrants and homesteaders." Millie's brow furrowed in thought. "There are a few other possibilities, though." Her gaze locked with Noah's. "The rectory being one, if Noah's of a mind to take in a boarder."

Beth's glance swung to Noah. His face reddened.

"It's a possibility, I suppose," he said. "We do have that spare bedroom off the kitchen." He looked to Beth. "Millie and I'll have to discuss it."

"And what's there to discuss?" His aunt folded her arms across her chest. "I'd say it's a perfect solution for us all. Emily's taken to Beth. Beth'll have a place to stay in town that I know her parents will feel comfortable with. I'll have some feminine companionship. And we'll all have some much needed company to brighten our lives."

Warily, Beth glanced from Millie to Noah. There was something unspoken being communicated between them, and she wasn't so certain she cared to be the cause of it.

"Well, yes, it could be a wonderful idea," she said, "but there's no hurry on deciding. I don't start working with Doc until Monday. And, in the meanwhile, I've time to look elsewhere."

Noah sighed, lowered his head, and rubbed his eyes. "Look elsewhere if you want, Beth. But Millie's right. The Lord knows I leave her alone with Emily most of the time. If your presence here will be a comfort to her, then I'm more than happy to have you." He managed a weary smile, then shoved back his chair and stood. "This is between you two ladies. I'm fine with it."

Millie looked up at him. "Time to be off again, is it?"

"Yes. The carpenter's coming to discuss a few problems he sees in the bell tower plans."

"Will you be home for supper?"

"I hope so." Noah turned to Beth. "I enjoyed our meal together. Whether you decide to live with us or not, don't be a stranger."

She smiled. "I won't. You can be assured of that."

After Noah departed, Millie rose and lifted a dozing Emily from her chair. "Let me put her down for her nap. We need to talk. I'm so excited that you'll be boarding here. You're a blessing sent from the Lord, not only for me but for us all!"

Beth made a move to protest she hadn't decided anything yet, then gave the attempt up as a lost cause. When Millie Starr got an idea into her head, woe to anyone who stepped in her way. And besides, the consideration of staying here was growing more and more appealing.

Living in close proximity with Noah would soon ease the unfamiliarity between them. In no time they'd be back to the easy camaraderie they had once shared. And most important of all, she could begin to be the helpmate he seemed to need. Beth refused to stand helplessly by and see his grief destroy him. Though her own heart was shattered beyond repair and even the idea of getting emotionally involved with another man repulsed her, she'd not desert Noah if he needed her.

No, she'd not desert him, any more than she'd turn from her own kin in their time of need.

For the rest of the day, Noah could barely keep his mind on his work. The notes he had made earlier that morning for Sunday's sermon looked like gibberish. Nicholas Blacklock, the town carpenter, had seemed to be in an argumentative mood, and by the time he was done marking up the bell tower plans, Noah had totally lost track of the man's point. Then Leona Gates, who worked at the mercantile, called to question Noah's order for paint to match the bell tower and annex to the rest of the church.

Repeatedly distracted by memories of his encounter with Beth MacKay, Noah was finally forced to ask Nicholas to return tomorrow and temporarily cancel the paint order. The sermon would have to wait for another day as well. The resulting solitude, however, did little to assuage the rush of thoughts and emotions churning chaotically in his head.

Beth . . .

Her image filled his mind. Rich, raven-black hair piled luxuriously atop her head. Luminous, soulful brown eyes the color of molasses. Smooth skin, washed with the hue of light honey and kissed with the tenderest of blushes.

His mouth quirked. Molasses . . . honey. One would think he saw her as some delectable morsel to devour. And she, his good friend Conor MacKay's daughter. And he, a widower old enough to be her father! Well, *almost* old enough anyway, with a span of thirteen years separating them.

With a frustrated sigh, Noah leaned back in his chair and closed his eyes. He was acting like some love-struck lad, but he had just never seen Beth like he had seen her today. She'd been a gangly ten-year-old when he had first come to Grand View and had matured eventually into a pretty girl before leaving for medical school. But the change in those years away had been amazing. Now she was a slim, elegant, exquisitely formed woman.

Noah didn't think he had ever seen a more beautiful woman.

Yet more than just her outward beauty attracted him. Her sincere interest in Emily touched his heart, as did her kindness and consideration for Millie. And there was still something more—a certain air of mystery about her, a fleeting glimpse of a deeply hidden pain, and frequent, sharp flashes of keen intelligence and insight.

Even in the short time he had spent with her today, Noah sensed that Beth MacKay was a deeply troubled soul, yet a soul equally brimming with talent and a capacity for goodness and love. He couldn't help but be drawn to her. No one could, he wagered.

What unsettled Noah, though, were emotions that encompassed more than just a friendly interest and attraction. In the instant their gazes had first met in the kitchen, the keenest blade of physical longing he had ever known lanced through him. Sheer, unmitigated lust had seized him in its gut-twisting grip.

With a groan, Noah lowered his head into his hands. What had happened in that instant to turn his heretofore brotherly affection for a young woman he had all but seen grow up into one of such depraved considerations? And why, oh why, knowing his feelings for what they were, had he agreed to allow her to stay with them?

Was he so arrogant in his priesthood he imagined he was immune to temptations of the flesh? Though he had been tempted before, nothing had ever affected him as strongly as what he felt for Beth today. He must beware. Complacency was a quagmire that could draw one in so gradually one might never recognize the trap until it was too late. And he had grown so weary, so increasingly unsure of himself and his judgments of late . . .

Still, who was he fooling in his silly imaginings? Beth loved him as a brother and always would. She was a good, pure young woman. There was no danger she'd encourage him, and rightfully so.

Shame filled him. Noah lifted his head and gazed heavenward.

"Father, forgive me. Forgive me."

Even as he uttered the prayer, the longing ache left him and peace engulfed him. Beth's image faded.

A passing temptation, no more. To be expected in a man—even a priest of God—who had been more than two years without his wife. But that was all it was. A passing temptation.

Not reason enough to deny Millie a companion, Emily a dearly needed friend, and Beth a place to stay.

4

Let no man deceive himself.
1 Corinthians 3:18

Abby rapped lightly on the frame of the open bunkhouse door. "May I come in?"

Glancing up from the traveling trunk she was packing, Beth nodded. "Sure. I was going to come to the house in a while anyway."

"To tell us what your newest plans were, and where you were going?"

At the mild reproof in her stepmother's voice, Beth paused. She quashed the swell of guilt that immediately filled her, refusing to allow emotions she had long ago mastered to take control.

"Yes, of course I was planning on telling you. Not that I'm going much farther than Grand View at any rate." She resumed placing neatly folded pairs of stockings and other unmentionables into the trunk. "I've found a place to stay in town, with Millie and Noah Starr."

51

"The Starrs? Really?"

"Mamie Oatman's boardinghouse was full. She agreed to put me on her waiting list but couldn't really say when my name would come up. So she suggested the Starrs. Seems Millie at one time had considered taking in a boarder."

"So you intend to move in with Mamie as soon as one of her rooms opens up?"

"That's the plan." Beth turned to retrieve her small velvet jewelry box and caught sight of Abby's frowning gaze. Here it comes now, she thought.

"Are you sure it's wise moving in with Noah? Considering how strongly you used to feel about him, I mean?"

"*Used* to feel about him," Beth was quick to correct. "That's all that matters."

"So you've no feelings whatsoever for him now?"

With a sigh, Beth laid her jewelry box in the trunk, then turned and leaned against it. "I care for him as a friend. That's all. And I'm very concerned for him. So's Millie."

"So am I, and your father, and all the rest of the family." Abby tilted her head and smiled gently. "But I'm equally concerned about you, Beth."

"Why?" Beth's eyes narrowed. "Do you imagine me still hopelessly infatuated with Noah? Well, you couldn't be more wrong. When I gave up the hope of ever marrying or having children to pursue my medical education, I also gave up on Noah."

"But now you've obtained that medical education. You're a doctor. And you're back home, close to Noah and about to get even closer to him by living in his home."

"Are you forgetting about Millie?" Though Beth tried to contain it, her irritation was beginning to rise. "I daresay both Noah and I will be quite adequately chaperoned. If you're worried about anything illicit, that is."

"No, of course I'm not worried about either of you." Abby exhaled a frustrated breath. "It's just . . . just that Noah's so lost and vulnerable right now. And you . . ."

There was something in the tone of Abby's voice—doubt, wariness, perhaps even some woman's intuition—that filled Beth with unease. "What about me, Abby?" She met the older woman's troubled gaze with a steady one of her own. "You sound as if you think I'm lost and vulnerable, too."

Her stepmother locked gazes with her. "Aren't you? There's something about you, Beth. Something different. Something not right."

"You haven't seen me for five years, save for those few days you and Pa stopped in the city after your mother's funeral last year. Did you think I'd still be the same girl I was all those years ago?" She gave a harsh laugh. "Well, I don't know of anyone who gets through medical school unscathed, especially no woman. Especially not one who's not only a woman but one of mixed heritage."

"I'd wondered about that, about it all," Abby said quietly. "But you never mentioned anything in your letters. It was almost as if . . . as if you were trying to protect us from the truth."

"I was." As the memories assailed her, Beth's voice grew taut. "What could you or Pa have done about it anyway? And I wasn't about to give Pa a reason to hightail it out to New York and bring me back home. I'd made my own bed. And I wasn't going to rise from it until *I* was ready."

"But at what cost, Beth? At what cost to your spirit? Your soul?"

"My spirit will heal, Abby. What counts is I didn't let them beat me." She shook her head fiercely. "No, not any of them."

"What happened, Beth? Can't you tell me? Now that you've beaten them, now that it's all over. Now that you're safe, back home."

"I'm not ready to talk about it, Abby." Beth managed a wan smile. "I need more time."

"Would it be easier, do you think, talking to your father? He's in his study, working on the accounts. I could fetch him."

Horror flooded Beth. She grabbed Abby's arm, gripping it tightly.

"No! I don't want to talk to Pa about it!" If he knew. Oh, dear God, if he knew, it'd surely break his heart!

"It's all right." Abby covered Beth's hand with her own. "You're correct, of course. It isn't the time. I see that now."

Hot color flushed Beth's cheeks. Just as she had feared, she had far too easily given herself away. The sooner she was gone from Culdee Creek, the better.

"Pa's got enough on his mind, Abby." Rallying the professionalism she had fought so long and dearly to achieve, Beth leveled a cool, impersonal gaze on her stepmother. "No need burdening him with my petty problems. Especially problems, now that I'm home, that'll most likely work themselves out."

Abby nodded, gave Beth's hand a quick, reassuring squeeze, then released her. "I'm sure you're right. Just know that, no matter what, your father and I love you and will always be here for you."

"I know, Abby. I know."

And Beth did know. Unfortunately, the knowledge of her parents' love didn't comfort her like it used to. Her troubled spirit needed something more. Problem was, Beth didn't know what that something was, or how to find it.

❦

"While you were home, packing up your things," Millie said to her the next morning as Beth's brother carried her trunk into the rectory, "I got your room cleaned up all spic and span. I also took the liberty of making your bed with one of my comforters, but you're welcome to add your own things whenever it suits you."

"I'm sure it'll do me just fine as you've furnished it," Beth replied, following Evan into her new room. "After all, I doubt I'll be spending much time in it—what with the medical practice demands—except to sleep, anyway."

"And you're more than welcome to share the parlor and kitchen with us anytime you wish, too," her new landlady continued. "I want you to feel at home here, you know."

"Thank you. I'm sure I will." Beth paused to indicate where her brother was to place her trunk. "And I want you to feel free to call on me for assistance when I'm here. My cooking skills may have gotten a bit rusty since I've been gone, but I'm certain they'll come back quickly enough. Abby was too good a teacher for me to have forgotten much."

"Pshaw, honey. You're paying room and board. I wouldn't expect you to help out with any chores on top of that."

"Nonetheless, you said you wanted me to feel at home. And I won't feel at home if I can't help out."

Millie grinned. "Well, we'll see. We'll see."

Evan came to stand before them. Though Beth was of a good height for a woman, he still towered over her. She stared up at him.

"Is there anything else you'll be needing, little sis?" he asked.

"Not that I can think of. Thanks, big brother."

"Reckon I'll be on my way then. Pa wanted me to stop by O'Brien's and pick him up some liniment. That fall he took tripping over Erin's roller skates bruised him up worse than he cares to admit."

Beth shook her head. "Pa should come in and see Doc. He might have chipped a bone or something. And Erin had better learn not to leave her skates in the middle of the hallway."

Evan chuckled. "Oh, from what I heard, Erin's not going to be doing any roller-skating for a long while to come. But then, she won't have any free time to go skating anyway, what with school starting up soon and *all* the picket fences to whitewash."

"You mean she's going to paint not only the main house's front-yard fences but yours and Devlin's, too?"

"Yep. She's been warned a couple of times already about those skates. Reckon this was the last straw."

Millie laughed. "Well, tell Erin when she's done with Culdee Creek's, she's more than welcome to come and paint ours. Noah hasn't time nowadays to do much upkeep around here, and our fence needed a good whitewashing the beginning of the summer."

"I'll be sure to tell Erin." Evan nodded to Millie, then tweaked Beth on the nose. "Better head on out. See you later, little sis."

"Bye, Evan."

The two women watched him depart, then turned to each other. "I'll leave you to get moved in," Millie said. "I've still got a few finishing touches to make to the chicken potpie we're having for lunch. But just as soon as you're tired of putting things away, come on out to the kitchen, and we'll have a nice cup of tea."

Beth smiled. "Sounds like a wonderful idea."

Millie bustled out, leaving Beth alone in her new room. She looked around. Graced with two windows that met at the joining of two walls, the room was bright and airy. A door leading outside also took up a portion of one of the windowed walls. White, rose-strewn lace curtains swayed in the windows. The walls were painted a soft, deep rose and matched the dark rose-and-pink chenille bedspread.

The bed was of white enameled iron topped with brass knobs. A cane-backed wooden rocker, draped with a hand-knitted lap robe, stood near the windows. A tall, dark walnut bureau topped by an oval beveled mirror graced the only other free wall. A rose, green, and white hooked rug lay beside the bed atop the polished hardwood floor, and several gilt-framed prints hung on the walls.

It was a thoroughly pleasant and functional room. Beth looked with longing at the rocker. She could easily imagine herself curled up in it many an evening after a day of hard work, reading anything that didn't pertain to subjects medical. Indeed, after years spent with her nose buried in topics addressing body parts and noxious diseases, she longed for a stirring tale of action and adventure or of lands far away.

First things first, though. Her belongings must be put away in the bureau, her comb and hairbrush laid out, her books set in place on the small bedside table. Then, with Millie's permission, she wanted to explore the rest of the house. Perhaps Emily might even enjoy coming along.

A half hour later, Beth walked into the kitchen. Millie was stooped over the sink, gasping for breath.

Beth hurried to her. "What's wrong? Are you ill?"

Sliding an arm about her shoulders, Beth helped Millie to straighten, then gently guided her to a kitchen chair. "Sit, now. You look as white as a sheet."

Millie all but fell into the chair. Her brow beaded with sweat; her breath came in sharp, shallow gulps. Beth watched her for a few minutes and, when Millie didn't improve, decided it was time to get her to bed.

"Can you walk to my bedroom if I help you?" she asked. "It's not far."

"I . . . I'll be . . . all right." Millie motioned weakly. "This'll . . . pass. It always does."

Even as she spoke, her color began to return, her breathing to improve. "See? I'm feeling better . . . already."

"Maybe so. Still, I'm not convinced this is as insignificant as you pretend it to be."

Millie shrugged. "It's most likely my heart. I had the rheumatic fever as a girl, you know."

"Did you now?"

Her suspicions rising even higher, Beth took one of Millie's hands. Sure enough, the nail beds were blue, the tips of the fingers bulbous—a sure sign of chronic heart trouble. An uneasy feeling filled Beth.

She released Millie's hand. "Well, that might well explain your episodes. Have you seen Doc about them?"

Millie's mouth tightened with determination. "No. I can live with this. No sense bothering him when there's nothing he can do about it anyway."

"Actually, there are a few drugs available that might help you a lot. One's called digitalis, from the foxglove plant. It helps to strengthen the heart."

"Do tell?" Millie cocked her head in sudden interest. "Well, maybe then I will pay Doc—or you, if you'll have me—a little visit. What with Emily growing and getting more active, I can use all the heart strengthening I can muster."

"We could go today. I'm sure Doc would see you, even if it is a Saturday."

Millie shook her head. "Leave the poor man be. He needs his days off. I've waited this long. I can wait until Monday."

Beth wasn't so sure of that. She feared Millie's heart was failing and her lungs beginning to fill with fluid for her to have such a violent attack with only a minimal increase in activity.

"Well, I suppose if you're going to insist on being so bullheaded about this," Beth said, staring sternly down at Millie, "I could see if Noah has better success in getting you to Doc's today. Of course, I hate to bother him, when I'm available, and—"

"No! Don't tell Noah." Once more, the color drained from Millie's face. "He doesn't know about my spells, and I don't want him to. He has enough to bear right now without adding this."

Seeing Millie's look of panic, Beth wondered what else she strove so mightily to protect Noah from. Anger rose in Beth. Perhaps Noah was a wee bit too caught up in his own misery to see what was going on around him.

"Well, I can't promise never to tell Noah," Beth said, laying a hand on Millie's shoulder, "but, like you said, no sense upsetting him, at least until we know more about what's causing your spells."

"If you're going to be my doctor"—Millie's eyes narrowed with grim resolve—"I expect you to keep my personal health matters private. They're nobody's business unless I care to make them that."

Beth sighed. "Fine. You're right, of course. I'll honor your desires. Sooner or later, though, we might have to have a very serious talk about letting Noah in on this."

"You think this is serious, and you haven't even examined me yet?

"I've seen enough to disturb me." She walked to the cookstove and took up the teakettle. Moving to the sink, Beth proceeded to pump water into the container.

"Let's plan on heading down to Doc's just as soon as the potpie's out of the oven," she said, placing the kettle back on the stove to heat. "In the meanwhile, I'll get Emily ready, bring her downstairs, and we'll have a cup of tea. By then, the potpie should be done."

"If you say so." Millie cast her an exasperated look. "Land sakes, but aren't you a MacKay through and through? Once you get an idea into your head, there's no changing you, is there?"

Beth grinned. "No, there isn't. Especially when it involves someone I care for. And I care about *you,* Millie Starr."

❧

Luckily, Doc was not only available but in his office when Beth rang him up. She quickly explained the situation.

"Millie could probably wait until Monday," he said, his gruff voice belying his concern, "but I agree she's gone long enough without treatment as it is. I'm going to have a stern talk with her about keeping this from me, you can be sure. She may well have made a big mistake taking a doctor into her house, if she thought to keep such secrets."

"I'd like to bring her over in about an hour. Will that be all right with you?"

Doc chuckled softly. "Even if it's Saturday, I've already seen two walk-in patients this morning. I can sure make room for an old friend like Millie."

"Good. I can help. I'm all moved in."

"Hopefully, Millie'll be the last patient for the day. But you're more than welcome to sit in on the visit."

"I'd like to. Thanks."

Beth hung up then realized that Nola Teachout, the central switchboard operator, might have been listening in on their conversation. She cursed her lapse of memory.

In New York City, the central switchboard was comprised of a large group of very busy women. Odds were strong they hadn't the time to listen in on conversations, much less recognize the speakers or their subjects. Here in Grand View, however, the amount of telephone calls necessitated only one switchboard operator. And that operator knew everyone.

Beth would have to be far more careful whenever she conferred with Doc or a patient over the telephone. The only consolation was that Nola was known to be a discreet woman who generally disdained gossip. Probably the main reason she was hired for the job, Beth supposed, and she offered up a prayer of thanks.

It was almost noon before they made their way to Doc's office. Millie entered first, with Beth following, guiding Emily's wheelchair through the door. To her surprise, a woman with a black eye and bruised cheek was just then walking out of Doc's examining room.

Beth parked Emily's wheelchair near the window, then turned back to the ebony-haired woman. "Why, Mary Sue Edgerton"—she extended her hand in greeting—"what a pleasant surprise. I haven't seen you in years and imagined you'd wed some rich, handsome man by now and moved away."

Mary Sue met her gaze, then averted it, flushing crimson. "It's Peterson. Mary Sue Peterson. And though I did marry the owner of the Grand View Bank, I didn't move away." She shot Doc Childress a quick glance. "Harlow will settle the bill on Monday, if that's all right with you, Doc."

He nodded. "That'll be fine, Mary Sue. Just have a care from here on out, will you? Next time you fall down the stairs, you might not get off with just a black eye and bruised face."

She managed a taut smile. "Yes, I was lucky this time, wasn't I?" With that, she all but dashed from the office.

Millie and Beth exchanged guarded looks then turned back to Doc, who was still staring after Mary Sue, a troubled expression on his craggy face. With great emphasis, Beth cleared her throat. Doc spun around and plastered a wide grin of welcome on his face.

"Well, what have we here, Millie Starr?" he asked, walking over to take her hand. "I hear you've been keeping secrets from me. Is that true?"

Millie's mouth quirked. "If I have, I've had good reason, John. You know I'm not one to come running for every ache and pain."

"And I appreciate that, Millie. Indeed I do. But this sounds a lot more serious than some little ache or pain." As he spoke, he led her into his examining room. "So why don't Dr. MacKay and I just have a little look-see?"

Millie cast a glance over her shoulder at Beth, who had gone to retrieve Emily and head her in their direction. "Suit yourself, John. Just be advised I haven't time for fancy testing or trips to see specialists in Colorado Springs. What can be done had better be done here."

"Well, let's just see what's going on first, shall we?" Doc asked, arching an eyebrow at Beth. "First things first, I always say."

Beth shot Doc a commiserating look, then wheeled Emily into the office and shut the door behind them.

5

We have redemption through his blood, even the forgive-
ness of sins.

Colossians 1:14

With a flourish, Noah finished the closing line of tomorrow's sermon and laid his pen aside. Not a moment too soon, he thought, glancing at the small desk clock. Half past six. Millie had probably served up supper already.

Just as well if they had gone on to eat without him. Noah shoved back his chair and stood. He had been so busy today, he hadn't had time to make it home for lunch, much less supper. Still, he knew Millie would have a plate prepared for him, kept warm in the oven.

He slipped on his black coat, straightened his clerical collar, and grabbed his hat. There was a smudge of dirt on its black grosgrain band, and Noah rubbed it off before donning the hat. After extinguishing his out-of-date but still functional kerosene lamp, he headed home.

The rectory was brightly lit, smelled of fried chicken and apple pie, and was filled with the sound of laughter. Splashing noises rose from the kitchen. He smiled. Supper was most definitely over if Emily was now getting her bath.

Noah deposited his hat and jacket on the rattan coat tree just inside the front door. Then, rolling up his shirt sleeves, he entered the kitchen. Three pairs of feminine eyes lifted, acknowledged him, then returned to their bathing duties.

"Busy day at the church?" Millie asked, sending a small sailboat back into Emily's splashing vicinity.

"Yes. For some reason, Sunday's sermon was a bear to write."

"But you're happy with it now?"

He nodded. "Yes, pretty much. I'll go over it once more in the morning before services." His glance moved to Beth. "All settled in and comfortable?"

"Yes." Cheeks flushed, dark tendrils of hair curling damply around her face, she smiled up at him from her spot on the floor beside the tinplated washtub. "My room's perfect. Absolutely perfect."

"Good."

Noah walked to the stove and retrieved his supper. As if to make up for the lunch he had missed today, Millie had piled his plate high with several pieces of crisply fried chicken, a generous mound of mashed potatoes and gravy, and a mess of fresh green beans seasoned with bacon. He carried it to the table, whereupon sat his napkin, silverware, and an empty coffee mug. After filling the mug from the pot on the stove, Noah sat down and dug in.

As he ate, he watched the two women with Emily. His daughter loved playing in water, and it provided such wonderful exercise that hardly a night passed that Millie didn't prepare her a bath. In the water, as his aunt supported Emily on her tummy, his daughter's spasmodic motions didn't seem quite so strange. Noah could almost imagine she was swimming, swimming like any other child. For a few minutes, he could dream of how it should have been. Then, as always, he'd wrench himself back to reality, feeling guilty for not fully accepting Emily as she was, for not wholeheartedly thanking the Lord for His gift, as unexpectedly tragic as that gift had turned out to be.

At the renewed swell of misery, Noah's appetite fled him yet again. He pushed aside his plate. Mug in hand, he leaned back in his chair, content to banish all thoughts and further self-recriminations and just mindlessly watch life continue around him.

"You hardly ate anything," Millie said, glancing at his plate. "Unless you had a very big lunch—which I doubt—you need to finish your meal, Noah Starr. You can't stand to lose any more meat on those already scrawny bones. As it is, most of your clothes already hang on you."

To appease her, Noah picked up a piece of half-eaten chicken and began to chew on it. "Is this more to your liking?" he asked after swallowing a mouthful of meat that, as well cooked and seasoned as he knew it always to be, still tasted like dried bones to him.

His aunt scowled. "A little more, but I won't be satisfied until you eat at least half of the food on that plate."

Beth, who had been intent on pouring water over a giggling Emily's head, chuckled. "Better get to work, Noah, or you'll be here all night."

He grinned. "I recall a few episodes like that as a boy. There was a time when I absolutely despised peas, and I wasn't allowed to leave the table until I ate all of them off my plate. Took me a couple of hours tossing them one by one out the window when my parents weren't watching, but I finally completed the mission."

Millie scowled all the more fiercely. "You watch yourself, boy. Lucky for you, Emily's not quite old enough to understand all that yet. But soon enough, you'll have to take care what foolish notions you put into her head with such tales. Mark my words. Soon enough."

"I'm doing as I was told, aren't I?" He waved a chicken bone now cleaned of meat in the air. "Same as I'd expect of Emily."

"Her appetite's not the problem." Millie paused to pinch one of the little girl's chubby cheeks. Then, leaning back, she gestured to Noah's plate. "Now let's see some of those mashed potatoes sliding down your gullet."

Noah shot Beth a long-suffering look, then dug in. At the teasing give and take just now, his appetite had improved a bit. Indeed, he was rather enjoying himself. As he ate, he realized the Lord had answered his prayers. In the warm, companionable atmosphere of the kitchen, Noah's earlier misgivings about Beth had all but evaporated. She seemed so at home, so much a part of the family, that he could almost imagine her as a sister or, leastwise, the girl she had once been.

Almost. Beth was too beautiful to forget her potent appeal completely. But if he considered her as a fine young woman and never allowed his thoughts to progress further, he'd be safe enough. Instead of allowing his mind to turn to more carnal pursuits, he would instead just rejoice in her beauty and be happy for her. Indeed, after all she had gone through as a child, Beth deserved every happiness possible.

"Millie"–Beth's voice intruded suddenly into Noah's musings–"why don't you go on up to bed? Noah and I can finish Emily's bath, then get her tucked in."

Noah looked to his aunt. For the first time tonight he noticed how exhausted she appeared. Her face was pale and shadows were smudged beneath her eyes. Remorse at his utter selfishness filled him.

"Yes, you do look tired," he said. "Go on up to bed. We can finish in here."

Millie sighed wearily. "That does sound most appealing. Can I trust you, though, to clean at least half that plate if I leave you?"

Noah laughed. "Of course you can. You know you can trust me."

"Trust that all the food doesn't end up out the window, but in your stomach?"

"Most certainly. After all, you've got Beth as a witness."

Millie eyed him for a moment. "Yes, I suppose I do. And if you can't trust a doctor and a priest, who can you trust?"

"My sentiments exactly." Noah pushed back his chair, stood, and came around to where his aunt sat beside the tub. "Come along, m'lady." He grasped her elbow and pulled her to her feet. "Allow me to escort you to your bedchamber."

As soon as she was standing, Millie laughingly jerked her arm away. "I'm not that decrepit, you young whippersnapper, that I need an escort to my room. You just sit yourself back down and finish off your supper. That's all *you* need to do."

Millie paused only long enough to shoot Beth a grin, then turned and marched from the kitchen. When she was gone, Noah walked back and took his seat.

"She can get a bit feisty at times, Millie can," he offered by way of explanation. "She's always been one independent woman. She's had to be, to move all the way out here as a young woman of twenty in the late 1860s when my uncle got it into his head to start up a church in the middle of the Colorado high plains. Talk about some hard times, not to mention the Indians weren't all that friendly in those days, either."

Beth shrugged, then applied some shampoo to Emily's hair. "By then, the Indians had seen enough to realize the threat the settlers presented. The massacre at Sand Creek wasn't that many years earlier, you know."

"They were some of your mother's people, weren't they? The Cheyenne, I mean, who died at Sand Creek?"

"Yes, they were." Beth didn't look up, apparently intent on scrubbing a squirming Emily's head. "My mother was a year old. She and her mother were the only ones in their family to survive the massacre."

"If they'd lived long enough to see it, wouldn't your mother and grandmother be proud of what you've accomplished?"

Beth lifted her gaze to meet his. "And what exactly have I accomplished? That I was nearly able to hide my Indian heritage and pass for a white woman? That I so successfully learned white ways that I could attend a white man's medical school?"

Noah stared at her. He had thought she had shared her heart with him countless times when she was a girl. But Beth had never spoken of the pain of her Indian heritage, not even while she was growing up.

"I suppose I blundered pretty insensitively into that, didn't I?" he asked after an awkward silence. "I just never realized how proud you were of your Cheyenne heritage."

"Why would you realize it? I didn't think about it much myself until, far from the support of my family, I was faced with the unexpected bigotry I encountered back East. Those people, after all, had never encountered Indians, much less suffered at the hands of them, like we out here have." She gave a harsh laugh. "I earned more than just a medical degree while I was gone. I earned a degree in people, too, and I can't say as how I liked much of what I learned."

She glanced down, picked up a folded washcloth, and handed it to him. "I'm ready to rinse Emily's hair. Why don't you hold this over her eyes? It'll help keep most of the soap out of them."

Noah got up from his chair and placed the washcloth he had taken from Beth over his daughter's eyes.

"Close your eyes, sweetheart. We're going to rinse your hair now."

"Dadadada," Emily chirped, nodding her head and squirming in the tub.

With his free hand, Noah gently grasped her shoulder to steady her. "Better get this done with as quickly as you can." He looked up at Beth. "Emily isn't overly fond of getting her hair rinsed and can raise a ruckus if you take too long at it."

"So Millie warned me." Beth grabbed a pitcher. "She said to use this to hasten things along."

The next fifteen minutes were spent finishing up Emily's bath, then drying and dressing her in her diapers and nightgown. Leaving Beth to tidy the kitchen, Noah carried his daughter upstairs to bed. He tucked her into her crib, rubbed her back until she fell asleep, and then, his thoughts returning to Beth, headed downstairs.

He had no intention of letting her earlier slip of the tongue pass. He knew enough about pain to realize it didn't ease until you named it and faced it, enlisting the good Lord's aid in the doing. He could help Beth; it was his calling and when it came to helping others, he was very good at it.

Problem was, he wasn't all that good at helping himself anymore.

"Blithering idiot and stupid fool! That's what I am, and no mistake!"

As Beth worked to clean up after Noah and Emily had departed the kitchen, she repeatedly berated herself for her unfortunate slip of the tongue. It had been hard enough to hide the pain she felt at helping Millie care for Emily. Millie, though, was ill and needed her help. Besides, Beth knew she'd have to get over her self-protective aversion to children sooner or later. But whatever had possessed her to anguish over medical school and the problems she had encountered there to Noah? The priest was an astute man, sensitive to the deeper issues that frequently lay beneath the surface. And he cared, truly cared. Odds were, he wouldn't let her barely veiled rancor pass.

With a groan, Beth sank into a chair at the table and buried her face in her hands. What was she going to do now? Lie?

"No." Savagely Beth shook her head. "I'll not add lying to all my other sins. I'll not. I'll just tell Noah it's none of his business, that I don't wish to talk about it, and that'll be that."

Fortified with that resolve, she went back to work. By the time Noah returned from tucking in his daughter, Beth had set the kitchen aright, save for the dirty bathwater. And though the sight of her host's handsome face did momentarily unsettle her, Beth's determination rose immediately around her like the walls of a stone fortress.

Noah said little as he helped her dump the contents of the tub outside. After placing the tub in the enclosed porch, he strode back into the kitchen.

"Want a cup of coffee?" he asked, heading straight for the cookstove. "It'd go right nicely with a big piece of apple pie."

The last thing Beth wanted to do was settle down at the kitchen table for a cozy little chat. "No, thanks. I think I'll turn in."

A fresh mug in one hand, a steaming pot of coffee in the other, Noah turned. "It's not all that late." His glance strayed to the small clock on the cupboard. "Why, it's only a bit after eight. I haven't had much chance to talk with you since your return. Please stay a while longer so we can catch up."

"Fine." Beth wondered if he could hear the exasperation in her voice. "Just know right off I'm not talking about medical school or anything else personal."

He motioned her to sit at the table, then took his own seat. "If that's what you want, that's fine with me. You did first bring up the subject, though." Noah poured out a mug for Beth, then refilled his. "Most times I find people don't broach something unless it's really eating at them. And most times those things need some talking about to set them right."

Beth stirred a spoonful of sugar into her coffee, then sipped it tentatively. It was rich and strong, just as she liked it. With a sigh, she set the mug, and the excuse of drinking it, aside.

"Maybe so, Noah." She lifted her gaze to meet his. "I'm just not ready to talk, that's all. I'm sure you, of all people, can understand that. I'd imagine you're not all that ready to talk about Alice, are you?"

Pain darkened Noah's eyes. Pain and a knowledge of what she was trying to do.

Remorse flooded Beth. "I'm sorry, Noah. That was cruel. You deserve better than those lowdown mean tactics." She laughed, the sound rough and rasping in the quiet kitchen. "It *is* a good tactic, though, when your back's against the wall. Lash out, take someone else off at the knees before they can discover your weak spot and cripple you. Funny thing was, I learned that at medical school, where people supposedly go to become caring and compassionate healers."

"Sounds like medical school was a pretty hard place."

"Yes, it was." Beth took another swallow of her coffee, then lowered it to stare back at the man across from her.

71

If he thought she was going to bite on that open-ended statement, he was sadly mistaken.

Noah took a sip of his coffee, then averted his gaze. Beth filled the silent seconds studying his profile.

It was still an impressive visage. His nose was straight and strong, his jaw solid. Dark blond brows shaded his deep-set eyes, and the shadow of a beard washed the lower half of his face. There were new lines, though, deep furrows of pain and tension on either side of his mouth. And the gray lightly threading his temples added to the perception of age.

Yet Noah was only thirty-six. Beth knew not only his birthday but also the year he was born. She had committed those details to memory long ago, along with all the myriad bits of information she had managed to glean about the Reverend Noah Starr. A girl in love did that. And Beth had once been a girl in love.

"What will your sermon be about tomorrow?" she asked, choosing the first thought that entered her mind rather than dwell an instant longer on such maudlin—and pointless—daydreaming.

Noah's mouth twitched, perhaps in amusement, perhaps in defeat. It didn't matter. Beth knew she had won the battle of wills.

"I thought I'd talk about forgiveness. Seems like something we all need to work on."

"Do we now?" Beth cocked her head. "And what sort of insightful message do you have on that topic?"

Noah chuckled. "Well, I won't go so far as to claim any great insights. I do better just asking questions, stirring things up. Then I send everyone on their way to work it all through on their own."

Beth leaned forward, resting her forearms on the table, cradling the warm pottery mug between her hands. "And what sort of questions do you plan to ask about forgiveness?"

He shrugged. "Maybe something like why, after we've imagined we've forgiven someone, the old pain and anger come creeping back in anyway. Makes you question if you truly forgave in the first place."

"I've had that happen. Bet you have, too."

"Oh, yes. Indeed I have." Noah paused to take another drink of his coffee. "It distressed me greatly, too. Then one day at prayers I began to think more on the matter, and I realized remembering and feeling the pain all over again isn't the same as failing to forgive. Remembering a hurt is something God gave us to protect ourselves so we don't make the same mistake again. But remembering isn't the same as indulging in renewed thoughts of vengeance."

Something dark and anguished twisted within Beth. Matthew had begged her forgiveness, and she had thought she had given it. But late at night sometimes, in the dark, aching loneliness, she wasn't always so sure.

"Then what are we to do," she asked, in spite of her intent to keep a safe emotional distance, "with all the anger and feelings of impotence, of pain? If we give it all up to God, why doesn't He take it and forever put it from us?"

"I wish I knew, Beth. Forgiveness is a gift. And like many of His gifts, sometimes God gives it to us in all its fullness right away. And then, other times, the Lord lets us wait on that forgiveness a bit."

Beth frowned. "Shouldn't something so all-fired important to God come easier? He's the one, after all, who puts such store on forgiveness."

"Yes, He does, doesn't He?" Noah smiled. "Some lessons, though, can only be learned in struggle—lessons about ourselves, about others, and about the kingdom of heaven. Like most things, in the end it all comes down to trusting in God and allowing Him to work in us in His own good time."

"Seems to me, if God wanted anything to work swift and sure, it'd be forgiveness. Leastwise, the business of forgiving others."

The priest smiled wryly. "As opposed to what—the forgiveness of oneself?"

"Yes. That's the hardest thing to forgive. Ourselves, I mean."

"And why's that, do you think?"

Beth opened her mouth to explain, then caught herself just in time. Noah was a sly one, that he was. He had played his waiting game well. He had almost gotten her to reveal what she had earlier been so adamant about not revealing.

"I don't know." She locked gazes with him, refusing to back down. "Why don't you tell me? After all, you're the expert on forgiveness."

"I'm no expert, Beth," Noah said softly. "Far from it. After all, I just ask the questions. With the Lord's help, everyone has to find their own answers."

"Hogwash!" Beth couldn't help getting angry, very angry. "When it comes to forgiveness, aren't all the answers the same?"

As if unable to bear her scrutiny or the challenge burning in her eyes, Noah looked down at his mug of coffee. "I'm not so sure they are, Beth. Leastwise, if they were, I think we'd all come to that forgiveness a lot quicker than we do."

Noah lifted his glance to hers, and Beth saw the most heartrending look of confusion and pain. Her anger fled, banished by the rising concern she felt for him.

"Then maybe, just maybe," she said, though she didn't know how such words came to her, or even how much she really believed them, "that's why the Lord gives us each other to learn from. In coming to understand others, we arrive finally at an understanding of ourselves. And in forgiving others, we learn at last how to forgive ourselves."

6

*We wait for light, but behold obscurity; for brightness,
but we walk in darkness.*

Isaiah 59:9

On Monday morning Beth was up bright and early. Her first day of work with Doc Childress and her first day of service to the people of Grand View! She was so excited she could hardly contain herself.

After her morning ablutions, she dressed, piled and pinned her hair atop her head, and headed for the kitchen. Noah, in black trousers, shoes, and a collarless clerical shirt, was already there, adding wood to the cast-iron cookstove. At Beth's entry, he rose, a smile of welcome on his lips.

"Well, good morning, Dr. MacKay." He briefly scanned her, then nodded his approval. "You're looking quite prim, proper, and professional this morning."

Beth laughed. Her navy skirt and pin-tucked white, high-collared blouse, adorned with a pert little black bow tie, was pretty much her usual wear. Never one for frilly clothes, Beth felt far more appropriately dressed–and comfortable–in simpler garb.

"Sure beats the overalls and boy's shirts I used to love wearing," she said. "And plain clothing's more sanitary and presents a reassuring appearance to a patient. Besides, I gave up long ago trying to dress to catch a man's eye."

"My dear, you could catch a man's eye dressed in a flour sack."

Beth couldn't help it–a flush swept up her neck and warmed her cheeks. Though she knew she shouldn't let the compliment affect her so, convinced as she was Noah only meant it in the kindest of ways, Beth was discomfited nonetheless. Masculine attention, especially the admiring kind, was the last thing she wanted.

"I doubt Doc would take kindly to having his new colleague appear in such garb. Might send his patients hightailing it all the way to Colorado Springs for a new doctor."

Noah grinned. "You're most likely right. Still, the thought does present some delightful images."

"Shame on you, Noah Starr!" Beth couldn't help a giggle. "And you a man of the cloth!"

He shrugged, took the coffeepot from the stove, and removed the filter basket. He filled the pot with water and put it back on the stove to heat. Then, walking to the cupboard, Noah took down a tin canister of coffee. After filling the coffee mill, he carried it to the table, sat down, and began grinding.

"Reckon I don't know how to give out the compliments anymore," he observed mildly. "I promise never to mention a flour sack in your presence ever again."

Beth gave a snort of disbelief. "Or, leastwise, until the next opportunity arises. You don't fool me. Unless my memory fails me, if some prank was played at a church picnic, you were always the first suspect."

Noah smirked. "Well, somebody had to stir a little life into those picnics. If the church's Ladies' Social Club had anything to say about it, we would've spent an hour in prayer before the meal, then set down to eat in total silence before sending everyone on their way."

"Yes, I do recall some of those ladies were a bit stodgy when it came to innocent fun," Beth admitted. She gestured toward the coffee mill Noah was still grinding. "Are you planning on pulverizing those beans to dust? If not, by the sound of the mill, the coffee's ready to make."

With a jerk and rueful shake of his head, Noah grabbed the coffee mill and stood. "Sorry. For a minute there, my mind had wandered back to you and the flour sack."

If it had been anyone else but Noah, Beth would've suspected a man on the lookout for a flirtation or even more. But this was Noah, and she was well aware of his teasing bent.

"Perhaps it's time," she said, "we get started on breakfast. Shall I go up and fetch Millie to help?"

Noah shook his head emphatically. "No, let her sleep. She hasn't been looking all that well in the past few months, and I'm worried about her."

Beth bit her tongue and glanced away. So Noah wasn't as oblivious to Millie's declining health as he may have appeared to be. And Millie's heart wasn't in good shape. With just chest percussion and stethoscope auscultation, along with a history of her symptoms, Doc had quickly ascertained Millie's heart was enlarged, weakening, and failing to adequately remove the excess fluid from her lungs. He had put Millie on digitalis that very day Beth had brought her to see him. Only time would tell if they had begun treatment in time.

"Perhaps it's just the strain of caring for Emily as she grows bigger," Beth offered. "And now that I'm here, I can help ease some of her load."

"Though I appreciate your offer, it's not your responsibility. It's mine."

The priest filled the coffee filter basket with the freshly ground beans and inserted the percolator tube. Then he walked back to the stove and put the contraption in the coffeepot.

For a long moment, Beth watched him stand there, shoulders stiff, his back to her. He was correct—Emily and any and all of Noah's other problems weren't her responsibility. Besides, what possible good would be served involving herself in their lives? Indeed, in anyone's lives? That wasn't the reason she had returned to Grand View. She had come back to begin anew and rediscover what she had lost of herself during those grueling years of her medical training.

"Yes, you're right," she agreed quietly. "Emily and Millie aren't my responsibility. I imagine I'll be busy enough helping Doc take care of all the folk in Grand View." Beth paused to glance around the kitchen. "So what's the plan for breakfast? I need to get over to the clinic, but I could sure use a good meal first to fortify me for the day."

"Well, there's eggs, milk, and bacon in the icebox." He indicated the four-foot-high carved hardwood box beside the sink. "The bread's over there on the sideboard, in the breadbox."

Beth arched a brow. "So are you hinting I should make breakfast?"

"I can do it, but it'll have to wait until I finish with Emily. I hear her starting to make noise upstairs. If I don't get to her right away, she'll wake Millie."

"Well, then get on with you." Beth made a shooing motion in the direction of the hall leading to the stairs.

"I think I can remember how to fry up some bacon and eggs."

Noah grinned. "I was hoping you'd say that. Not that I'm asking so as to take advantage of you, or anything . . ."

"Of course not." Beth rolled her eyes. Then with a laugh she turned and headed for the icebox.

֍

An hour later, Beth walked into the clinic. Helen was already at her desk. Three patients—an elderly man Beth didn't recognize, Mrs. Nealy, the blacksmith's wife, and a middle-aged woman with a small, crying child on her lap—had already arrived and were ensconced in the waiting area. Beth paused to meet each of their curious gazes before walking over to Helen.

"So, is Doc in?" She placed her hands on Helen's desk and leaned forward.

Helen nodded. "Yes, ma'am. He came in about fifteen minutes ago."

"And what are these patients' complaints?"

"Well"—Helen glanced down at her notes—"Mrs. Nealy's got problems with her hips again. Mr. Herring thinks he's going deaf. And Mrs. Stout's boy, Abraham, just keeps crying and pulling at his left ear. He also has a fever of 102 degrees." She glanced at the watch she wore pinned to her blouse. "And in a half hour, the patients with appointments will start coming in. We've four scheduled this morning and another four this afternoon."

"Any house calls for today?"

Helen shook her head. "Not today. Plenty tomorrow, though, plus clinic appointments."

Beth straightened. A pretty routine day, it seemed. "Guess I'll go see what Doc's up to then."

79

"Here." Helen handed her a chart. "That's the Stout boy's. Doc should see him first." She pointed to a note she'd clipped to the chart.

No money. Will pay in trade. Beth frowned and, after pausing to knock on the door, walked into Doc's office.

At her entrance, John Childress looked up. Laying aside his pen, he smiled. "Well, well, here bright and early for your first day, are you?"

Beth closed the door behind her, then came to stand before his desk. "Helen says this is our first case." She handed the chart to him. "I'd bet on a left otitis media. And as you can see, they have no money."

The older man took a look at Helen's note, then laid the chart on his desk. "Ah, yes. The Stouts. Fine, upstanding family. They've got five children, and the father works at the creamery washing out the milk cans and cleaning up. Mrs. Stout takes in ironing and laundry."

"Is there anything else I should know before we see them then?" she asked. "Medically speaking, I mean?"

Doc paused to scratch his jaw. "Well, they're good, God-fearing folk and try to feed and clothe their children as best as they know how. They attend the Episcopal church—sit way in the back so you probably didn't notice them yesterday—and their oldest girl, Luanne, just graduated this past June and was a straight-A student at Grand View's high school. The three older boys are showing promise, too. And the baby, well, if he takes after the rest of his—"

"So there's no other medical problems or family medical history that might influence this case?" Beth interrupted.

Doc arched a graying brow. "No. It's important, though, that you learn something about these people. They're not just diseases or illnesses, you know."

She had offended him yet again. When would she learn to hold her tongue? If Doc put such store in all this extraneous trivia, that was his choice. She'd just have to keep quiet and endure until she was finally free to see her own patients in her own way.

"Yes, I know they're more than diseases or illnesses," Beth hurried to explain. "Guess I'm just so eager to begin today that I'm being a bit abrupt. Go on. Tell me whatever else you need to about the Stouts."

"That's pretty much it, I suppose." He managed a rueful smile. "Reckon I'm getting a bit slow at times. And I've known most of these folk for years. Can't expect you to pick up everything about them the first time you meet them."

The child—Abraham—had a clear-cut case of an infected middle ear. That was all Beth needed to know. Their social history was hardly of any bearing on her diagnosis and treatment plan.

"Well, shall we call them in then?" Beth chose to say instead, indicating the door. "I can fetch them if you'd like."

Doc grinned broadly. "By all means. I've a real hankering to see some big-city doctoring. Never too old to learn something new, you know."

Beth smiled in return. "No, you never are."

As the weeks passed and a wide variety of patients passed through the clinic, Beth became reacquainted with all the folk she had once known and learned a lot about the newcomers to Grand View, too. More than she really cared to know, if the truth be told. But from that first day until the day, a month later, when Doc announced she was free to start seeing her own patients anytime she wished, Beth had carefully guarded her tongue—and her frequently divergent opinions.

81

It wasn't that Doc wasn't a good physician. He had a diagnostician's gut instincts, a solid if somewhat out-of-date knowledge base, and years of experience that had served him well. And he truly cared about his patients. They in turn loved and revered him for his years of devoted service to the town.

But even with two physicians in the growing town, there were still so many unmet needs. Efficiency and time management were of the essence. And Doc squandered far too much time in patient visits with pointless social conversation. Once she took over the practice, Beth intended to make a lot of changes. For now, though, all she could do was try to make some progress with her own patients.

Plenty of folk, however, seemed reluctant—if not downright against—being seen by a woman doctor. Even once Helen was given the go-ahead to make appointments for her, Beth averaged only one patient of her own a day.

"Just give it time, my dear," Doc Childress said to console her one afternoon two months after Beth had returned to Grand View. "I knew folk would be hesitant at first. Let's face it. You're young, fresh out of your internship, and you're a woman. And they've known me for years and trust me. It'll just take a while—"

"But I can't support myself for long on the fees generated by one patient a day!"

Doc had stepped into her office as she was restocking her cabinet. He came around to sit at her desk. Beth shot him a frustrated look over her shoulder, then turned back to her task.

"At the very least, I've room and board to pay. And I'm not bringing much money into the practice, either!"

"I know. That's not a concern of mine, though. I knew it'd take a while. I can meet your basic expenses for the time being. Besides, I'm willing to bet Millie and Noah will give you time, too. One more mouth to feed won't break them, either."

"That's not the point." Beth could feel her voice going tight, her anger rising. "I have my pride, and I won't accept charity. If I can't pay my bills . . . well, I guess I'll have to move back in with my parents!"

Doc chuckled. "Land sakes, my dear. Don't make that sound like a fate worse than death. From what I hear, Conor and Abby would be tickled pink to have you back home to stay."

Beth sighed in exasperation, closed her eyes, and shook her head. "What else can I do, Doc? I'm about willing to start treating livestock if that's what it takes."

"If you feel a calling to that, I suppose helping out some of the ranchers and farmers with their animals couldn't hurt. Once they'd a chance to see you in action . . ."

She opened her eyes and glared at him. "You can't be serious."

It was Doc's turn to sigh. "Okay, it was just an idea." He lowered his gaze. "Have you taken any of the patients up on coming to supper? And besides attending Sunday services, have you gotten out and socialized? That's another way to build relationships and keep yourself foremost in people's minds."

"I don't think that's wise." Beth clamped her lips. "It's best to maintain a certain professional distance."

Doc gave a snort of disgust. "I can't believe I'm hearing that from you, Beth MacKay! You've grown up here. A lot of these people knew you since you were a child. And this isn't some big, impersonal city where you rarely run into your patients. It also isn't some place you plan to stay for a few years, then move on. You've got to build trust, and that takes a while. You've got to build lifetime relationships."

Beth went back to stocking bandages in her cabinet. "I find I do my best work when I keep myself a bit removed from my patients. Emotions can cloud judgment and good diagnosis. Maybe in time, when I've had more experience . . ."

"Pshaw!" Doc slammed his fist so hard on the desk it made Beth jump. "That's the biggest load of hogwash I've ever heard, and from a physician, no less. What are they teaching in medical school nowadays?"

"A whole lot more than when you went, I'd say!" She wheeled around, her hands fisted on her hips.

Doc stared up at her. "Seems to me when you forget you're taking care of a human being with needs, fears, hopes, and dreams, you might as well stop calling yourself a doctor. We're called to care for the whole person, not just his or her symptoms and medical data. And if we don't, in the course of our treatment, also touch their hearts, then we haven't done our job."

"I'm an excellent doctor. I graduated at the top of my class."

"In the end, the patients decide who the good doctors are and who're the bad. You can't fool them for long."

Tears stung Beth's eyes. She blinked them away. She hadn't cried during all those years in medical school or during her internship. Why was she so near weeping now?

"So you're saying I'm not a good doctor because the patients don't like me. Is that it?"

A sad, solemn look darkened his eyes. "No, Beth. I'm not saying you aren't a good doctor. I'm just saying you still have some things to learn to be an excellent doctor."

"Well, you'll forgive me if I don't care to give your words much credence. I know how to build rapport with patients. I listen to them. In the end, though, it's my education, my knowledge, that they've come for.

And it's my professional responsibility to use it the best way I know how."

"Suit yourself." Doc rose from behind the desk. "I've worked long enough with you now to know your medical judgment is next to faultless, your treatments right on the money. I can live with your style of patient care if you can. But you asked for my input, and I gave it."

I've gone and started another fight, Beth thought in frustration. Will I never learn?

"I'm sorry if I got a little defensive there." She managed a conciliatory smile. "I guess I'm still finding my way, still searching for my own 'style' as you called it. But I'll give your words consideration. I promise."

"Beth, maybe I shouldn't be saying this, but it seems to me you've got some things . . . some personal pain . . . that's getting in the way here. If you ever want to talk . . ."

Once more the tears welled; she was on the verge of spilling her guts, but this wasn't the time or place. She was a professional, after all.

She wheeled around to hide the traitorous tears. "Thank you. I'll keep that in mind." She made a great show of checking her watch. "Will you look at that? Time for lunch."

Taking great care not to let Doc see her face, she hurried to her desk and picked up her hat and pocketbook. "Mind if I take an extra hour off? I don't have any appointments this afternoon, and Millie could probably use the help."

"Take the whole afternoon off if you want. I can manage, and if there's some emergency, it'll be easy enough to ring you up at the rectory."

Beth nodded curtly, then all but fled for the door. "Thank you. I'll do that then."

85

Noah shrugged on his coat and grabbed his hat from the coatrack. As he did, a knock sounded at the door. He left the hat where it was hanging and opened the door.

Conor MacKay stood there.

"Come on in," Noah said, smiling in greeting. "If you've come to see Beth, though, she isn't here. You'd do better to head to the clinic."

"I didn't come to see Beth," Culdee Creek's owner muttered as he doffed his Stetson and walked in. "I came to see you, if you've got a few minutes to spare."

"I've always got time for an old friend. I was just getting ready to pay George Wilson a call, but it can wait a while longer." Noah closed the door behind Conor. "Where would you like to talk? Would the kitchen suit, or do you prefer my office? If it's the kitchen, I'm thinking Millie's still got a piece left of her famous apple pie, and the coffee's always hot."

Conor shook his head. "No, thanks. I'm not much in the mood for food, and I've already drunk more coffee this morning than Abby likes me to have in a day." He used his hat to point in the direction of the kitchen. "We can sit in there, though."

Noah paused to remove his jacket and hang it back on the coatrack, then followed Conor into the kitchen. He took a seat across from his friend, leaned his forearms on the table, and waited.

Conor wasn't long in getting to the point. "It's Beth. Abby and I are concerned about her."

Noah wasn't surprised. If he had so quickly ascertained Beth harbored some secret pain, her parents would've surely noticed it even earlier.

"What's bothering you? About Beth, I mean?"

"Well, she came home as thin as a rail, and that's not like her. Then, though she stayed a week at the ranch, I couldn't quite shake the feeling she couldn't wait to get away from us. And the day Beth told Abby she was moving in with you, Beth let slip she'd been through some pretty rough times in medical school. Times she felt she didn't dare tell us about, for fear we would've gone out there and brought her home."

"Which you would've, wouldn't you, Conor, if you'd thought anyone was threatening your little girl?"

Culdee Creek's owner smiled thinly. "Yes, I reckon I would've."

"And Beth's got your pride and determination. Can you blame her for not telling you all that was going on?"

"No, I can't blame her, but what did it cost her, Noah? What happened to her?"

Noah leaned back and sighed. "I can't say, Conor. But you know if Beth ever comes to me with the truth, I'll do my best to help her."

"I know. That's why I thought I'd better tell you this. So you could keep an eye out for her." He paused, scratched his jaw, and eyed Noah consideringly. "I've never told you much about Beth's past, have I? I mean, not much more anyway, than she was born out of wedlock when I hired on Squirrel Woman to take care of Evan after his mother ran off with that music teacher of hers?"

"That's pretty much it," Noah said. "That and Beth and Abby didn't hit it off well when Abby first came to Culdee Creek to be your housekeeper and Beth's teacher."

"Well, there's more, and it might have a lot to do with Beth's pain right now." He glanced over at the stove. "Maybe I will take you up on that cup of coffee after all."

Noah scraped back his chair, rose, and headed for the cupboard. After grabbing a mug, he walked to the stove and poured out another cup of coffee. "Go on," he then urged his friend as he placed the mug before him and again took his seat. "What else happened to Beth that I don't know about?"

"Well, after Squirrel Woman died of smallpox when Beth was two years old, I ran through a passel of house-keepers." He smiled wryly. "Seems I wasn't the most pleasant of people to be around in those days. Then when Beth was seven, a woman named Maudie came to work for me. She was young, pretty, and wanted something. That something turned out to be me. When she finally realized I'd no intention ever of wedding her, she devised a scheme to win my heart through my daughter."

Conor grimaced. "Maudie treated her so sugar sweet, even I began to suspect something. I finally had to send the woman away. She knew, though, there was only one sure way to punish me for rejecting her, and she used Beth to do it."

Noah could feel his blood run cold. "She used a seven-year-old girl to get back at her father?"

Conor nodded slowly. "Maudie took Beth to school that last day she worked for me, claiming she just wanted a chance for a final good-bye. Once there, though, Maudie somehow managed to slip into the schoolhouse while the children and their teacher were outside at recess. She stole the big gold pocket watch Sullivan–the teacher–always kept on his desk. Beth, of course, was the one accused of taking it."

"Did Beth see Maudie take the watch?"

"Yes, but I didn't find that out until much later." Conor dragged in an unsteady breath. "Her teacher made her stand before the whole class while he called her a bas-tard and half-breed little thief. He beat her across her knuckles until they bled. And, when even that didn't extract the answers he wanted, Sullivan locked her in a small, dark storage closet next to the woodstove. He left her there for six hours, the stove burning hot all the while, until I came to fetch her.

"By the time I carried her out of the closet, Beth was half dead from the heat and lack of water. And when I got her home, she wouldn't talk for five months."

Noah's heart clenched at the sudden swell of pain. It explained so much about Beth's prickly pride and what seemed to be an underlying sense of rejection and unworthiness. Though he knew Conor loved her with all his heart, she would always be his illegitimate, half-breed Indian daughter. Perhaps somewhere, in some deep, hidden place, that realization still hurt Beth. It also made her vulnerable to the cruelty of others. Cruelty she had most obviously suffered during medical school.

Noah took a swallow of his coffee, then met his friend's tormented gaze. "It helps knowing that. Helps a lot."

Conor's mouth quirked sadly. "I don't like talking about that time in Beth's life. Especially knowing it was all my fault. But I thought you should know, in case Beth ever mentions it." He sighed. "Much as I hate to admit it, my little girl's all grown up and I can't protect her anymore. Fact is, she might not even like coming to me with all her problems."

"I can't promise Beth'll come to me, either."

"No, she might not. But just in case, I wanted you to know." Conor rose. "I hope it is you, though. You'll know how to handle it."

Will I? Noah thought. There were times he wondered how effective he was anymore. It was hard to help others when your whole life—and all it had ever stood for—seemed to be crumbling before your eyes. Still, he had to keep on trying, hoping that sooner or later all would be made clear.

Noah rose to his feet. "As I said before, I'll do my best for her. You know that."

Conor MacKay nodded. "Yes, I know."

7

We are perplexed, but not in despair; persecuted, but not forsaken; cast down, but not destroyed.

2 Corinthians 4:8–9

Once she was out in the crisp October sunshine, Beth didn't head straight for the rectory. As upset as she was, just one concerned, caring comment from Millie and she was sure to break down and bawl her eyes out. No, it was best to keep to herself until she could regain control. A good, brisk walk would do her a world of good.

Beth strode down the boardwalk along Main Street. A few riders passed by–a farm wagon full of potatoes fresh from the fields and the town fire truck out for a spin, filled with what looked to be the entire elementary school. They waved and called out to her and everyone else who looked their way.

She managed a halfhearted wave and smile; most of the children didn't know her anyway. Then Doc's words came back to her. *This isn't some big, impersonal city where you rarely run into your patients. . . . You've got to build trust. . . . You've got to build lifetime relationships. . . . And if we don't . . . also touch their hearts, then we haven't done our job.*

Touch hearts . . . Beth shook her head in irritation. Why was everyone so bent on getting involved in everyone else's life? Were they blind to the potential pain of rejection? She, on the other hand, had learned her lesson early and well: Don't open your heart to strangers, or they'd sooner or later use and abuse it. People weren't to be trusted. Neither, it seemed, Beth added bitterly, was God.

Well, leastwise, not most people. Beth knew she could trust her family. And she supposed Millie and Noah would never knowingly do anything to hurt her. Still, Noah had hurt her when he had wed Alice, even if he hadn't done it on purpose. The pain of that was all over now, though. And as long as he never learned the truth about her and Matthew . . .

"Hello! Where are you going at such a fast and furious pace?"

Beth lurched to a halt. In the street next to her, a black buggy slowed to a stop. Noah sat in the two-seater, dressed in his hat and clerical garb.

Beth glanced around. She had walked past Gates's Mercantile and was almost to Mr. Herring's house at the edge of town. She grinned sheepishly.

"Guess I was so engrossed in my thoughts, I lost track of where I was headed."

Noah patted the empty seat beside him. "Well, jump in. I was just heading home after paying George Wilson a visit, and as I turned back down Main Street, I saw you."

"No, thanks." Beth shook her head. "I've got some thinking to do. I'm not ready to head home yet."

91

"Well, a nice, relaxing ride out into the country would do me a world of good, too. And I promise not to talk, if you're not of a mind for talking."

Beth thought on his offer for a moment, then nodded. Why not? "Okay, but only if you promise not to ask any questions."

Noah grinned. "I promise. If you don't want to talk, we won't. Now, climb on in, m'lady."

Beth did just that.

They rode along in silence for a time. Though the breeze was cool, the sun was warm. Beth found herself gradually relaxing and even reveling in the sight of the scenery around them.

To their right, the hills smoothed southward into low, undulating masses, the rich, dark soil easing to sand. Frost-browned prairie grass parted before the ever-churning onslaught of the buggy's steel-spoked wheels. North of them, pine-tree-studded bluffs rose from the land, stark sentinels of the rolling hills.

A lone red-tailed hawk soared overhead on the blustery currents. Occasionally a brown ground squirrel, his long, sleek tail flitting behind him, darted from some tunnel in the earth. But other than those creatures and the ever-present pronghorns, little else was stirring today.

Beth exhaled a long, deep breath, leaned back against the buggy's padded seat, and sighed. This was her home, the land she knew and loved through all its vagaries of season and weather. It played no games, bore no secret agendas, and treated all the same, no matter the race, creed, or gender. Out on these high, windswept plains, the Front Range of the Rocky Mountains rising behind her in the distance, Beth felt whole, at peace, safe.

She felt safe with Noah, too. He had always accepted her, respected her, and made her feel loved and worth-while. Well, Beth amended quickly, not quite as loved as she had wished he would love her, when she had finally grown into young womanhood, but that hadn't been his fault. To the best of his ability, Noah had always been honest with her. That was better than most men had treated her ever since.

She shot him a sideways glance. He smiled as he drove along, his gaze riveted straight ahead, one foot braced against the front panel, his arm resting on his slightly raised leg. The lines of tension that so frequently tightened his face had softened a bit. He appeared to be enjoying this ride as much as she. Did he, as well, enjoy her presence as much as she was enjoying his?

With a grimace of disgust, Beth flung that foolish question aside. It was beginning to border on the ridic-ulous how often and easily her mind turned to roman-tic notions, notions she had long ago rejected. Medicine was her only love, her lifelong calling.

But even that wasn't going well. Doc had all but told her she was an inadequate physician. Though for entirely different reasons, his comments cut as deeply as had those of her fellow medical students and instruc-tors during the years of her training. Would she never measure up in the eyes of her male colleagues?

Beth told herself that it shouldn't matter what others thought, that it only mattered what she thought. Yet peace and self-acceptance eluded her, and she couldn't understand why.

Does Noah, Beth wondered, ever encounter such questions in his own life? She supposed he had all he needed in God and the Bible. But Noah had suffered greatly when he lost Alice. He'd continue to suffer, too, all the days of Emily's life, knowing she'd never be able to run and play like other children or even live an independent life. How, indeed, did his faith sustain him anymore?

Beth had seen too much needless pain and suffering, had encountered too much cruelty and hypocrisy, to believe in a merciful God. How could Noah continue to believe?

She turned to him. "Would you mind if I asked . . . asked a rather personal question?"

A smile quirked the corner of Noah's mouth. "Depends. If I answer it, do I get to ask you one in turn?"

Beth thought for a moment, then shook her head. "Never mind. I withdraw my question. It's not fair for me to ask you and not be willing to have you do the same. And I'm not."

"Oh, Beth." Noah sighed. "What happened to you back East to change you from that trusting, open, happy girl you used to be? None of us here purposely have done anything to hurt you, yet your fear of us is all but palpable."

Beth didn't know how to answer without sharing more than she cared to reveal. She looked away, all the old, angry emotions rising again. "I told you. I withdraw my question. Can we let it go at that?"

"What's your question, Beth?" he asked softly, gently. "Ask me anything, and I'll answer you the best I know how."

"No." Fiercely, she shook her head. "It wouldn't be fair."

"Fairness has nothing to do with it. You're hurting. I can see that. You're suspicious and afraid. Well, if it takes me baring my soul to break down those walls of yours, then I'm willing to risk it."

"Why?" She turned back to Noah, tears of confusion blurring her vision. She furiously blinked them away. "Why would you do that?"

"Why else?" His brown eyes shone with love. "Because maybe, just maybe, if I take the first step toward you, then you'll someday take one back to me. Back to me and all the people who've always loved you."

She looked down, unable to bear the intensity of his gaze. "It was nothing really anyway. My question, I mean. I was just thinking about all you'd suffered in losing Alice, then what's happened to Emily. And I wondered how you keep your faith so strong."

With a tug on the reins, Noah halted the buggy. He wrapped the lines around the brake arm, then turned in the seat to face her.

"What makes you think my faith is particularly strong right now?"

Beth stared at him. "You're still a priest, aren't you? You're still here, serving your congregation, going about your work every day."

He smiled sadly. "Sometimes you go on in spite of yourself. Because people need you. Because you hope with all your might that sooner or later the darkness will lift and the Lord will be there right where He has always been all along. When you lose faith, you go on out of sheer, stubborn determination and a lot of hope."

"If God has deserted you, one of His most faithful servants," Beth said grimly, "then He's not a God I care to serve."

"Ah, Beth, I don't really think God's deserted me."

Noah scooted close and took her hands. He looked into her eyes, and Beth saw his anguish—and his conviction.

"Well, leastwise not in my mind anyway," he admitted. "In my heart, though . . ." He shook his head with a savage intensity. "It doesn't matter. Great and holy feelings are wonderful gifts from God, but there are still times when you just have to hang on with all your might.

95

And that's what I'm doing—holding on with all my might and putting my trust in the Lord."

She could see the pain, the torment Noah was in. But she could see his courage, too. His sheer, stubborn trust and love for a God who she wasn't so sure could ever be deserving of him.

"You've held on for two years like this, haven't you?" Beth released a slow, deep breath. "I admire that in you, Noah. I truly do."

"And your admiration's deeply appreciated," he said with a wry chuckle. "It's been a lonely road, to be sure. It's not like I can share this with most people. Folk don't like to know their pastor's in such dire straits."

"Well, they won't be hearing it from me." Beth cocked her head. "Have you thought about marrying again? That might help in so many ways. You'd have someone to share your doubts and fears with. You'd have someone to help you with Emily, be a mother to her, and . . . well, you'd have a wife," she finished lamely.

Noah looked away. "No. I don't want to remarry."

She opened her mouth to ask him why, then clamped it shut. She had pried enough.

"You'll accept friendship, though, won't you? Because if you will, I'd like to offer you mine," Beth said, wondering even as she did if, when it came to Noah Starr, friendship in itself wasn't a pitfall-ridden country.

Noah turned back then, his eyes crinkling at the corners. "Of course I'll accept friendship, especially yours. Nothing would give me greater pleasure."

For a long moment, silence fell between them, and they sat there, staring into each other's eyes. And, as they sat there, a fierce, sweet joy warred with a growing uncertainty in Beth. It—this—was yet more uncharted territory. She must not forget he had hurt her before and could well do so again. To be Noah's friend, his confidante, perhaps even his special solace when there was none to be found elsewhere was taking a big chance.

As they remained there, though, something changed between them. The light in Noah's eyes flared; his grip on her hands tightened. Beth's heart commenced a rapid beating.

Just then, the horse's head flew up. The animal gave a snort of surprise and lurched forward.

Noah released Beth's hands and grabbed at the reins. Before the horse could take two steps, he had the animal back under control. He pulled it to a halt.

"Well, so much for my problems," he said, grinning at her. "Anything you'd care to share about yours?"

Her hands still gripping the carriage for support, Beth stared back. "Me? No, not really. After hearing what you had to say, I'm thinking my problems aren't all that serious." She shrugged surprised at the sudden wave of relief that swamped her. "Nothing, at any rate, that a little time and effort won't put right."

"Then I helped you anyway, didn't I?"

She thought about it for a moment. "I guess you did." Beth shot him a narrowed glance. "You're a sly one, that you are, Noah Starr."

He chuckled. "I've been called that a time or two, but really, it's just the healing that comes from two people talking and finding understanding in each other. Knowing they're not alone or so very different." As if a sudden idea had struck him, Noah paused. "And you know something else, Doctor?"

"What's that?"

"You're pretty sly yourself. In getting me to talk about myself, you've helped me. I don't feel quite so sad or hopeless anymore."

Happiness welled and spilled over within her. "Really, Noah? I helped you?"

"Yes, Beth," he said, his voice husky with emotion. "You did."

&

Noah dropped Beth off at the rectory, put up the horse and buggy, then headed straight for his office in the church basement. He checked his desk for any messages and found none. A letter, however, had been propped up in the most conspicuous place possible, against his worn Bible.

Briefly, Noah noted the return address was from his old seminary, then shoved the letter into his jacket pocket. He'd read it later. Right now, he had more pressing matters to attend to. He needed to spend some time with the Lord.

As soon as Noah walked upstairs and entered the church, a familiar sense of holiness, of entering a sacred space, engulfed him. No matter how dark his thoughts, how tormented his heart, he realized with the deepest gratitude that God never left him.

He made his way to the altar and knelt before it. Gazing up at the cross, he clasped his hands before him and prayed.

"It hasn't gotten any better, Lord," Noah whispered, his low voice echoing softly in the empty church. "I'd thought it had. I'd thought I'd gained mastery of it, but today . . . today when I held her hands and we spoke of friendship . . . well, You know as well as I my feelings quickly transformed to those of lust."

His mouth curved at one corner. "It was You, wasn't it, who spooked the horse? I felt Your hand in that, and I thank You. Still, we both know I can't expect You to rescue me each and every time my mind takes such carnal turns. This is my battle. Trouble is, the more I get to know Beth, the more time I spend with her, the more I want her."

He bowed his head, resting it against his clenched hands. No, God wouldn't continue to rescue him. God expected him to work this problem—this heart-wrenching temptation—out himself. And the best, well, the easiest, tactic was to turn one's back on it and walk away.

Walk away from Beth . . . Send her away . . .

Noah shook his head. "And how am I to do that, Lord? How would I explain that to Beth, to Millie, to Conor and Abby? After what Beth and I shared today, how could I continue to call myself her friend and do such a thing? It would hurt her, Lord. Surely that's not what You want?"

But if not that, then what did God want him to do?

As if to free the answer from the depths of his brain, Noah pounded his clasped hands against his forehead. No answer came, however. He still faced the same frustrating dilemma: harbor temptation in his own house or risk wounding an innocent woman by sending her away for something she hadn't willingly or knowingly caused.

No matter how he looked at it, Noah could see no solution. Even worse, though, he was beginning to wonder what kind of man he was becoming.

"So," Millie said as she stirred the mashed sweet potatoes, then poured the mixture into a baking pan, "you *are* going to the Fall Social tomorrow evening, aren't you?"

Beth looked up from the pork roast she had just finished sliding onto a platter. It smelled heavenly, seasoned as it was with bread crumbs, rosemary, and garlic. "To tell you the truth, I decided to pass on the social.

My newest medical journal just arrived, and I thought I'd spend the next couple of evenings reading it."

"Pshaw!" Millie paused to spoon brown sugar over the sweet potatoes, then shoved the pan into the oven to brown for a few minutes. "It's not healthy to hole up in your room every night after supper and study. Why, at the very least, you'll get eyestrain and need spectacles."

"I read by the oil lamp. The light's very good. I won't get eyestrain."

"Well, then," Millie said, "have you given any thought to the fact that as a doctor in this town, you've a duty to get out in public on a social as well as professional basis? The more folk see you out and about, the more they get to know you as a fine human being as well as an excellent doctor, and the better it'll be for your practice."

Beth scowled. Had Millie been talking to Doc Childress? It sure sounded as if she had. Still, she had a valid point. But a valid point, Beth amended swiftly, if and only if one was inclined to go along with Doc's view anyway.

"I don't know, Millie." She shook her head. "I've never been the sort to line up with all the other single ladies on one side of the hall, bat my eyes, and hope some brave man will saunter over to ask me to dance. And since I'm not even in the market for a husband, it wouldn't be fair—"

"Noah can escort you!" As if a flash of inspiration had struck her, Millie grinned and nodded vigorously. "That way you can stick with him all evening, not look as if you're there to meet other men, and still get out and show your face in public. Everyone will see your efforts to mingle socially, you'll make new friends and acquaintances, and all at no cost or embarrassment to yourself. It's a brilliant plan, if I do say so myself!"

Just then Noah walked in. Closing the front door behind him, he doffed his hat and coat, then made his way into the kitchen. At the sight of his aunt's beaming face and Beth's skeptically arched brow, he halted.

"And what have you two ladies been up to here?" He smiled in mild anticipation. "Anything I can assist you in?"

"As a matter of fact, nephew dear, you most certainly can." Millie marched over and, taking him by the arm, turned him to face Beth. "Tomorrow's the Fall Social. You were planning on attending as usual, weren't you?"

Noah eyed his aunt, a puzzled furrow forming between his brows. "Well, yes. You know I try to go. It's good for folk to see me in other places than just church."

"And that's exactly why Beth should be there, too, wouldn't you say? To demonstrate some community involvement?"

"Yes," he agreed cautiously, meeting Beth's gaze, "I suppose so."

"Then it's settled," Millie proclaimed, victory ringing in her voice. "You'll escort Beth to the Fall Social!"

8

*Ye shall be sorrowful, but your sorrow shall be turned
into joy.*

John 16:20

As soon as Beth headed off to bed, Noah
guided his suddenly energetic aunt back
to her chair at the kitchen table. "Folding the laundry
can wait," he said gently but firmly. "We need to talk."

"Really?" Millie slipped from his grasp. "And, even
so, what precludes me from folding laundry as we talk?
A woman, you know, can do more than one thing at a
time."

"Especially," Noah agreed, sending her a wry look
as she dragged the basket of clean shirts, socks, and
petticoats over to the table, "when one of those things
is talking."

She plopped back down in her chair, extracted an
armful of clothes, and deposited them on the table.
"Well, you're the one so all-fired intent on having a talk,
not me."

Noah sighed in exasperation. "And that's only because you're so all-fired intent on suddenly playing match-maker."

Millie feigned a look of shock. "Me? Just because I thought you wouldn't mind helping Beth a little in learning how to fit in better in town? It's not as if you don't always attend the Fall Social at any rate."

"So that's all it was? You using me to ease Beth's way with the town folk?"

"What other motive could I possibly have?" She paused to arch a brow. "You're not sweet on Beth are you? I can't think of any other reason you'd have turned so nervous and jumpy, not to mention down-right suspicious."

Noah scowled. His aunt had the most unsettling talent for turning the tables on anyone who dared accuse her of meddling. And this was one topic he didn't want Millie to examine too closely.

"That's not the point, and you know it!" To distract her, he pulled out a letter from his pocket. "Just got this today. From my old seminary."

Millie laid aside a pair of folded socks and took up two others. "And what do they have to say?"

Noah shrugged. "Don't know. Haven't opened it yet." That said, he slit the envelope, extracted the letter, and read it.

An opening—a position teaching sacred theology—had occurred, and the dean was offering him the position. Excitement filled Noah. He had always dreamed of returning to teach at the New York City seminary. He had the qualifications, thanks to his advanced degrees and stellar seminary performance, especially in theological studies. And each time he had gone home to New York on his rare vacations, he had always visited his old school and renewed acquaintances with his former professors. In his dreams, however, he had

103

always seen himself as a lot older, grayer, and more experienced.

"Well, spit it out. What does the letter say?"

The tone of impatience in his aunt's voice wrenched Noah back to the present. He lifted his gaze.

"They want me. The General Theological Seminary has offered me a teaching position."

Millie stared at him for a long moment.

"I didn't know you'd ever written them asking to be hired. I thought you were content with this ministry, with Grand View and its people."

"I am content, and I didn't write them," Noah said. "But the more I think about the offer, the more promising it sounds."

"Promising? How?"

"There'd be no routinely long hours. I'd have a regular schedule. I could do so much more for you and Emily with a job like that." Noah leaned on the table. "Let's face it. I neglect you and Emily something terrible. You can't depend on me. The needs of the congregation always come first."

"And what's so bad about that? Isn't that why you became a priest? To see to the needs of your congregation? And I married a priest, too. I knew what the life was like, what I was in for."

"Still, it's not fair to you. And it'll become increasingly unfair to Emily, too, as she gets older. She has . . . special needs. She always will."

"And the Lord will provide, just as He always has." Millie reached over and took Noah's hand. "First and foremost, honey, you're called to do the Lord's will and serve His people. You must never forget that."

Frustration filled Noah again. "But you're one of the Lord's people, and so is Emily. And you're family, too. I owe you—"

"Land sakes, Noah Starr!" Millie slapped his hand for emphasis. "Have I ever once complained about how you treat me? I just worry about you and your health, that's all. I'm happy here. Happy to do my part for the Lord in assisting you in any way I can. But if you're unhappy here or feel called to take this new job, then you go right ahead and do it. Just don't do it for me."

A deep affection welled in Noah. His aunt had always been there for him as his confidante and mentor, a wise woman filled with the knowledge and love of God. But it seemed as if he was always the one doing the taking, and she the giving. Just once, he wanted to give to her.

But if this call to teach at the seminary wasn't a call from the Lord, then accepting the position would be wrong. And Millie would never let him do such a thing, just to give back to her.

"Okay," Noah said with a sigh of resignation. "I'll think on it. I'll give it some prayer."

Millie nodded. "Yes, you do that, honey. And make sure, when it's all done and thought through, that it's the Lord's voice you're hearing, and not just your own."

Her nervousness rising with each passing second, Beth fastened the last button on the gathered, elbow-length sleeve of her princess-style, brocaded silk dress. The color suited her well, a deep crimson trimmed with a darker crimson beaded silk ribbon at the modest V neckline and at her shoulders down over her bust to the hem of her skirt. The five-gore skirt ended in the back with a slight train and rustled deliciously when she moved.

She pulled a few additional tendrils from her full, upswept hair and curled them briefly with the heated curling iron. At the very least, they'd help soften what she had always considered her strong-jawed face. As if it mattered anyway, Beth thought, making a face at her reflection in the dresser mirror. Who was she trying to impress, after all?

Certainly not any of the local bachelors. But there were always the town ladies, she supposed. If a wife happened to think well of her, it wouldn't be long before the woman would have her entire family in to see the new lady doctor.

"Yes," Beth muttered, nodding with firm resolve. "I definitely need to impress the ladies of Grand View."

With that conviction to bolster her, she turned from the mirror, picked up her handbag, and strode from the room. Noah, Millie, and Emily, already dressed in a bonnet and warm coat, awaited her in the kitchen. At the sight of them, Beth's steps faltered.

"Oh," she said, "I didn't realize I was keeping you all waiting. I'm sorry."

"Land sakes, honey," Millie replied, a note of awe in her voice, "but aren't you a wondrous sight?" She turned to her nephew. "Isn't Beth absolutely breathtaking? Isn't she?"

Noah's mouth quirked, and Beth noticed he couldn't take his eyes off her.

"Yes, Millie. Beth's absolutely breathtaking." He walked over and offered his arm. "I may not get through the night alive, what with the most beautiful woman in these parts on my arm, but I'm honored to be your escort, m'lady."

Beth blushed—she couldn't help it. "And I'm honored in turn, kind knight, to be with you." She leaned close. "Just promise not to leave me alone tonight. That's all I ask."

Noah arched a brow. "Even if you're besieged with hordes of men begging for a dance?"

Beth rolled her eyes. "Especially if hordes of men besiege me. Not that I'm expecting that to happen, of course."

Millie laughed. "Mark my words, missy. You're going to be in for a big surprise tonight. You are indeed."

"Well, in that case," Beth said, eyeing Noah with rising dismay, "maybe I'll just stay home and—"

"You'll do no such thing!" All but dragging Beth across the kitchen to the entry, Noah paused only long enough to grab her cloak and toss it haphazardly over her shoulders. "Millie's right, and you know it. You can't hide from Grand View's social life forever."

With that, he opened the door and pulled her outside. "Stay there and don't move. That's an order, Doctor."

Her mouth agape at Noah's take-charge attitude, Beth watched him head back inside, grasp Emily's wheelchair, and guide it through the door. Millie followed, closing the door behind them.

"Go on ahead, m'lady," he ordered. "Millie, why don't you come around and join Beth? I can follow with Emily. That way I can also more easily head off any sudden bolts for freedom."

As Millie joined her and they set out, Beth laughed and shook her head. "You're incorrigible, you know? You're acting as if I'm some wild filly about ready to hightail it out of here."

"And aren't you?" the priest asked, bringing up the rear. "Thing is, as fine a filly as you are, I'm not of a mind to let you go. Not every night a man like me gets a chance to escort a fine filly like you to a dance."

"As if I believe that. You could have your pick of any single lady in Grand View."

Noah's glance swung to Millie. "See? What did I tell you?" he demanded of his aunt with a grin. "We're not even halfway to the town hall, and already Beth's trying to cut me loose."

"That's not true!" Beth protested, laughing. Thanks to Noah's teasing banter as they walked along, she was finally beginning to enjoy herself. "If it wasn't for you, Noah Starr, I would've never agreed to going in the first place."

He pretended disbelief. "Well, we'll see then, won't we?"

As they crossed Main Street, the music started up, floating to them on a sharp, chill breeze. Beth could make out a piano, an accordion, two fiddles, a banjo, and a harmonica. The sound of feet pounding rhythmically on the hall's hardwood floors rose to mingle with the music.

Beth smiled. As a girl at Culdee Creek, she had loved the periodic socials held in Grand View. They had been a welcome respite from school and what seemed to be endless ranch work. She would come with her parents, then immediately flee to join the other girls, giggling and casting come-hither looks at the boys across the room. Those nights had always ended far too soon.

This time, however, she came to the town social as a grown woman, a doctor with a changed outlook. Gone were romantic hopes and dreams. Tonight Beth came only for professional reasons.

She paused on the boardwalk fronting the town hall to await Noah and Emily. Then, pushing open the door, she motioned for all of them to go inside. No sooner had Millie walked in and Noah had shoved Emily's wheelchair in after her, than he turned and walked back out.

"M'lady?" he said, once more offering Beth his arm. "Best not waste the power of first impressions, since you seem so set on having me appear as your escort this evening."

Beth grabbed Noah's arm and clung to it tightly. "First impressions are indeed powerful, but just don't forget about me the rest of the night, will you?"

His smile faded. "It's your call, Beth. I'll stay with you for as long as you need me."

Her heart gave a lurch, then commenced a rapid pounding. *For as long as you need me.* . . . She dragged in an unsteady breath. And what if I'll always need you, Noah? What then?

"Fair enough." Beth forced a wobbly smile. "For as long as I need you, then."

With that, they entered the town hall. It was bright inside, full of people. The din of pounding feet, music, talk, and laughter engulfed Beth in a wild riot of sound. She must have clutched Noah's arm even tighter, because he glanced down at her and smiled reassuringly.

"It really hasn't changed much, the Fall Social, I mean," he said, "save that a lot more people attend now."

As he guided her to the donation table, Beth scanned the room. Orange, yellow, and brown streamers festooned the corners, then all came together to join in the center of the room. Shocks of wheat, adorned at their bases with pumpkins, gourds, and dried flowers, were stacked about the room. A long table, loaded with food, stood beneath a bank of windows. And on a small, raised platform across from the door sat the band, industriously playing their music.

Mary Sue Edgerton—Beth quickly corrected herself—Mary Sue Peterson, sat at the donation table with a man Beth didn't know. He was older than Mary Sue, easily twenty years older if Beth didn't miss her guess, with steel-gray hair and a rather hard-eyed, calculating look. He was a heavyset man, and his nose was large, somewhat bulbous, and red like that of a drinker. He wore a finely tailored suit, high-buttoned waistcoat, and snow white, high-wing collar and black bow tie.

Noah guided her to the table. "How are things going tonight, Harlow?"

"Brought in fifty dollars for the kitty so far," the man said, his voice deep and raspy. With an arched brow, his gaze swung to Beth. "And who is this lovely lady you're escorting, Father?" He shoved back his chair and stood. "I don't believe I've made her acquaintance."

"That's Dr. MacKay, Harlow," Mary Sue was quick to offer. "Don't you remember? I told you—"

The man grabbed Mary Sue's hand. "Is it really, my dear? Well, proper manners being what they are, I'd still appreciate a formal introduction."

Mary Sue winced, then blushed. "Oh, of course, dear. Forgive me." She went quiet then, all but seeming to disappear into herself.

But Beth met Harlow's gaze with a cold one of her own. She didn't like this man; something about him filled her with revulsion.

Noah spoke up in the awkward silence. "Beth Mac-Kay, this is Harlow Peterson, Mary Sue's husband and owner and president of Grand View's bank. Harlow, this is Dr. Elizabeth MacKay, Conor MacKay's daughter."

The big man executed a flawless bow, then extended his hand. "I'm very pleased to make your acquaintance, my dear. It says a lot for Grand View's progressive outlook to have a lady doctor."

She took his hand for a brief shake, then released it. His palm was clammy, soft, not at all like the work-hardened, masculine hands she had grown up knowing.

"Actually, Mr. Peterson," Beth said, "the West was one of the first places willing to accept women physicians over forty years ago. If anything, Grand View's behind the times."

His pale blue eyes narrowed fleetingly; his mouth tightened. Then, with a sharp laugh, he sat back down.

"Well, perhaps you're right, Dr. MacKay. Any way you look at it, though, I'm all for progress. Ask anyone. Ask Father Starr, for that matter."

110

"You brought the bank to town," Noah agreed amiably. "That's progress, to be sure."

An uncomfortable silence fell between them again. Beth's gaze met Mary Sue's and saw that her eyes glimmered with tears. Beth's glance lowered to Harlow's hand, still clasped, tightly it seemed, around Mary Sue's.

Anger swelled and Beth almost said something. Caution and good sense, however, quickly prevailed. She turned, smiling her sweetest smile at the big banker.

"Would you mind lending me your wife for a few minutes, Mr. Peterson? I've a few womanly things I need to discuss with her and would hate to bore you two men with them."

Harlow laughed and released Mary Sue's hand. "Of course. I'm certain Father Starr and I can find something to talk about while you two lovely ladies discuss your 'womanly things.'" He glanced to Noah. "Can't we, Father Starr?"

Noah shot Beth a quizzical look, then nodded. "Most certainly we can. Just don't get lost in the crowd, Beth. I'm looking forward to a dance, you know."

"I'll be sure and find you soon." She looked to Mary Sue. "Are you ready?"

Mary Sue all but leaped to her feet. "Yes. Yes, of course." She looked to her husband. "I won't be long. I promise."

He motioned expansively. "Take all the time you need, my dear. I can handle the donations quite well alone. I am, after all, the one with the head for numbers."

As Mary Sue cleared the table and came to stand beside Beth, Beth took her arm and marched off into the crowd. Neither woman spoke until they reached the punch table.

"Care for something to drink?" Beth asked.

Mary Sue nodded. "Yes, please."

111

After ladling out two cups of mulled cider, Beth glanced around. The walls were crowded with people either talking or watching the dancers. At the end of the hall the band and tables of food held sway. The only place for a private talk seemed out of doors.

"I'd like to talk," Beth said. "Would you mind if we went outside?"

"That'd be fine." Cup in hand, Mary Sue headed toward the side door.

Once they were outside, the darkness and relative quiet engulfed them. Beth chose and discarded several opening gambits—no purpose was served in offending or jumping to conclusions. Still, there was something about Mary Sue and her husband's relationship that just didn't seem right. . . .

"I was wondering—"

"Oh, what a relief to get out into the cool air!" Mary Sue exclaimed at the same time. She set her cup on the railing, clasped her arms to her body, threw back her head, and heaved a great sigh. "It was so stifling in there, and Harlow was getting so tense. He's having problems with some employee at the bank right now, and I know it's been eating at him."

She turned to Beth. "He probably seemed quite irritable tonight, and he really isn't that way. I just wanted you to know, as I realize how lasting first impressions can be."

"He did seem rather upset with you. And I saw the tears in your eyes, Mary Sue."

The other woman reached over and patted her arm. "You're so sweet to care, Beth. I may call you Beth, or do you prefer to be addressed by your title?"

Beth was tempted to tell her she preferred her title, if for no other reason than to maintain what she deemed the doctor-patient professional distance. Somehow, though, she sensed that was not the way to gain Mary Sue's confidence.

She shook her head. "Beth's fine. And I do care. Why, I feel like I've known you nearly all my life."

Mary Sue laughed ruefully. "I suppose you have, even if I haven't been on the best of terms with the MacKays for most of it."

"Time's change, and so do people. And now you're married to someone who looks to be a very prosperous, powerful man." Beth took a sip of her cider. "How did you meet Harlow, and when did you wed?"

"About five years ago. That's when he arrived in Grand View, full of plans to set up its first bank." A far-away look filled her eyes. "I was twenty-six then and deathly afraid I was doomed to spinsterhood. Harlow, however, never seemed to mind my age. He was a recent widower, you know, and had just moved here from St. Louis. Three months after we met, he asked my parents for permission to court me. Three months later, we were married."

Mary Sue paused for a moment. "Harlow loves me in his own way. He can hardly stand to see me out of his sight. That's why I work as his personal secretary, you know. And if any cowboy dares to cast me an inappropriate look . . . well, Harlow soon sets the young man straight."

"And you don't find that stifling?"

"No." Mary Sue shook her head. "Not at all. It's just because he loves me so much."

"And is that what you truly believe, or is that what Harlow wishes for you to believe?"

For a long moment, Mary Sue stared at her. Then apprehension began to tauten her features. "I . . . I don't know what you're talking about. Harlow's not–" She paused, clasped her arms about her once more, and

113

averted her gaze. "It's getting rather cool, don't you think? Perhaps it'd be best if we go back inside."

Beth realized that Mary Sue, at least tonight, wasn't about to share anything more. "Yes, I suppose so. The men will be wondering what happened to us."

"Everyone's talking about you and Noah, you know. With you staying at the rectory and all, I mean."

"It's only temporary," Beth said stiffly, her guard rising. "Until Mamie Oatman has an opening."

"Maybe so." Mary Sue shrugged. "It doesn't matter to me at any rate. I'm married, after all. But some of the single ladies are certainly gnashing their teeth over you. And after tonight, when word gets out Noah escorted you to the Fall Social . . ."

"We're friends, and nothing more." Beth gestured toward the door. "Shall we head on inside?"

Chuckling softly, Mary Sue picked up her cup from the railing. "Oh, I believe you, Beth. Really, I do. Still, tongues will wag and people will talk. Just be ready to take it. That's all. Just be ready."

Noah was surprised how well escorting Beth to the Fall Social had gone. As he walked back to the church after his monthly haircut at Sam Edgar's barbershop the next day, he almost wanted to laugh out loud. He had spent the evening with her, danced a few dances, and apart from enjoying himself immensely, he hadn't felt any untoward feelings for her. Perhaps at long last his prayers had been answered.

Noah squinted in the bright sunlight. Down the street, a crowd appeared to be forming near the entrance of the town hall. The Ladies Quilting Society was meeting there today, and Noah wondered whether they were having some display of their handiwork. If so, strange that Millie hadn't mentioned it.

Just then a man shoved his way through the throng and sprinted down the street in the direction of the clinic. Noah quickened his pace. Had perhaps someone been taken ill?

As he reached the people milling about outside, someone recognized him. "Father Starr," a voice called. "Come on in. Hurry. It's your aunt."

Millie. Noah elbowed his way past the crowd and found several of Millie's quilting compatriots fanning her. Millie sat in a chair, gasping for breath, sweat beading her brow.

"Millie, what's the matter?" He took her hand.

She looked up at him. "Just a little sp-spell," she gasped. "It-it'll p-pass."

"Let me through," Doc Childress said just then, his deep voice rising from outside the hall. "Everyone step aside."

As Doc cleared the crowd, Noah saw Beth accompanying him. Both wore concerned expressions, and both hurried to Millie.

"What happened?" Doc asked. Beth pulled a stethoscope and some kind of cloth apparatus from her black bag. She handed it to Doc. He waved it aside. "You do it. I'll get the history."

Millie looked from one physician to the other. "I was busy helping set up the luncheon we always have midway through our quilting bee, and I suddenly couldn't catch my breath." She managed a wan smile. "I'm already feeling better, though."

Doc bent close. "Have you been taking your medicine?"

She shot Noah a furtive look, then glanced back at Doc. "Yes. Of course I have."

"Then we need to reevaluate, maybe increase your dosage."

"Fine," Millie muttered, her mouth set in an obstinate line Noah knew no amount of persuasion would ease. "Now enough of airing my private affairs in public. We can talk more about this at my next appointment."

"No," Doc said. "I want to see you sooner than that. Like today."

"But I've got this—"

"Today, Mildred Starr." Doc straightened. "Now, let Beth take your pulse and blood pressure."

As Beth checked Millie's vitals, Doc turned to Noah. "Will you see she comes to the clinic just as soon as she's fit to walk again?"

Noah nodded, a troubling presentiment filling him. "You know I will."

9

*If the salt have lost his savour, wherewith shall it be
salted? it is thenceforth good for nothing.*

Matthew 5:13

Beth finished examining Millie. "You can
get dressed," she said as she stepped back
from the table. She turned and put away her stethoscope, then walked to her desk, sat, and began to write
up the results of her examination.

November first. Beth stifled a groan. It had been only
two months since they had first started Millie on the
digitalis, and already it wasn't working as well. Just as
Doc had feared, they'd have to increase her dosage.
Problem was, they couldn't increase it much more without risking life-threatening side effects.

"Well, Doc," Millie said when she was fully dressed.
She walked over and took the chair in front of Beth's
desk. "What's the verdict? Am I going to make it?"

Beth laid aside her pen. "Your heart's not responding
as well to the digitalis. We need to increase the amount
you're taking."

"Pshaw. Is that all it was? And here I thought I was on death's door." She gathered up her handbag from the desk and stood.

"Millie, sit back down. Please."

Millie frowned, but did as asked. "There's more, isn't there? And it's not good."

"It might not be. I'd like you to see a doctor in the Springs. He has a lot of specialized experience in cardiac conditions. He might be able to provide us with additional options." ·

Millie shook her head. "I don't have the time to be gallivanting off to Colorado Springs. Besides, what could I tell Noah that wouldn't get him to worrying about me?"

"One way or another, you can't hide it from him much longer. You need to tell him, Millie. After what he saw today, he's going to ask questions. Hard questions of the both of us. And bound as I am by my oath to keep your medical affairs private, I'm going to have to send him straight back to you."

Millie looked down. "And what do you suggest I tell him that won't add to his burden, his pain? Things were just starting to improve for him since you came to us and all. I just want Noah to have a little happiness again, before . . ."

She knew, Beth realized. Knew that even the miracle of medicine could only do so much, for so long, for her failing heart.

Beth rose and came around her desk. Kneeling, she took Millie's hand. "Just tell him what you know. That your heart's not in good shape, but that Doc and I are doing everything we can for you. Hence, why we're sending you to that physician in the Springs, why we're increasing your medicine. And as far as the rest, tell him what he already believes. That your life, as it has always been, is in God's hands."

Noah sat in the waiting room outside Beth's office, gazing out the window. In the past half hour, the clouds forming over Pikes Peak had moved eastward. Only occasional glimpses of sky and sun peeked now through the growing cloud cover. The wind gusted in sporadic bursts, sending the dirt flying. If Noah didn't miss his guess, a storm was on the way.

A patient, Mrs. Nealy, left Doc Childress's office. She stopped and nodded to Noah, who stood in response.

"I'm sure Millie will be just fine, Father Starr," the woman said. "Still, if you need anything, you know where to come."

"I appreciate your offer, Mrs. Nealy," Noah replied. "And I'll definitely keep it in mind, too."

They stood there in an awkward silence until Mrs. Nealy reached out to squeeze his hand.

"Well, I'd best be going. Got to bring in the wash, what with this weather coming in."

"Yes, best you do."

She released his hand, turned, and left the office. It was quiet once more, save for Helen's occasional shuffling of papers and the rhythmic scratching of her pen.

Noah went back to his seat. How long did it take to do an examination? Was Millie sicker than he feared? She hadn't been her usual self for months now. More tired, less cheerful. He should've made her see Doc or Beth a long while ago.

The door to Beth's office clicked open, and Noah leaped to his feet.

"You can come in now, Noah," Beth said.

He couldn't read anything in her expression. She kept it flat—a doctor's inscrutable mask. Well, he'd soon have the truth out of the both of them.

119

Noah followed Beth into her office, closing the door behind them. Millie turned to smile up at him, then averted her gaze. There was something about that forced, automatic action that didn't set well with him.

Beth motioned to another chair against the wall. "Why don't you pull that over and have a seat. Millie's got a few things she'd like to tell you."

As soon as he was in his seat, Noah turned to his aunt. "What is it, Millie? What's wrong with you?"

Millie looked briefly to Beth, then pursed her lips and met Noah's concerned gaze. "I've heart trouble. Goes back to when I had rheumatic fever as a child. And now . . . now it's getting worse."

"Worse?" His fear rising, Noah looked from Millie to Beth and back to Millie again. "How much worse?"

Millie glanced at Beth beseechingly. "You tell him, honey. You can explain all that highfalutin doctor stuff better than I can."

Noah inhaled a deep breath. "Yes, please. But just someone tell me what all this means."

"It means"—Beth leaned forward on her desk—"Millie's heart is failing. It's not strong enough to pump the blood around her body as well anymore, and one of the places it affects is her lungs. Hence, why she gets breathing problems when she overdoes it."

"Doc said something at the town hall about medicine, and was she taking it. Is this heart medicine?"

Beth nodded. "Yes, it is. It's called digitalis. It helped Millie for a while, but now it isn't enough."

"Then do something else." He knew his voice was sharp, demanding, but he didn't care. The way Beth was talking, and both she and Millie were looking . . .

"We will. Before you brought Millie to the clinic, I conferred with Doc. We're going to increase her dose of digitalis. We'd also like for her to see a physician in the

120

Springs who has considerable experience with cardiac problems. Maybe he can give us some more ideas."

"And if he can't? Give you more ideas, I mean," Noah asked softly. "What then?"

When Beth didn't answer right away, Millie reached over and took Noah's hand. "Then we put it all in the good Lord's hands, honey. We pray, and we wait. Sooner or later, He'll give us our answers."

Noah looked down at his aunt's hand. It was age-spotted, and the veins stood out from the thin, sinewy flesh. But it was a beautiful hand nonetheless, work-hardened, dependable, gentle, loving. Just like Millie. *Just like Millie . . .*

She wouldn't live forever. She was already in her early sixties, and life out here was hard on a woman. But Noah hadn't expected to lose her so soon. Not when he still needed her so desperately.

Tears stung his eyes. He was afraid he'd shame himself by crying, so he pulled his hand from Millie's, rose, and walked over to stare out the window.

"This is one time," Noah said, shoving his hands in his trouser pockets, "I'm not so certain I want to know what the Lord wants. If He decides it's time to take you . . . well, I don't know what I'll do."

"Noah, honey," his aunt began, shoving back her chair. "It'll be all right. One way or another, the Lord will see to that."

He wheeled about and lifted a hand to stay her. "Don't, Millie. I-I'm sorry, but I need some time to think about this. To be alone."

With that, he turned and hurried from the office, leaving the two women staring after him.

It took every ounce of willpower for Beth not to get up from her desk and go after Noah. Only the knowledge that Millie was her patient, first and foremost, held her in her seat, wearing the most professional demeanor she could muster. Still, Millie must have read something in Beth's eyes or in the way her hands fisted on her desk.

"Go to him," Millie urged, sending her an encouraging smile. "I'm okay. It's Noah who needs you now."

Beth dragged her tortured gaze from the open doorway. "Are you sure? I feel like I'm deserting you in your hour of need."

Millie shook her head. "I've all I need, all I've ever needed. The love of the Lord and the love of family and friends. Who can be richer?"

Gazing into the other woman's eyes, Beth saw the conviction shining there. Who else, indeed, could be richer if one still truly believed in a merciful, loving God? But even if Beth knew the Bible well, thanks to Abby's instruction and Noah's sermons all those years of her growing up, she no longer believed. How could she, after all that had happened to her back East?

She pushed back her chair and stood. "Well, then let me first escort you home. You were my last patient for the day at any rate." Beth came around, helped Millie up, and led her from the clinic.

The walk back to the rectory was slow, and Millie tired quickly. The increasingly windy weather didn't help any, but in time they made it home.

Mary Sue Peterson, who had been at the quilting bee and had volunteered to watch Emily while Noah and Millie went to the clinic, was there, waiting with the two-year-old in the kitchen. Upon Millie and Beth's arrival, she jumped up, hurried to Millie's other side, and helped her into Beth's room.

"Thank you . . . ever so much," Millie said between breaths, "for watching Emily. I hope . . . hope Harlow won't be upset. You taking off from your . . . other duties, I mean."

"As far as Harlow knows, I'm still at the Quilting Society meeting. It's one of the few social activities he allows me on my own, as the Peterson family's community contribution. But helping out our priest's aunt in a moment of need should set just as well with him, too." Mary Sue managed a taut smile. "To keep up our outstanding image in the community, I mean."

Beth shot Mary Sue a sharp glance. The edge of bitterness in her voice was not easily ignored, especially since she was normally quite reticent when it came to anything regarding her husband or her marriage.

"Well, I'm glad you were here to help with Emily," Beth said as they entered her room. She let go of Millie's arm and quickly turned back the bedcovers, plumped up the pillows, then returned to Millie's side. "Here. Sit on the side of the bed so we can get off your shoes and jacket. Then you lie down for a nice nap."

"Bring Emily in here so I can watch her," Millie said. "Since you need to find Noah and all."

Mary Sue turned to Beth. "If you need to speak with Noah, I can stay until you return. Millie can't really rest if she has to keep an eye on Emily."

Beth eyed her uncertainly. "Well, that would help, if you're certain Harlow won't mind."

"For all the help you and Millie have been to me, I think I can risk it."

"I'll try not to be long." Beth assisted Millie onto the bed, paused to slip off her shoes as Mary Sue removed her jacket, then both women helped Millie to lie down. After tucking her in, Beth lowered the shades, then followed Mary Sue from the room.

"Thank you once again for your kindness." Beth laid a hand on Mary Sue's arm. "I truly appreciate it."

Mary Sue smiled. "It's my pleasure. I feel like, after all these years, we're finally becoming friends. And that feels very good."

Beth squeezed her arm before releasing it. "Yes. It does." She headed to the coatrack and donned her jacket. "I think Noah's at the church, so if you need me before I return—"

"Get on with you." Mary Sue made a shooing motion. "We'll be fine."

Beth hurried out into the late afternoon storm. Large, fat flakes were tumbling down from a roiling sky, and even as she strode along, the temperature seemed to drop. She flipped up the collar of her wool jacket, hunkered down into its warmth, and stepped up her pace.

The closer she drew to the church, however, the more her steps slowed. When Noah had first fled her office, comforting responses had formed on her lips. But now, as the time to face him drew near, all her fine phrases and clever consolations had evaporated into thin air.

She had always hated this part of medicine—addressing loss, handling grief. Nothing she ever said seemed to offer much solace.

This time, though, it was different. This was Noah who was in pain. This was Millie who might be dying. More than anything, Beth wanted to be of help to them.

As quietly as she could, Beth opened the church's front door and walked inside. Strange, she mused as she closed the door behind her, how quiet, how suffused in holiness a church seems when it's empty. As the sun sank slowly toward the cloud-shrouded mountains, a single ray angled its way through one of the stained-glass windows. Just when the stained glass had replaced the plain, clear windows, Beth didn't know, but the effect was breathtaking as the rapidly waning light suffused the interior with a soft rose, emerald, lavender, and cobalt-blue glow. And it was there in the puddle of color that washed the front pews that Beth found Noah.

He sat in the first pew, his shoulders hunched, his head bowed. Just sat there, unmoving, his body rigid as if he fought some fierce, interior battle.

Beth hurried forward. Gone were her earlier doubts. Gone was her personal need to be the all-knowing, infallible physician. Nothing mattered but Noah. Being with him, helping him by sharing his pain.

Beth slid into the pew beside him. He glanced up slowly, the look in his eyes bleak, hopeless, even confused. Beth's heart twisted.

Scooting close, she wrapped her arms about him. With a groan, Noah came to her, resting his head on her shoulder, clasping her about the waist.

"Why, Beth?" he whispered. "Why Millie? Why now?"

"And why not now? Why not Millie?" she asked. "None of us knows how long we have on this earth, nor can we extend the moment one second longer than what's decreed. You know that."

"I don't know anything anymore!" he cried in anguish. "It's almost . . . almost as if God's taking some perverse pleasure in tormenting me, in pulling the rug out from beneath me every time I finally seem to get my bearings again. How much more does He think I can take?"

"It's not necessarily God's doing." No matter how angry she still was with the Lord, Beth refused to vent her own unsettled feelings just now. She stroked Noah's head. "I think it's just life. Sometimes the bad just keeps coming for no reason. But you can't lose hope that the bad will eventually pass, and the happiness will return. You can't lose hope."

"Why not? I don't think God would care one way or another."

125

She had never heard him talk like this. If he, a man of God, could fall to such depths in his despair, what hope was left for the rest of them? Surprisingly, the realization frightened her.

"I'll tell you true, Beth," Noah said. "I'm near the end of my rope in losing those I love."

"You haven't lost Millie yet."

"But it doesn't look good for her, does it?"

She licked her lips and looked away. "No, not for the long term it doesn't. There's only so much we can do for her."

"It's my fault, you know. If she hadn't had to work so hard to keep up the rectory and take care of me and Emily . . ."

"Don't." Beth took Noah by the shoulders and pushed him back to look into his face. "Don't start whipping yourself for what couldn't be helped. And do you seriously think you could've kept Millie from doing what she did for you anyway? Do you?"

"No. I suppose not."

"None of us can be less than what we're meant to be, and Millie has always been a loving, giving person." She smiled. "And you, you're the heart of the town, the salt that savors us all."

His mouth twisted. "Well, at this moment, I feel like my salt has lost its savor. I don't feel of much use to anyone, especially not to Millie."

"But you will when it's needed. You can't help being what you are, either, Noah Starr."

"And what are you, Beth MacKay?" As he spoke, Noah's eyes warmed with affection. "What do you think you were meant to be, meant to give?"

Her hands fell from his shoulders. "I don't know." She sighed and shook her head. "I used to think I was meant to be a healer, someone everyone would look up to. But now . . . well, now I'm not so sure anymore."

"You're a good doctor, Beth, and getting more and more respected by the day. Why, a lot of people make mention of you and how thorough you are with them and their children." Noah cocked his head. "Why would you doubt that, or yourself?"

"I don't doubt my medical abilities. I'm just beginning to realize there has to be more than book knowledge and precise technique. Leastwise, if one really wants to be a good doctor. A good doctor has to understand the heart. Has to be willing to open her own heart."

"And risk it, too."

Beth nodded. "Yes. Just like you did with Alice, and like you do every day with Millie and Emily and the people of Grand View. But that scares me, Noah. When I think of the pain of losing someone—the pain you're going through right now—I want to run away and shut myself off from people."

"Yet if you did, what a loss it'd be. We need you, Beth. Doc needs you. And you need us."

She smiled. "Just like we need you, and you need us?"

"Yes, I suppose so," Noah agreed reluctantly.

"We can do this together, you know." Beth scooted close and took his hand. "Just as Millie won't be alone in this, neither will you. I'll be here. I'll help you in every way I can. And so will my folks. You know that."

Noah's head dipped. For a long moment, he was silent. Then he looked up, meeting her gaze.

"I appreciate that, Beth," he whispered hoarsely, his eyes glimmering with unshed tears. "More than you may ever know, I truly and deeply appreciate that."

10

God is the strength of my heart, and my portion forever.
Psalm 73:26

On December 2 the MacKays threw a huge birthday party for Sean, who had turned the strapping age of twelve. It was held in the evening, after school had let out for the day. Besides all the MacKays and all of Sean's sixth grade class, the Starrs were invited as well.

Millie had been to the physician in the Springs, but he had little more to offer than an increase in her medication. For a while the greater dosage did improve most of her symptoms, but as time went on, she began to tire easily again. Still, nothing Beth or Noah could say would deter her from coming to the birthday party.

The main house was in sheer chaos, but it was a happy, life-filled kind of chaos, so everyone tolerated it in good humor. Millie especially reveled in the festivities. Finally, though, with school on the morrow, the cake- and homemade-ice-cream-stuffed children began to trickle homeward.

As Abby, Conor, and Sean saw the children off, Beth helped Claire and Hannah put to right the wreckage. The men gradually adjourned to the parlor for some whiskey and male talk. Once they were out from underfoot, the cleanup went far more quickly.

After all the exhausted but happy MacKay children were put to bed upstairs, the women gathered in the kitchen. Abby put on a kettle of water for tea and set out cups. Claire washed, Hannah dried, and Beth put the clean plates and cutlery away. Millie, worn out from all the excitement, watched from a chair pulled up at the table.

"Did I mention I'd received a letter from Ian today?" Claire piped up from her place at the sink.

Beth's head jerked around. She and Claire's younger brother had formed a fast friendship when Claire had first wed Evan and had come with Ian to Colorado from their home in Scotland. Though Beth and Ian had once imagined they were madly in love, in time their youthful ardor had cooled to a comfortable friendship.

Three years older than Beth, Ian had lived at Culdee Creek until she had gone off to medical school. Then one day, out of the blue, he announced to his sister he was returning to Scotland, and there he remained to this day.

"No, you didn't mention you'd received a letter," Beth said as she came to stand beside her sister-in-law. "What did Ian have to say? How is he? And did he ask after me?"

Behind her, Hannah chuckled. "And why would he ask after you in particular? By now, I'd imagine Ian has all but forgotten about you, what with all those bonny Scottish lassies to choose from."

Beth shot her cousin's wife a black look. "He'd ask about me because I was his best friend, that's why." She turned back to Claire. "Well, what did Ian have to say?"

"Och, he's verra fine. He's still in Culdee and working that land he bought. He's raising Highland cattle, has a large vegetable garden, and he's quite proud of his snug little croft house. And"—she paused for dramatic effect—"he's mentioned a wee lass who he claims to be verra fond of."

As Beth stared in shock, the other women laughed. "Ian? Ian's going to get married?"

"Well, I couldn't say." Claire turned back to her sink full of soapsuds and extracted the last plate. She rinsed it, handed it to Hannah, then pulled the plug, draining the sink. "He didn't mention marriage, after all. Just that there's that wee lass."

Beth wasn't certain how she felt about Ian being in love with some other woman. It wasn't as if she wished to marry him, but he could've at least checked with her first. They had always shared everything when they were children. Besides, what did Ian really know about women anyway?

"When you write him back," she said, "tell him not to do anything until he writes me. I need to be certain this is the proper woman for him."

"And why don't ye write and tell him that yerself?" Claire asked, grinning at Beth as she wiped her arms on a towel. "He's not likely, at any rate, to listen as well to his older sister as he is to ye."

"I suppose you're right." Beth thought about it a moment longer, then nodded her head. "I'll write him tonight and post the letter first thing tomorrow."

"How are things going with you?" Abby asked a short time later after Hannah and Claire had left for their own houses with their families. Millie had gone to nap upstairs with Emily and the other children while the men finished one last game of checkers. "We don't seem to see you all that often, and I think about you a lot."

Beth glanced at her stepmother. "My practice with Doc is picking up now. For a time, I'd some problems scheduling enough patients. Then, on Doc's advice and with Millie's prodding, I started getting more socially involved in town. Now, slowly but surely, the patients have started coming." She smiled and added a spoonful of sugar to her tea. "At this rate, I'll soon have more work than I know what to do with."

"Good. I'm glad to hear that's working out." Abby leaned her forearms on the table, cradling her own tea between her hands. "And what about your stay with Millie and Noah? You've been there how long now? Three months? Any word when Mamie will have an opening in her boardinghouse?"

Beth knew where this was leading, but smiled anyway. "Nope. Mamie finally found a room for the hotel maid, but the Russian man's family can't come now until next summer, so he's next on the list. Guess I'll be staying on at the Starrs' indefinitely. What with Millie's medical problems, Noah needs me now more than ever."

"You and Noah seem to have settled into a comfortable relationship."

"Yes, we have. We're good friends."

"And are you content with that? Just being friends, I mean?"

"Yes. Why wouldn't I be?"

Abby shrugged. "Oh, I don't know. Sometimes living in close quarters can stir old feelings, causing them to rise to the forefront."

"Or," Beth countered, "they can dampen them just as easily, too."

"Well, I was just wondering. Not having seen you much of late, I guess I started making up all sorts of stories in my mind."

Guilt plucked at Beth. She knew her stepmother really did enjoy having her visit. "I've been very busy, Abby. I'll try to get out to Culdee Creek more often, though, from here on out."

"Your father would like that. He worries, too."

"Then tell him not to. I'm fine and getting better all the time."

"Are you truly, Beth?"

Beth nodded, the surety of her words filling her with a strong sense of peace. She felt cherished again, valued, and fulfilled at so many levels. Being home, among the people and land she loved, was indeed helping her to heal. Not that she didn't still have a long way to go, but at least now there seemed some hope.

And hope was something she hadn't had in a very long time.

By Christmas, Millie was faring so badly that Beth and Noah decided she needed additional help during the day. Noah promptly nominated Beth to broach the subject with his aunt.

"Men," Beth muttered in disgust to Emily as they awaited Millie's rising one Saturday morning. "They think they're all so brave and then run off with their tails between their legs first chance they get. As if offering any woman some extra help would ever be taken as an insult!"

"What's that about men and their tails between their legs?" Millie asked just then as she walked into the kitchen. "I didn't quite catch all of that."

Beth wheeled around in her chair, almost spilling her coffee. With a practiced eye, she swiftly scanned the older woman's appearance. Despite the fact she had just risen from what should've been a good night's rest, Millie looked haggard. Her hands and feet were swollen. Her lips were slightly blue-tinged, and her skin was pale.

"Oh, it wasn't anything." Beth made a dismissive gesture. "I was just talking to myself." She paused. "So, how did you sleep?"

"Okay, I suppose. Had to sit up a couple of times to catch my breath, and that dratted cough . . ." Millie sat down heavily at the table. "I'll be fine after my first cup of tea, though."

Beth rose, took up the kettle she'd had steaming on the stove, and made a cup of tea. Then she took a seat across from Millie. "There's something I'd like to talk with you about," she said, deciding there was no sense in delaying the inevitable. "I'm thinking it might be a good idea to hire on some help for a while."

Millie took her time stirring sugar into her tea before looking up. "Some help, you say? Don't think I'm up to the work around here anymore, do you?"

"Well, I suppose I could pretend to some other reason or dance about the truth, but I won't. No, you're not up to the work around here anymore, and you know it. Emily, for one, is getting too big and heavy for you to handle. And overtaxing your heart when there's no reason—"

"Was this your idea or Noah's?"

"Both of ours. But you know as well as I it's as important for Noah as for you, that you start taking it easier. He worries himself sick over you."

"Yes, I know he does." She sighed, then took a sip of her tea. "And only for Noah's sake and Emily's will I do it. Who did you have in mind? I can't bear a nervous, flighty sort of woman in my house. She'll have to be neat and clean and pay attention to details. I won't compromise my standards, no matter how sick I get."

Those stringent requirements would eliminate half the women Beth had in mind. And, since she had only three potential candidates . . .

"Well what about Luanne Stout? She's a good, strong young woman and right now is just helping her mother with the washing and ironing they take in. She's intelligent and a high school graduate. I even heard she'd like to attend college someday but hasn't the money."

Millie appeared to consider the idea. "That might work. The Stouts are God-fearing folk. And if the money would help Luanne get ahead some day . . ." She nodded. "Have her come by so I can talk with her."

Beth couldn't believe Millie had seized on the suggestion so quickly. But then Millie always liked helping people, and if any family in Grand View deserved some additional opportunities, it was surely the Stouts.

"Good." Beth pushed back her chair and stood. "I'll pay the Stouts a visit first thing after I fix you and Emily some breakfast."

"Did Noah already leave then? And did he eat anything?"

"He made himself some toast and coffee. Not the heartiest of breakfasts, but more than he used to eat."

A faint smile teased the corners of Millie's mouth. "He's fattening up right nicely of late, isn't he?"

"I hadn't really noticed," Beth replied, grateful she had been stooping down at that moment to fetch the fry pan from the cupboard.

It wasn't exactly a lie, she thought, her cheeks reddening. She didn't spend a lot of time looking at Noah. They were both too busy, after all, to see each other all that much.

"Yes," Millie said, "he's looking back to his old self. Just hope Luanne Stout knows how to cook. Can't be having Noah backsliding after all the work I've put into him."

⌘

The month of January blew in with its usual bitter weather and heavy snows. But the lowering clouds and sub-zero chill rarely lasted more than a few days before the sun would once more break through. Brilliantly blue skies and blindingly bright, glinting snow, accented by the dark green of ponderosa pines, would then provide ample reward for the earlier periods of gloom. The snow would soon melt, Grand View's broad dirt streets would transform into muddy trails and, to everyone's chagrin, buckboards and buggies would mire and sink.

Beth found all of the ongoing seasonal happenings reassuring and familiar. It was nice to trust in something, in the midst of so many things in life that couldn't be trusted. Like Millie's health, which had steadily gone downhill in the past few weeks. Her breathing had gotten so bad she could barely climb the stairs to her room. Beth had insisted Millie take her bed, while she slept in an army cot to be near Millie whenever her breathing spells got bad at night.

They hadn't hired Luanne any too soon, and the girl turned out to be a blessing. Not only was she a good cook and housekeeper, but Luanne adored Emily. Millie seemed to find her greatest relief from her breathing difficulties whenever Luanne and Emily went to her bedroom to entertain her.

It was the best that could be done, Beth supposed one sun-drenched mid-January day as she finished her last chart and filed it away. Not good enough for any of them watching Millie's slow decline with its inevitable outcome, but there was a certain peace about it nonethe-

135

less. A peace beginning with Millie and spreading outward to touch them all.

"The hardest part isn't in the dying," Beth recalled Millie telling her a week ago. "I love the Lord so, my heart leaps with joy thinking I'll soon be with Him. Oh, to lay my head on His breast, to feel the strength of His love enfold me as I've never known it in this life! What pains me, though, is the thought of leaving you and Noah and Emily behind. Of the anguish it'll cause you." Millie smiled sadly. "It's always the hardest on those left behind in this vale of tears. The loss of a loved one creates such a gaping wound in a heart, a wound that, at best, can only heal a bit at its edges."

"Yes," Beth agreed softly, "some wounds don't ever heal, do they?"

"No, they don't." From her place on the bed, Millie's hand settled on Beth's shoulder. "With time, though, and the Lord's guidance and love, we can turn that loss, that pain, to good."

Beth couldn't choke back an outraged protest. "What possible good could ever come from losing someone you love? God doesn't need that person. *We* are the ones who need our loved ones. Yet God gives them to us, then, just when they've insinuated themselves into our hearts, He takes them back." She shook her head with a savage vehemence. "It's not fair. It's just not fair!"

"No, it might not seem fair, but many are God's reasons, and we must trust in Him. He is always with us, in the pain as well as in the happiness. Indeed, in many ways, He seems nearest in our sorrow."

Beth frowned. "That doesn't make Him seem like a God who wishes us to be happy."

"On the contrary, honey. The Lord would wish us always to be happy in Him. He just knows we tend not to think of Him very much when things are going well. It's almost as if in our joy, we feel it's our just deserts.

136

But in our sorrow—a sorrow, of course, never of our *own* doing," she added with a grin, "we finally turn to Him and bitterly complain at the unfairness of it all." Millie shook her head. "It's all turned upside down. All that's good comes from God. All that's bad, the sorrow and the pain, is but a natural part of life—or rises from our own sin and failings."

Beth smiled ruefully. "True enough, I suppose. It's our human nature to take credit where we wish and discard the rest."

"Yet God is everywhere, in the sorrow and the joy. He is all we can ever depend on, and we must strive always to seek Him and cling to Him. The rest"—Millie shrugged—"well, the rest—family, friends, our meager accomplishments—are but way stations on the road home. They are never, however, home. At their best, they help gladden our hearts and strengthen us on the journey."

"That's why I don't want to lose you! You gladden my heart and strengthen me on my journey. As you do for Noah and Emily, who need you even more desperately than I."

The older woman smiled. "They needed me for a time, but I think the Lord has finally provided them with a new friend. A friend who can fill those empty spaces in their hearts even better than I."

Beth frowned. "I don't understand. Who could ever do more for them than you, Millie?"

"You, of course." Millie laughed. "Already you're all but a mother to Emily. And Noah . . . well, I'm a woman. I can see what's growing between you and him. You're the one, honey, who'll finally heal the wound of Alice's loss."

Warmth flooded Beth's face. "I . . . I think you're mistaken. There's nothing between us. And I give you my word we've never acted unseemly with each other."

"I know that. I trust Noah, and I trust you. But I also know what I've seen." Millie cocked her head. "Are you trying to tell me now that you don't care for my nephew? Is that it?"

Beth released an exasperated breath and looked away. "Yes. I mean no! Who wouldn't care for Noah? He's so kind and good, and . . . and . . ."

"Then what's the problem? You like him and he likes you. What could be more natural?"

"It doesn't matter how I feel about him." Beth turned back to face Millie. "He's far too good for a woman like me!"

"And why's that?"

"Because . . . because I'm tainted. I've sinned. Sinned grievously. And someday Noah will find out." She shook her head fiercely. "When that day comes, I don't want him to feel as if I tricked him, that I was leading him on to think I was better than I really was." And, even more importantly, Beth added silently, I don't know what I'd do if, when he learns the truth, he rejects me.

"Do you love him, honey?"

Hot, traitorous tears sprang to Beth's eyes. "No," she said, clamping her mouth shut. "No!"

Millie chuckled. "I don't believe you. You've always loved him."

Beth gasped. "If you're talking about that schoolgirl crush I once had for him, that's been over a long while now," she muttered, growing irritated at being boxed in at every turn. "Besides, what does it matter anyway? Noah doesn't love me."

"On the contrary. He just doesn't realize the true depth of his feelings for you. But you're kindred souls, honey. You belong together. Remember that when I'm gone. Don't let your fears keep you from the man of your heart."

Remember . . .

Beth shook her head, shoved her desk drawer closed, and stood. Since that day she and Millie had talked, little else had been on Beth's mind. Was it really possible? Did Noah have deep feelings for her?

Though he might care for her as a friend, Noah had never once given her a reason to suspect his feelings went any deeper. Millie's imagination, fired by her need to put her affairs in order, was just working overtime. And finding a mother for Emily and a wife for Noah was one of her most pressing concerns.

Besides, the reason why she could never become Noah's wife hadn't changed. She was an impure woman. She wasn't worthy, and nothing could ever change that.

11

Do all that is in thine heart; for the LORD is with thee.
2 Samuel 7:3

At half past ten on a bitterly cold, late January night, the kitchen telephone rang. Beth, who had just settled onto her cot, leaped up and hurried from the bedroom. "Hello?" she said, trying not to talk so loud as to disturb Millie. "This is Dr. Mac-Kay. What can I do for you?"

"It's John," Doc Childress's gruff voice rumbled through the lines. "I need you over at the clinic. Can you come?"

"Of course." Beth's heart increased its rate, as it always did when an emergency occurred. "I'll be there in five minutes." She hung up, hurried back into her room, and began to dress.

Millie turned over in bed, facing her. "Who was that?"

"Doc." Beth pulled on her skirt and fastened it. "He needs me at the clinic."

"Would you like me to come, too?" Millie weakly shoved up in bed. "In case you require an extra set of hands?"

It is so like her, Beth thought, to think of everyone else even as she can barely get around anymore. "No." She shook her head. "We should be fine. And if it gets bad, I'll call you and you can send Noah over. Okay?"

Panting for breath, Millie laid back. "O-okay. Guess I'm better off anyways . . . just staying put." She managed a tremulous smile. "You're such . . . a blessing to us all, you know."

Beth slipped her stocking feet into her boots. "As you are to us." She walked over, took the older woman's hand for a quick squeeze, then released it. "Are you all right? I can fetch Noah if you feel you might need someone while I'm gone."

"No. Let the dear . . . boy sleep. I'm fine."

"I'd better be on my way then."

"Bundle up . . . nice and warm, honey. The wind sounds like it's . . . blowing pretty fierce . . . out there."

"I will," Beth called over her shoulder as she headed into the kitchen. "I will."

Two minutes later, impelled by a strong tailwind and the frigid weather, Beth raced into the clinic. Doc's office door was open. Inside, she could hear the voices of a man and woman, the woman hysterical, the man angry. She quickly removed her jacket, mittens, and wool scarf, and hurried into the office.

"Ah, Dr. MacKay," Doc said, rising from behind his desk as soon as he saw her. "Just in time to assist me with the examinations."

She scanned Doc's patients. They were Harlow and Mary Sue Peterson. Harlow boasted a rapidly purpling bruise on his left cheekbone. Mary Sue clasped her right arm closely to her.

Beth looked to Doc. "What happened?"

"Seems Harlow and Mary Sue had a minor disagreement," Doc said. "Unfortunately, it was at the top of their staircase. They lost their balance and both fell down the stairs."

The observation, that Mary Sue had a most disconcerting habit of falling down the stairs, was on the tip of Beth's tongue, but she chose not to share it. The true cause of the injuries would come out soon enough with an examination.

"I assume you'd like me to examine and treat Mary Sue, while you see to Harlow?" she asked, plastering on her most stone-faced, professional demeanor.

Doc nodded. "Yes, I think that'd work best." He glanced from Mary Sue to Harlow. "If that's acceptable to the both of you, of course."

The big banker looked at his wife. She refused to look back. "Yes, I suppose so," he said finally.

Beth touched Mary Sue on the shoulder. "Can you stand, or do you need help?"

"I . . . I can stand." Mary Sue climbed to her feet and without a backward glance stalked from the room.

Once inside her office, with the door closed firmly behind them, Beth indicated the examination table. She pulled over a stool for Mary Sue to step up on, waited as she settled herself, then glanced at her arm.

"You're holding that as if you think you broke it. May I have a look?"

"Suit yourself." Mary Sue's lips trembled. "If it isn't broken, though, then I miss my guess."

As gently as she could, Beth examined her lower arm. The radius, midway up from the thumb, was indeed fractured. She gently lowered Mary Sue's arm back into her lap.

"You're right. One of the bones in your lower arm is broken. We need to get your arm out of that sleeve so I can fix it."

After helping Mary Sue do that, Beth walked to the supply cabinet and took out gauze and several rolls of gauze-impregnated plaster of paris. She placed them on a small table and rolled it over next to Mary Sue, then filled a bucket with water.

Beth expertly set the broken bone and wrapped the arm with the gauze. She soon had the plaster of paris rolls soaked enough to begin applying them. When the cast was on, Beth put Mary Sue's arm in a sling and helped her from the examination table to the chair placed before her desk. She then took her own seat behind the desk and scribbled out a prescription.

"This'll help the pain." Beth handed Mary Sue the script. "You'll have to wait until morning, though, to get it filled. If you think you need it, I can give you a few pain pills to tide you over until then."

"I'll be fine." Mary Sue took the prescription.

"You'll need to prop the casted arm on a pillow and keep it elevated for the next day or so to minimize the swelling. And if your fingers should become cold or numb, you must return immediately to the clinic. The resultant swelling from the injury can sometimes cut off the circulation, especially when it comes up against a stiff cast."

"Fine. I'll be sure to do that."

Beth frowned. It was evident Mary Sue wanted to get out of here as quickly as possible. There were some questions that needed answering, however, before Beth would let her leave.

"This isn't the first time this has happened, is it?" She leveled a piercing stare at the injured woman. When no answer was forthcoming, Beth leaned closer. "Is it, Mary Sue?"

"No, it isn't." Mary Sue wouldn't look at her.

"Did you and Harlow both fall down the stairs together, or was it only you?"

"I slapped Harlow . . . well, maybe I hit him," Mary Sue said. "Hard enough anyways to leave that bruise. That's when he finally lost his temper. He hit me back. I lost my balance and fell down the stairs."

"So it was an accident? He didn't push you?"

Mary Sue met her gaze. "And why would you think Harlow would purposely hurt me? I've never implied such a thing. Never!"

Though the woman tried to mask her panic, Beth couldn't help but catch a note of it in her voice. "No, you've never implied anything of the sort," Beth said, trying to speak soothingly. "However, I'm trained to look below the surface of things. Not long after I arrived here, you came in with injuries sustained after a fall down the stairs. And the first time I met Harlow, I noted how he treated you. Disdainfully, almost cruelly. I saw him squeezing your hand so hard at the Fall Social it brought tears to your eyes. And then there's the edge of hysteria I hear in your voice and see in your eyes sometimes when you think someone's getting too close to the truth."

Mary Sue laughed unsteadily. "And what might that truth be?"

"The truth that Harlow beats you."

The blood drained from Mary Sue's face. She half rose from her chair, hesitated, then sank back into it. Cradling her casted arm against her, she dragged her gaze up to Beth's.

"He'll deny it. Then when he gets me back home, he'll beat me again." Mary Sue bit her lip and looked away. "And there's no one who can stop him or would want to."

"I want to." Beth's hands clenched on her desk. "No one has the right, just because they're married, to treat another cruelly."

Mary Sue shook her head. "And what could you do? No one would believe you any more than they'd believe me. Harlow has a reputation to uphold in this town. He's seen as a good, God-fearing man who attends church regularly."

"I could talk to Noah for you. Maybe he could–"

"No!" Mary Sue's eyes filled with tears. "It's too shameful. I couldn't bear for anyone else to know."

"Noah would be discreet. You can trust him. And it'd just be you and Harlow coming to see him in the privacy of the rectory."

"Y-you don't understand. It's my fault. If o-only I was a better wife . . ." Mary Sue began to sob.

Beth stood and came around her desk to take Mary Sue into her arms. She didn't know what else to do. What Mary Sue had said was perhaps true. Even if people knew what Harlow did to Mary Sue, most wouldn't interfere.

But she wasn't most people. She was Mary Sue's doctor and sworn to heal. Moreover, she was sworn first to do no harm, and allowing these beatings to continue was prolonging the harm.

Still, what could she do if Mary Sue demanded she not tell anyone? What was of more importance–the responsibility to keep her patients' secrets, or defending them, even if in the doing she must break confidentiality?

Beth released Mary Sue and stood. "Wait here. I need to confer with Doc about a few things. I'll be back."

"Y-you won't tell him, w-will you?" Through her tears, Mary Sue looked pleadingly up at Beth.

"I'm pretty sure Doc's already figured out what happened," said Beth. "Harlow shouldn't have brought you here tonight if he hoped to hide the truth from us."

"He got afraid once he realized he'd probably broken my arm." She smiled wanly. "He's not a cruel man, Harlow isn't. He just gets so frustrated sometimes, and it doesn't take much to set him off."

"Well"—Beth laid a hand on her shoulder—"let's just see where this leads, shall we? Will you permit me that much anyway?"

"Okay."

Mary Sue's acquiescence was barely audible, but it was all Beth needed. She swept from the room, closed the door, and walked to Doc's office. Her knock was soon answered.

"How's Mary Sue?" Doc asked.

"Her right radius sustained a simple fracture. I set it, then casted it. She's waiting in my office." Beth glanced at Harlow, who was sitting before Doc's desk, his head turned in their direction. "I need to confer with you. Privately."

Doc looked back at the big banker. "I'll just be a few minutes. Dr. MacKay has some questions." He closed the door and motioned Beth to the waiting area.

"How extensive were Harlow's injuries?" she asked, wasting no time getting to the heart of the matter.

"Just the bruised cheekbone. Nothing else."

"Doesn't look like he took a tumble down the stairs with Mary Sue?"

"It'd be highly unlikely."

"Did he perhaps change his story of what happened?"

Doc shook his head. "Nope. How about Mary Sue?"

"I'm not at liberty to say, but you're welcome to draw your own conclusions."

He gave a snort of disgust. "Oh, I was beginning to draw my own conclusions a ways back."

"Then what do we do?"

Doc inhaled a deep breath. "This sort of thing is tricky. I'm no lawyer, but from what I've heard, a woman doesn't have a whole lot of rights in such matters. Best that Mary Sue could do is divorce him."

"I'm not sure she's ready to take such a step. And she doesn't want Harlow to know she told me what really happened."

"Well"—Doc scratched his jaw—"the only thing I can do then is confront Harlow with my suspicions, based on the extent of Mary Sue's injuries and, in comparison, how minor his were. See if, for starters, I can get him to confess to some marital discord."

"If you can do that, maybe we could get them to talk to Noah. Otherwise, I'm going to push Mary Sue to leave that monster."

"Now, hold on." As Beth turned away, Doc grabbed hold of her arm. "Let's take this slow and easy. Harlow may have his troubles, but he's not a monster. He needs help as much as Mary Sue."

"Maybe so, but Harlow's life isn't in danger if Mary Sue continues to stay with him. Mary Sue, on the other hand . . ."

Doc sighed. "I know. Let's bring Harlow into your office and discuss this. Let me do most of the talking, though. In your present state of mind, you're as likely to blow up as Harlow is."

"Fine," Beth muttered, knowing Doc's assessment was probably accurate. Right now she was so mad at Harlow Peterson she was tempted to give him a matching bruise on his other cheek.

When the banker was seated in Beth's office, his chair on one side of the desk with Doc, while Mary Sue sat on the other side with Beth, he soon admitted to the fight. "It was an accident, though, that Mary Sue tripped and fell down the stairs," he said. "I didn't push her. I'm not that sort of a man."

"Then you admit to having some marital problems?" Doc asked. "Problems that aren't getting any better?"

"Oh, I wouldn't say that." Harlow cast a glance at his wife. "Would you, honey?"

147

Mary Sue wouldn't look at him. "I-I'm worried, Harlow. I'm afraid of what might happen next time."

"Well, you *did* get pretty riled up tonight. And you haven't been yourself in a long while."

Beth saw Mary Sue's hands clench knuckle white. She bit back her own scathing reply and seized on the opening that Harlow, in his attempt to foist all the blame on Mary Sue, had given her.

"Perhaps it's time for you and Mary Sue to seek some outside help." She locked gazes with the big banker. "Perhaps it's time you and Mary Sue have a talk with Father Starr. Being the God-fearing man that you are, I'm sure you hold the sanctity of your marriage vows in the highest esteem and would do whatever it took to protect and honor them."

As if he were considering a possible trap, Harlow's eyes narrowed. "I'd prefer first to try and work out our differences privately."

Beth's smile was thin and unyielding. "I think it's past time for that, Mr. Peterson, when injuries occur. Don't you agree?"

Fury blazed in Harlow's eyes, but he nodded. "I suppose so, Dr. MacKay." He turned to Mary Sue. "Well, shall we be going, my dear? I think we've imposed on the good doctors' time long enough as it is."

"Yes, it is getting late, isn't it?" Doc Childress climbed to his feet. "Time enough tomorrow to make arrangements with Father Starr."

Beth stood. Harlow Peterson wouldn't like what she had next to say any more than he had before, but Mary Sue was her patient. She intended to do everything she could to protect her.

"One thing more. Due to the extent of Mary Sue's injury, I'm concerned about possible circulatory and neurological complications for the first twenty-four hours or so. With your permission, Mr. Peterson, I'd like her to stay in the rectory's spare bedroom tonight. That way I can check on her periodically to make certain there's no permanent damage."

Harlow frowned and looked to Doc. "Is this really necessary? I'm quite capable of taking care of my own wife."

"Yes, I'm sure you are," Doc said agreeably. "Still, sometimes the signs are very subtle and noted only by the trained eye. I must add my concurrence to Dr. Mac-Kay's recommendation."

"Fine. Okay." The banker rolled his eyes and sighed. "First thing tomorrow morning, though, I intend to—"

"That'd be a wonderful idea," Beth said. "I'll alert Father Starr you'll be stopping by. You can talk with him then and set up some times for more extended visits."

Harlow hesitated, shooting his wife a questioning glance. "Is that acceptable to you, my dear?"

"Yes. I trust Dr. MacKay to know what's best for me."

He retrieved his hat from the desk where he'd placed it, nodded, then turned on his heel and stalked from the room. When the front door closed behind him, Beth smiled at Mary Sue.

"I hope you don't mind my forcing your stay at the rectory tonight. I just thought it best you both have a time to cool off."

"Rather," Mary Sue offered dryly, "you thought it best *Harlow* have a time to cool off. But it's okay." She stood. "Shall we go? It's getting late, and tomorrow promises to be a trying day."

"Yes, let's be on our way." Beth indicated the door. "It's best we all get as much sleep as we can, to prepare us for tomorrow."

᷂

Thankfully, their arrival at the rectory didn't wake Millie. Beth soon had Mary Sue tucked in Millie's old bed upstairs, her arm propped up on several pillows. After checking Mary Sue's fingers for adequate circulation, she left the woman to her rest.

Though hesitant to disturb Noah at midnight, Beth thought it best to inform him he had an extra houseguest. She rapped softly on his bedroom door and was soon rewarded with the sound of footsteps. A few moments later, Noah opened the door.

He was barefoot, clad in trousers and a hastily and lopsidedly buttoned shirt. His hair was tousled, his expression still groggy from sleep. It took all Beth's control not to grin at his boyishly endearing appearance.

"What's wrong?" Noah asked. "Is Millie worse?"

"No. Millie's fine and sound asleep. I just wanted to alert you to the fact Mary Sue Peterson's using Millie's room tonight." She pointed two doors down. "*That* room."

A dark blond brow arched in puzzlement. "This sounds like a longer story than can be told standing out here in the hallway. Why don't you put on a pot of water while I finish dressing? I'll meet you in the kitchen shortly."

"I didn't mean to keep you from your sleep," Beth said by way of protest. "It can wait until—"

He held a silencing finger to his lips. "Downstairs. Five minutes."

Beth knew no purpose was served in arguing further. Besides, all this talk might wake Emily, not to mention upset Mary Sue. She nodded, then turned and headed back down the hall to the stairs.

Five minutes later, Noah joined her in the kitchen. The kettle was already on the stove and the coals were stoked back to a nice little fire. Beth glanced up from the mugs she was setting on the table.

150

"I'm sorry to have awakened you," she hurried to explain, keeping her voice low. "I just thought you should know, since it's your house, and I didn't want any embarrassing surprises in the morning."

Noah smiled wryly as he took a seat at the table. "Nice of you to remember it's my house *after* you invited in a houseguest. Still, I know you wouldn't have done it unless you thought it necessary. And, if I don't miss my guess, this smacks of something that might well involve me at any rate."

"Well, yes, it might. Since Harlow has agreed to pay you a visit tomorrow, and you'll soon see the extent of Mary Sue's injuries, I guess I'm not really revealing anything you won't soon know for yourself."

Beth pulled out a chair as quietly as possible and took a seat. Although Noah had combed his hair, rebuttoned and tucked in his shirt, and put on shoes, the image of him when he had first opened his bedroom door kept coming to mind. Beth couldn't shake the feeling of intimacy between them, of trust and respect. It was almost as if, bit by bit, they were growing closer, more comfortable with each other. But Beth tried to clear her mind of such thoughts. She had a patient to take care of.

"Mary Sue and her husband had a fight tonight. It resulted in Mary Sue falling down the stairs. She suffered a broken arm. Harlow now sports a bruised cheekbone."

Noah frowned. "I've heard rumors they were having marital difficulties. Sounds like those difficulties have escalated now, though, to some dangerous heights."

"Doc and I got Harlow to agree to come see you tomorrow. In the meanwhile, I thought it best Mary Sue spend at least tonight away from her husband."

He nodded. "Might not hurt. I'd imagine they both need a little time to think things over."

151

"If it was up to me," Beth muttered, "I'd like to see Mary Sue leave that brute for good. I don't hold out much hope Harlow Peterson's the kind of man to change his ways."

"The Lord willing, there's always hope. Harlow's got his problems, but he's a man of his word. And he gave his word to cleave to Mary Sue through good times and bad."

"That may be," she said, "but those bad times might eventually also be the death of Mary Sue."

"We won't let it come to that, you and I." Noah reached over and took her hand. "Now that the truth is out in the open, we can work together on this."

Beth smiled. Noah's hand felt good upon hers. His presence, this night in this kitchen, seemed so natural, as if it always had been meant to be this way. She could almost imagine what it'd be like to sit here with him every night from now on . . . as man and wife.

With a jerk, Beth recoiled from such a thought. All they could ever be was friends. Friends who might indeed be able to work together for the good of Grand View. But only to serve others, and never, ever, themselves.

12

When I was a child, I spake as a child, I understood as a child, I thought as a child: but when I became a man, I put away childish things.

1 Corinthians 13:11

With a rising sense of frustration and futility, Noah watched Harlow Peterson, Mary Sue in tow, storm from his office. Their meeting had not gone well.

Apparently fortified by a good night's sleep and the leisure to think on what had transpired the evening before, Harlow wasted no time setting the record straight. Over the past year, he claimed, his wife had become increasingly irrational, her mood swings frequently culminating in violent outbursts. Last night was only one of many.

Mary Sue, instead of defending herself, had begun weeping silently; nothing Noah said or did could extract any comment from her. His exasperation rising, he had then been forced to direct all his efforts at Harlow.

And Harlow had refused to accept any blame in the events leading to last night's battle. He was only trying to defend himself, he said, when Mary Sue lost control and began striking out at him. Her fall down the stairs was her own fault.

The final insult to Noah's intelligence, however, had been when Harlow claimed it was only because he was a good Christian that he even tolerated his wife's presence in his home anymore. Noah lost the last of his rapidly shredding patience and accused Harlow of being a hypocrite and a fool. No decent man–Christian or not–treated a woman, much less his wife, in the manner Harlow treated Mary Sue.

Now as he sat alone in his office contemplating the aftermath of the disastrous meeting, Noah deeply regretted his heated words. It just tore at his heart, though, how beaten down and hopeless Mary Sue had seemed. He had known her for almost thirteen years. She was no longer the woman she had formerly been.

True, Mary Sue had once been a spoiled, spiteful young woman. But she had also possessed a sparkle and wit and passion for life. With her lush ebony hair and flashing, vibrant blue eyes, Mary Sue had been the belle of Grand View. Though she had tried and failed to win the heart of every MacKay man at Culdee Creek at one time or another, she had otherwise never lacked for suitors.

As the years passed, however, Mary Sue considered and cast aside all potential mates. Maybe the rest of the men had been, in her estimation, beneath her. Whatever her reasons, spinsterhood was fast approaching when Harlow Peterson came to town. And though at first their marriage had seemed a happy one, rumors had gradually filtered even to Noah's ears. Rumors, until Beth MacKay's arrival, no one dared examine too closely.

Noah sighed and pushed himself up from his chair. He had been no better than the rest. He had hoped the Petersons would work out their marital difficulties on their own. It wasn't his business to pry into anyone's private life, especially when it might disrupt a holy union sanctioned in the eyes of God.

He couldn't ignore the situation anymore, though, Noah thought as he entered the kitchen and headed toward Millie and Beth's bedroom. Whether Harlow wished it or not, it was his duty as pastor to help Mary Sue and Harlow salvage what was left of their marriage, then teach them how to rebuild it into one pleasing to the Lord.

Millie was awake, reading her Bible. As he paused at the bedroom door to knock politely, she laid her Bible aside and turned toward him.

"Come on in, honey." Through her labored breathing, she smiled in welcome. "It's so unusual to see you still at home . . . this late in the morning."

"It's a long story," Noah said with a sigh as he pulled a chair up close to her bed. He hesitated, recalling that Luanne Stout was somewhere in the house. "Mind if I close the door?"

"Sure. Luanne's upstairs, though . . . playing with Emily. I don't expect her . . . down here anytime soon."

Noah climbed to his feet, walked over, and shut the door. "Well, I'd still feel better having some privacy. Besides needing advice, I just plain want to talk."

"So, what keeps you here . . . so late in the morning?" Millie asked when Noah was seated.

"Had a talk with Harlow and Mary Sue Peterson. It didn't go well."

"I'm sorry . . . to hear that."

"I lost my temper with Harlow." Noah shook his head. "I don't know what's the matter with me. Of late, I don't seem to have the patience and compassion I know I should."

"You've been under . . . a lot of pressure." Millie turned over onto her back. "It's not easy on anyone . . . seeing a loved one slipping away."

Noah glanced down. "What's wrong with me, Millie? If anyone should be able to accept death, it should be me. Death is but the final bridge we must cross to a full and eternal union with the Lord. But I can't . . . I can't see it that way anymore!"

"Why not, honey? What has changed . . . from what you used to believe?"

"Losing Alice shook me to the core of my being. And now to lose you, too. . . ." He shook his head. "I question God's mercy. I question His wisdom. I don't understand Him anymore."

"And when has any of that been necessary . . . in order to love and serve the Lord? Indeed, aren't we but arrogant fools . . . ever to presume to know the Lord's mind?"

"Perhaps we are, but what can I give to His people if I suddenly feel as if the Lord has turned His back on me and walked away?"

Millie chuckled softly. "I was just reading the story . . . about Jesus raising Lazarus from the dead. Lazarus and his two sisters . . . must have felt that same sense of desertion when Lazarus was sick and Jesus wouldn't come. I wonder what Lazarus thought . . . at the moment of his death? Did he feel betrayed by his friend? Or did he die in faith . . . certain even in his dying that the Lord's will . . . would be done, and that was all that really mattered?"

Millie paused to catch her breath and reached out to put her hand on his arm. "Because, for God's will to be done . . . in that instance, Lazarus *had* to die. In his surrendering to the unknown . . . of death, however, Lazarus was reborn . . . and the Lord was glorified." Her eyes shone with a joyous light. "That's why I surrender . . . to whatever fate the Lord wishes for me. In my loving surrender, I further God's will. My living–and my dying–glorifies Him. As will yours, in your acceptance and surrender . . . to whatever happens to me."

"But I need you, Millie! God knows that. You're my greatest mentor and friend. Who'll I come to, to speak of God and things eternal, when you're gone? I need your wisdom. I need your strength. I need your example to guide and inspire me!"

"Trust in the Lord, honey. He'll not long . . . leave you bereft. Perhaps, just perhaps, in His wisdom God has decided it's time for you to move on, to set aside childish things . . . and become the man of strength and maturity He has always wanted you to be. And perhaps, to do that, He must purge you . . . of your dependency on me, of the things of this world that have tethered you overlong. You want to fly . . . don't you? Fly to the Lord?"

"Yes. Yes, I've always wanted that, but instead of feeling closer to doing that, I feel . . . I feel . . ." Noah groaned and lowered his head, burying his face in his hands. "I feel as if I'm sinking farther and farther into the muck and mire of this life."

"Then stand fast. Never despair. The Lord may well . . . be working to bring you to a higher level of union with Him. But with each breakthrough there are always . . . crises of trust and faith." She touched his head. "It seems our souls stretch, grow best, that way."

Noah looked up at her. "I know that, Millie. Deep down, I know that. I just get so lost and confused sometimes. You help me so much to sort things through."

"You talk with Beth a lot these days. It gladdens my heart . . . to see you making a friend, and a close one, too."

He smiled, straightened, and laid his head against the chair's high back. "Yes, little by little I think Beth's coming to trust me. And I hope someday to learn the source of the great pain she carries so closely to her heart. That, I think, is the key to healing her wounds."

"You care about her, don't you?"

"Yes, I care," he said carefully. "I've known her for so long that she almost feels like—"

"That's not what I mean, Noah Starr, and you know it!"

The vehemence of Millie's words set off a spell of coughing. Noah stood, took up the glass of water at her bedside, and offered it to his aunt. Millie accepted the water and, by-the-by, the coughing eased. But she was not to be deterred.

"You love Beth. Don't you?"

The blood drained from Noah's face. His eyes widened; he swallowed hard. But even with Millie, he lacked sufficient courage to name the desires still raging hotly within him.

"Love her?" He laughed unsteadily. "Why would you ever think that? Beth and I . . . well, we're just friends."

Millie snorted with disbelief. "Same story I heard from her . . . after a mess of blushing and hemming and hawing. For pity's sake, why don't you two sit down . . . really talk to each other for a change? You might be very pleasantly surprised at what you discover."

"It's not as simple as that." Noah made an exasperated motion indicating the room with all of Beth's belongings scattered around it. "She's a boarder here, not to mention the daughter of my best friend. If you're wrong about Beth's feelings for me, my broaching such a subject could make for a very uncomfortable situation. Besides, I've no intention of ever marrying again. One heartbreaking loss of a wife was more than enough!"

"So I'm supposed to hang around a while longer just because you're too afraid to give life . . . and love another chance? Is that how it is?"

158

Noah stared up at his aunt in confusion. "Whatever does Beth have to do with you?"

"Oh, never mind." She waved him away. "Get on with you. It's impossible to talk to you . . . when you get this way. Just get on with you!"

He rose, paused as he struggled with something to say, then gave up. His aunt had turned her face away from him, but he could still see her tightly pursed lips and stern expression. Best to let her cool down a bit, then try again.

"Have it your way," he said, walking to the door. "You always do in the end anyway. I'll leave your door open, though, in case you need anything. And I'll tell Luanne I'm leaving. She should maybe bring Emily downstairs now."

"Yes, you do that, honey," Millie said, her voice softening a bit. "Will you be home for lunch today?"

"Probably not." Noah stifled a grin. As always, his aunt's bursts of temper never lasted long. "This morning's work has put me behind as it is. I'll try and make it home for supper, though."

With that, Noah turned and strode from the room.

The snow fell all day, covering the land with a thick, white blanket that only grew deeper as the hours passed. The sky took on the leaden color of a storm growing in strength and power. Clouds sagged with the weight of rising moisture, until it became difficult to see more than a few yards above or ahead. And then the wind picked up, howling wildly as it careened between buildings and down the streets.

Noah glanced up from the sermon he was preparing for tomorrow's service on Sunday, January 30, and frowned. January and February were traditionally the

159

most bitter, snow-laden winter months in these parts. The pending storm, however, promised to be one of the worst he had ever seen.

He laid down his pen and glanced at his desk clock. Half past three. Save for a few finishing touches, his sermon was done. Though he made it a policy not to take work home with him, today was an exception. The weather outside would only get worse. The thought of watching it from the warm, snug haven of the rectory with Millie, Emily, and Beth held great appeal.

It was frigid outside, well below zero, he noted as he paused to check the thermometer nailed beside the church's side door. Noah turned up his collar, hunched down in his coat's thick, woolen warmth, and made a dash down the street toward the rectory.

The dash, however, quickly slowed to a trudge through the knee-high drifts. By the time he stomped into the rectory's entry, he was coated from head to toe in thick, fat flakes.

"Oh, thank the Lord!" Luanne ran into the entry as Noah stood there, slapping off as much snow as he could from his clothing. "I was hoping you'd come home early, Father Starr. It's a long walk to my house, and what with the snow getting so deep . . ."

"Would you like me to hitch up the horse and buggy and take you home?" he asked. "I'd be glad to, you know."

"Well, if you wouldn't mind too much, Father Starr." Her expression brightened. "And then, on the way back, you could fetch Dr. MacKay, too. She hasn't come home from the clinic yet, but she sure needs to right soon, don't you think?"

"Yes, I think so, too." He hung his coat on the coatrack. "Let me just check first with Millie. And where's Emily?"

"Emily's in with Millie. They're both still napping."

"Okay. That should be all right. We'll only be gone about fifteen minutes or so." Noah took up his coat again, donned it over his woolen neck scarf, slipped on his gloves, and added a knit woolen cap to his head. "Stay inside here until I bring the buggy around. Then come on out with those two lap robes in the trunk there."

Luanne nodded. Noah shot her a quick smile, then headed around back to the stable. The horse was none too fond of the idea of going out into the near-blizzard conditions, but Noah was finally able to coax the animal into the buggy traces. He drove around to the front of the rectory, and Luanne dashed out to join him. As Noah urged the horse forward, she threw the thick, warm lap robes over their legs.

When Luanne was finally deposited safely at her home, Noah turned and headed back into town and down Main Street. The light was still on in the clinic, so he tied the horse outside, then walked in. Helen Yates sat at her desk.

"What can I do for you, Father Starr?" she asked.

Noah pulled his cap off his head and glanced at Beth's closed office door. "Is she still seeing patients?"

Helen's gaze swung to the door. "Oh, no, not anymore. Dr. MacKay always closes her door when she's not around. She left three hours ago on a house call to the Johnsons' farm. I assumed she'd already finished and had returned directly to the rectory. The Johnson boy—Samuel—had a case of the measles and was her last patient for the day."

Unease curled in Noah's gut. "Well, Beth's not home. Can you ring up the Johnsons and see when she left them?"

"Of course." Helen went to the telephone and turned the crank. After what seemed an interminable amount of time, she finally hung up the earpiece.

161

"No answer. Nothing. I wonder if the lines are down because of the storm."

"So we don't know if Beth's still at the Johnsons', waiting out the storm, or somewhere in between there and Grand View. Is that what you're saying?"

Helen's eyes grew wide. "Yes, I suppose that is what I'm saying. But surely Dr. MacKay would choose to stay where it's safest. She knows how bad the weather can get here in the winter."

"Yes," Noah said grimly, "but she's also prone to imagine, after living here all these years, that she can handle anything the weather cares to dish out." He did some quick mental calculations. "The Johnsons live about five miles northeast of here, don't they?"

"Yes." Helen nodded vigorously. "If you follow the bluffs, you should be able to run right into their place."

"Problem is," he muttered, "if Beth takes a different route home, I might miss her in this snow." He put his cap back on his head and pulled it low over his ears. "Could I impose on you to go to the rectory and stay with Millie and Emily until I get back? I took Luanne home to be with her family, and there's no one to stay with them now."

"I'd be happy to, Father Starr." She gathered up her paperwork and shoved it into her desk drawer. "Don't you worry about them at all. We'll be fine until you get back."

"I'm much obliged to you, Helen." Noah turned to go when she halted him.

"Be careful out there, Father Starr. And bring Dr. Mac-Kay safely back to us."

He glanced at her over his shoulder. "I'll try, Helen. Just say a prayer for the both of us, will you? We're going to need it."

"I'm sorry, Father Starr," Zeke Johnson, Samuel's father, said to Noah an hour later after a painfully slow ride out to their ranch. "Dr. MacKay left here over an hour and a half ago. She should've been back at Grand View by now."

"Well, that's the problem. She wasn't an hour ago when I left to ride out here."

"We asked her to stay the night and wait for the storm to blow over, but she insisted she needed to get back to town." Zeke shook his head. "And you know how head-strong those MacKays can get when they set their minds to something."

Unfortunately, Noah did. And Beth was a MacKay through and through.

"What direction did she ride out? And was she in a buggy or on horseback?" he asked.

Zeke lifted his arm and pointed. "Straight west she went, and on horseback. A big bay gelding."

"Thanks. I'd best be on my way if I'm to have any hope of finding her in this snow."

"God go with you, Father. The Doc's been good to me and mine. I don't want her to come to any harm."

Noah smiled tightly. "Nor do I, Zeke. Nor do I."

An hour or so after he rode out from Zeke Johnson's place and headed back in the general direction of Grand View, Noah lost his way. As the day waned into dark-ness, the wind and snow created whiteout conditions. At best, he could barely see to his horse's head. And, at the worst, he couldn't even see the horse.

Frustration and a growing apprehension filled him. He'd be lucky even to make it back to Grand View him-self, much less have any hope of finding Beth. Trusting his horse's instincts over his own, he gave the animal his head and just held on.

Lord, Noah silently prayed, let Beth have made it to town already. Let her be safe and sound back at the rectory. And if it's also Your will, let me make it back home safely, too.

The wind was icy, bitter, and his face, hands, and feet gradually became numb. He pulled the wool scarf from his jacket and tugged it up to cover his nose and mouth. After dragging the two lap robes high up onto his chest and tucking them snugly behind him, he wrapped the reins around the loosened brake arm and thrust his gloved hands beneath his armpits. By now the temperature was at least ten or twenty below zero. No telling what it'd drop to by the end of the night.

He knew he had to find some sort of shelter; there was little hope of surviving out in this wind. But the chances of happening onto any sort of building when he couldn't see more than a few feet in any direction would require more than luck. It'd require a miracle.

An ironic thought struck him. He had been so worried about losing Millie and had agonized over God's heartlessness in taking her from him, he had never once considered the possibility he could actually die before his aunt. But no one, save God, knew when the time of one's death would come. And death just might come for him this night.

The consideration didn't frighten Noah. Despite all that had transpired of late to test it, he still had his faith. His only regret was leaving Millie and Emily. And Beth. Sweet, alluring Beth. Who knows where their relationship might have led?

Noah chuckled, the sound more of a grunt through cold-stiffened lips. He must really be getting frostbitten, leastwise in the head, to imagine such a thing. He and Beth . . . What a dreamer he had become!

His horse's pace quickened suddenly, causing the buggy to lurch then skid on the frozen ground. The animal whinnied. From a place ahead and down to his right, Noah heard another horse whinny in reply. Excitement shot through him. He grabbed the reins from the brake arm and pulled back hard, halting his horse.

"Beth?" he shouted out into the wind and snow. "Beth, is that you? Beth, are you there?"

No answer came. Despair filled him. How could he possibly find anyone in this?

Then the other horse whinnied again. Noah set the buggy brake, wrapped the reins around the brake arm, and climbed down, heading through deep snow in the direction of the horse.

"Beth? Beth?" Noah cried out as loud as he could. "If you're there, answer me!"

For a fleeting instant, he thought he heard a sound, a voice, but then it was gone. Still, it was enough to guide him closer. For a moment the wind stilled. The snow dissipated, and he saw the horse. At the animal's feet was a dark form.

"Beth!" Noah whispered and fought his way forward.

13

Though your sins be as scarlet, they shall be as white as snow.

Isaiah 1:18

She was cold, unconscious. No matter how hard Noah tried to rouse her, Beth wouldn't respond. Finally, because there were no other options, and because he couldn't leave her out in the wind and snow any longer, Noah gathered Beth into his arms and carried her back to the buggy.

He wrapped her snugly in the two lap robes and laid her on the buggy floor, out of the wind. Then, gathering up the reins, Noah urged the horse on.

He had to get Beth to some sort of shelter as soon as possible, if there was to be any hope of reviving her. The blowing snow, however, refused to subside, and he couldn't see any farther ahead than he had before.

Anger filled him. Had he found Beth only to lose her?

Help me, Lord, he prayed, his entreaty both fervent and frantic. Help me. Don't let Beth die. Help me find some way out of this storm. Help me.

The wind screamed, tearing down from the heavens. The snow rose, fell, swirled endlessly as if in some crazy dance. And still Noah drove on, battling his growing despair.

Trust, he told himself over and over. Trust the Lord will make this all turn out for the good. He loves Beth. He knows what's best for her.

Tears stung his eyes before being whipped away by the icy wind. If You would, Lord, take me this night instead of Beth. Take my life and spare hers, because the thought of losing her—

Just then, the wind died once more. The airborne snow settled, drifting gently back to the ground. And, once again, Noah could see for some distance. To his left and not more than fifty feet away was a small house. It was dark, most likely abandoned, but shelter nonetheless. If the wind hadn't died when it did, he would've driven right past it and headed on into the darkness.

Noah turned the horse toward the house, praying desperately that the wind would hold for a few minutes more. And, by some miracle, it did. Just as he pulled up before the house, the storm unleashed its fury once more.

As if it had built in intensity in those few minutes of respite, the wind shrieked down now with a savage vengeance. Climbing from the buggy, Noah was nearly knocked from his feet. He grabbed hold of the buggy, which also threatened to topple over, and held on. Finally, when the wind eased a bit, Noah staggered to the house and pounded on the door.

"Is anyone home?" he shouted above the roaring maelstrom. "Is anyone home?"

No one answered. Noah tried the door. It swung open. He pulled out a packet of matches he always kept with him for lighting a stubborn altar candle, walked into the dwelling's dark interior, and struck a match.

It was indeed abandoned, empty save for a rickety table and some chairs, an old chest shoved into a corner, and tattered curtains at the windows. On the table sat an oil lamp. The house appeared reasonably weather tight, however, and possessed a cast-iron, potbellied stove.

Noah ran from the house, pulled Beth from the buggy floor, and slung her over his shoulder. When they were inside, he kicked the door closed. In the pitch blackness, he carried her to the stove and laid her off to one side. Then, feeling his way to the table and the oil lamp, he struck another match to illuminate the area.

After removing the chimney, Noah lowered the match to the wick and prayed the small amount of oil remaining in the fount would light. After what seemed an interminable amount of time, the wick glowed then flamed. Noah put the chimney back on the lamp and carried it to the stove, where he placed the lamp on the stovetop.

Ten minutes later and with the aid of the wood from a chair, he had a good fire going in the cast-iron stove. Noah then turned his attention to Beth. Unwrapping her from the blankets, he saw her coat, hat, and skirt were frozen and hard. He pulled off her outer garments, only to find her blouse and petticoat were also wet clear through.

Noah hesitated. If he removed those clothes, too, Beth would have scant remaining clothing left to insulate her. And she'd need more than the thickness of the two lap robes to warm her. She'd need his warmth as well.

He ripped off his jacket, hat, and gloves, which were as stiff and frozen as Beth's had been, and tossed them aside. The best that could be done, in addition to the heat slowly building in the woodstove, was to try to add his own body's warmth to Beth's chilled body. She'd do the same for him, he well knew, if the tables had been turned. And at such a time as this, saving a life was far more important than propriety.

With trembling fingers, Noah unbuttoned and removed Beth's blouse and petticoat. He shed his boots, shirt, and trousers just as quickly. Then, clad in his drawers, he snuggled up close to Beth and wrapped the lap robes around them both.

Her chilled flesh was uncomfortable, and Noah's first instinct was to pull away and hoard his own warmth, but he forced himself to press closer. If it required all his body's heat, if it drained the very life from him, he'd give it all to save her.

Her hands were like blocks of ice. Noah took them in his, trying to massage some circulation back into them. He pulled them up to lie between their two bodies. He laid his feet alongside hers. And all the while as he gently rubbed her back, he spoke to her.

"You're safe now, Beth," he whispered, his mouth pressed to her ear. "I'm here. I'll protect you. Just come back, Beth. Don't leave. I need you. Millie needs you. Emily needs you. Oh, sweet one, you're needed by so many. Don't leave us. Please, don't leave me!"

He talked and held her close as the night wore on. The little house warmed and, gradually, so did Beth. But she never woke, only dreamed on, caught in a place from which Noah feared he might never call her back.

In the wee hours of the morning, Noah finally fell into an exhausted sleep. And in his slumbering the storm passed through, leaving a ravaged land in its wake.

Something tickled Beth's nose. She rubbed at it and touched a rough blanket. Turning her face away, she snuggled against something warm, firm, and thudding most disconcertingly against her ear.

She frowned. It sounded . . . sounded just like a heartbeat.

Beth slowly opened her eyes. A thick, plaid lap robe half-covered her face. Above the blanket, she could see the beamed ceiling of a small and totally unfamiliar house. And beside her, that steady pounding went on and on. A chest rose and fell, slowly, rhythmically. An arm, a strong, masculine arm, pinned her to a *very* masculine body.

Recollection flooded back. She had been out in that horrendous snowstorm. Her horse had stumbled, and she had gone flying, striking her head on something hard.

That was the last thing she remembered. And now she was lying in a strange place, beside a strange man.

Ever so carefully, Beth pushed up to stare down at the man. Relief swamped her. Noah. It was Noah! She sighed and lay back next to him, reveling in the joyous realization. She was alive and safe with Noah. She was—

With an outraged gasp, Beth reared backward. Noah's chest was bare, and as her gaze swept downward, she realized he was dressed only in his underwear. As was she, she noted, turning her gaze to her chemise and long, lace-trimmed drawers. Whatever had happened?

Beth's glance scanned the room. It was bright outdoors, probably midday, and the sun glinted blindingly off tall drifts of fresh snow. Inside the house, she saw her coat and skirt flung in one direction, her blouse and petticoats in another. Noah's clothing lay nearby. At their head was a potbellied stove that radiated a faint heat.

The realization of what had most likely transpired struck her. Noah had rescued her last night, brought her here, and tried to save her life by warming her in whatever way he could. But how had Noah found her in that terrible storm? Indeed, how had he even known she was gone from town?

Taking great care not to disturb him, Beth disentangled one of the lap robes, wrapped it around herself so she was completely covered, then lay down beside Noah once more. A sweet joy filled her, twining about her heart until it squeezed with a fierce, aching pain. Noah . . . All that mattered was he had come for her, risking his own life in the doing.

She could love a man for such courage and devotion, if she hadn't loved him already.

Tenderly, Beth gazed at him. Her glance caressed his features, admiring his strong nose, his firm, full lips, the proud angle of his jaw, the smooth line of his cheek. He was so handsome, so dear.

Reaching up, Beth dared what she'd never dare if he had been awake. She ran her finger down the side of his face, across it, and then traced the line of his mouth. His cheeks were rough, his beard beginning to grow in. She reveled, though, in the maleness of it, the short, coarse hairs rasping most pleasantly beneath her fingertips. For this rare, glorious moment, he was hers to savor.

Noah stirred, shifted beside her. Then, ever so slowly, his lids lifted, and Beth was impaled by a clear brown gaze. As recognition seemed gradually to dawn, Noah's eyes warmed. He smiled.

"Beth," he said, his voice rusty with sleep. "God was good. He answered my prayers. He led me to you, then showed me the way to this house. He saved us both."

Beth didn't know what to say. The words caught in her throat, melted away in the emotions of the moment. God was indeed good. She was at Noah Starr's side, and she was content.

Clutching her blanket close, Beth snuggled against him. "Yes," she murmured at last and, for once in a very long while, meant it, "so it seems."

171

"Why did you leave the Johnsons', when you saw how bad the storm had become? If I hadn't known you were gone, if I hadn't gone out to find you . . . Well, you know as well as I you would've died out there."

"I wanted to get back to town, to you, Millie, and Emily. Millie's getting really bad, Noah. She doesn't have much time left." Beth exhaled a deep breath. "I wanted to be there for her, for you."

"But not at the risk of your life, Beth. No matter what happens, we'd never want you to risk your life." He cradled her face in his hand. "Do you really know how much you mean to us? Do you?"

Pain stabbed at her. Ah, if only Noah meant those words the way she needed him to mean them! But he was such a good, caring man, and would speak words like that many times in his life to many people. As he should. He was a man of God, after all.

Tears formed in Beth's eyes. "It was all I thought to give back to you," she whispered. "For all you've done for me."

"Beth, Beth," he crooned. Shoving to a sitting position, Noah pulled his lap robe up to cover himself, then wrapped his arm around her and pulled her close. "In truth, I've done so very little. I haven't even been able to aid you with that secret pain you carry so close. Yet how I've ached to help you with it."

She clenched her eyes shut. Fear swelled within her.

"If I told you, you wouldn't like me so much anymore." Her voice wavered. "Y-you'd think less of me and be so very disappointed. And I can't bear for you to do that. I just can't bear it, Noah!"

"There's nothing you can tell me that I haven't heard from someone, in some form, before. And when I listen, I am vowed to listen just as Jesus listened. With love and understanding. And even, if need be, with forgiveness."

172

Beth didn't want to tell him, but she was so weary of bearing her secret alone. Even if she lost Noah's affection and respect, perhaps he could at least show her the way to put the pain behind her. Show her how to find peace, acceptance, and maybe, just maybe, absolution. Absolution of her sins. Absolution from God.

"It happened in my final year of medical school," Beth said at long last. "I was getting maybe four hours of sleep most nights. The workload was heavy enough, and I put an even heavier burden on myself to keep up my class standing."

She tilted her head to look at him. "I was at the top of my class, as I'd been from the start and was determined to stay there. I was going to show everyone who had ever made a disparaging remark about me as a woman or an Indian that, in the end, I was better than any of them. But the strain got to be too much. I hadn't any friends and had made a fair share of enemies in the bargain. Too uppity, they said. A female who needed badly to be put in her place.

"In time, the isolation and loneliness became unbearable. I could hardly drag myself from bed in the morning. I fought constant exhaustion." She smiled grimly. "Then a handsome—and very wealthy—young intern took a sudden interest in me. At first, Matthew just seemed concerned. We'd go to the park near the hospital to eat our lunches together and talk. He made me laugh, something I'd almost forgotten how to do.

"Eventually, Matthew coaxed me from my dismal little flat to go to the opera with him, and then another time to the symphony. He showed me things I'd never seen before. Like a flower long denied sun and sustenance, I bloomed under his kind attention. He made me feel so alive, so womanly. In time, though . . ." Beth hung her head, suddenly ashamed to go on, to put the truth to words.

"In time," Noah finished gently for her, "you gave yourself to him? Is that what you're trying to say, Beth?"

"Yes"–her head jerked up, and she unflinchingly met his gaze–"I gave myself to him! But that's not the worst of it. A couple of months later, I discovered I was pregnant. I, nearly a doctor, had allowed myself to become pregnant! I felt like such a fool."

"And what did you do then? Did you tell him?"

She gave a strident laugh. "Oh, yes. I told him. At first, Matthew seemed happy, claiming he loved me and that we'd wed. But as he made plans to tell his parents and spoke of the fine life we'd have, I began to feel as if the jaws of a trap were closing about me. I realized that as kind as Matthew had always been to me, I didn't love him. Still, what choice did I have? The scandal would've ruined my medical career."

"Yet you didn't marry him, did you?"

"No, I didn't. Once his family discovered my Indian heritage, they wouldn't have anything to do with me. And Matthew wouldn't go against them."

"So he wasn't man enough to meet his responsibilities?"

"No, he wasn't." Beth looked away, playing over the events in her mind. Finally she turned back to Noah. "Luckily, the baby was due in late August. I was able to hide my pregnancy until I completed my final year of medical school. Then I insisted I had to return home for the summer.

"Instead, I left the city and found a place in a small town in upstate New York. I engaged a kindly, discreet physician to deliver the baby. And then I holed up in my tiny room, hiding there, afraid to leave for fear someone might see me." She paused, fighting the tears once more. "The baby came a few weeks early, stillborn but a perfectly formed, beautiful little girl."

174

Beth closed her eyes, the sheer, stark pain of that terror-filled night flooding her anew. Finally, though, she found the courage to go on.

"I'd thought that once she was born I'd take her to a foundling home and give her away. It was the only choice I had. I couldn't start my internship burdened by a child. Even with the money my parents sent for my tuition, there was barely enough left to support myself. And then there would've been the scandal . . ."

She dragged in a tear-choked breath. "But when I saw her, lying there so perfect and beautiful, my heart swelled with such love that I knew if she hadn't died, I could've never, ever, given her up not even for the sake of my medical career. But there was never any choice to make. I baptized her, then had her buried. Just in case God might take pity on my baby, I wanted to make sure she had a chance at heaven. If she'd lived, I would've even given up becoming a doctor for her."

"Ah, Beth. Beth." Noah kissed her on the forehead. "It breaks my heart to hear what you went through, all alone and so far from us, the people who love you. If I'd known, I would've come out there to help you, to do whatever you needed." He crooked her beneath her chin and lifted it, bringing her eyes level with his. "You believe that, don't you?"

Beth wanted to look away, but she didn't. "Yes, I believe you would've, but I just couldn't tell anyone. It was too shameful, and I couldn't bear to disappoint my father or Abby. I wanted them to be proud of me."

"They've always been proud of you, Beth, and would've anyway. They love you. Sure, it would've hurt them, because you'd been so hurt in the process, but they would've never stopped loving you."

"And what of you, Noah?" Beth forced herself to ask the question that carried an equal burden of pain. "Knowing what you know now, how do you feel about me? Do you still want me in your house, caring for Millie and Emily?"

He frowned in puzzlement. His hand fell from beneath her chin to rest lightly on her shoulder. "And why would you think my opinion of you has changed? Because you've made a mistake?"

"Because I've sinned and sinned grievously, that's why!" Despite Beth's staunchest efforts to quell her tears, they welled and coursed down her cheeks. "I engaged in an illicit union. I bore a child out of wedlock, for once Matthew turned his back on me, he never spoke to me again, not even to ask about the baby. And, I lost my faith in God. I—worst of all I hated God, Noah," Beth admitted at last, "especially after my daughter died. I raged at Him, called Him every name I could think of, and vowed never to follow Him again. Not because of what had happened to me, mind you, for I deserved my punishment. But because He had taken an innocent child"—momentarily, a sob choked off her voice—"taken her from her m-mother."

"Oh, Beth, Beth." Noah tenderly stroked her hair. "I think the Lord understood your anger and your pain and long ago forgave it. It's you who won't forgive yourself. Because of that, you imagine no one else—God included—will ever forgive you, either."

She rested her head on his shoulder. "But you don't understand, Noah. I knew better. I was raised better than that. Yet I willingly and willfully sinned anyway."

"Yes, you sinned. But God understands that. What matters now is that you confess your sins to Him, ask His forgiveness, then forgive yourself."

"You make it sound so simple."

"It *is* simple. Jesus Christ's death on the cross made it that simple." He smiled. "As for me, Beth, I'm hardly the one to judge you. My calling is to help, to teach, and to lead God's children back to Him. But never to judge. That's for Him, and only Him, to do."

A fierce, sweet joy rose in Beth. Suddenly, everything seemed possible, even returning to the Lord's loving arms. And Noah, dear sweet Noah, had shown her–in his own loving acceptance–the way.

"Do you know how much I love you, Noah Starr?" Impulsively, she sat up, leaned over, and kissed him on the mouth, then pulled back, stunned at her audacity.

His eyes widened. He stared at her, impaling her with the sudden intensity of his gaze. Then he raised his hand, moving it to cup the back of her neck. He pulled her to him, until her lips hovered but a hairsbreadth from his.

"Sweet, sweet Beth," he breathed huskily before closing the remaining, infinitesimal distance.

His mouth touched hers, slowly, leisurely, as if he wished to prolong the experience to its fullest. For a fleeting instant Beth stiffened, her mind refusing to register what her body recognized and accepted. Then, with a moan, she came to him, responding to his kiss with an eager, ardent abandon.

A fire ignited between them. A bittersweet recognition of their long-denied need swelled, then exploded. Joy rushed in to drench them in ever deepening waves of delight.

Then, from somewhere outside, noises intruded. Men's voices shouting in excitement. Heavy footsteps stomping on a wooden porch.

Beth struggled up from the pleasurable haze Noah's mouth and body had wrought on her. She pushed back, breaking their embrace.

"N-Noah! Someone's coming!"

Noah didn't seem to comprehend the implications of her words. He reached for her again, attempting to pull her back to him. Then recognition dawned. Hastily, his blanket clutched to him, Noah shoved to his knees.

The front door swung open. A man—tall and broad of shoulder, dressed in a thick jacket and black Stetson—strode in. At the sight of Beth and Noah, the man froze.

"Pa!" Beth cried with a crazy mixture of relief and horror, pulling the lap robe up to cover herself more fully.

14

*The LORD is nigh unto them that are of a broken heart;
and saveth such as be of a contrite spirit.*

Psalm 34:18

Noah locked gazes with Conor, and in his friend's eyes he saw relief and pained bewilderment. His heart twisted.

"It's not what you think, Conor," he said. "I went out looking for–"

Another pair of footsteps sounded on the porch. Then, from behind Conor, Harlow Peterson glanced around.

"What did you find, MacKay?" he demanded irritably. "Are they in here? If not, we need to–"

Harlow went silent as his glance took in Noah and Beth, quite obviously scantily clad beneath their individual lap robes. His eyes widened.

"Well, well. What do we have here?"

At the look of gloating triumph in Harlow's eyes, fury blazed in Noah. Fury at Harlow Peterson, but fury, as well, at himself. Whatever had possessed him to remain there on the floor with Beth after they woke, clinging to each other, kissing each other? No matter that it had felt so natural, so good, waking up to find her there beside him. What counted was the impropriety of it all. What if he had irreparably ruined Beth's reputation?

Conor must have seen the look in Noah's eyes, for he turned quickly to Harlow. "Why don't we step back outside while Father Starr and Beth get ready to go?" As he spoke, Culdee Creek's owner guided the other man out the door and back onto the porch. "Time enough for explanations later. We've got to head back to town." Conor glanced over his shoulder at Noah. "Why don't you get dressed, then join us out here?"

Noah nodded as the front door swung closed. He expelled a deep breath. "I'm sorry, Beth. This was all my fault."

"Oh, really?" Anger burned in her eyes. "And exactly where did you go wrong, Noah? When you risked your life to find me last night? Or was it, rather, when you removed our wet clothes and used the heat of your body to warm me? Or perhaps you're speaking instead of allowing me to kiss you?"

He reached over, grabbed his trousers, and proceeded to slip them on beneath his blanket. "We should've risen and dressed as soon as we woke. Conor's none too happy with us right now, and Harlow will soon be spreading all sorts of tales around town. He's sure to use this to his advantage, considering his current problems with Mary Sue. After all, a juicy scandal about us would take the heat off him."

"There's no scandal, and you know it, Noah Starr!"

At the sight of her, her cheeks flushed, her eyes flashing, her ebony hair a beguiling tumble about her shoulders, Noah paused in the task of fastening his trousers. Yes, there *is* a scandal, he silently answered her. Though

180

nothing but a kiss occurred, I wanted a lot more than that. I've wanted a lot more for a long while. It's just that this particular scandal, until today, lay hidden deep in my heart.

Noah grabbed his boots and socks, tugged them on, then found his shirt and did the same. "Well, we're not going to solve this or anything else right now. Best you hurry up and dress. I'll wait for you outside." He picked up his jacket, hat, scarf, and gloves, and headed out to the front porch, where Conor awaited him. Harlow had joined the other two men who had ridden out to find them as well.

"Thanks for getting Harlow out of there as fast as you did," Noah said. "I haven't wanted to punch a man in the face in a long while, but the way he looked at us . . . well, it made me mad."

"Yeah." Conor removed his Stetson to scratch his head. "I kind of gathered that. I didn't take too kindly to having my daughter's state of undress on display, either."

"There's a good reason we were like we were, Conor. I—"

His friend held up a hand. "Save it for later. Right now, we've got more pressing problems. When I left Millie four hours ago, she was in a pretty bad way, Noah. Doc and Helen were with her, but it didn't look good. We need to get you back to town as soon as we can."

Noah's gut clenched painfully. "Millie's dying?"

"I'm sorry, Noah, but it looks that way. Just hope she can hang on until we get back."

"I . . . I . . ." His mind racing, Noah glanced around. He caught sight of the extra horse tied to Conor's big black gelding. "Could I take that spare horse of yours and head on out? I . . . I want to get back to Grand View before it's too late."

Conor considered him a moment, then nodded. "Sure. By the way, we found your horse and buggy, plus Beth's

181

mount this morning. Seems they decided to head home on their own."

"Oh, yes," Noah replied, distracted now, "that's good." He pulled out his hat and gloves and put them on. "Please, would you explain to Beth where I've gone, and why? I don't want her to think I've deserted her, but I need–"

"Get on with you." Conor gave him a shove. "She'll understand. And we'll catch up with you soon at any rate."

"Thanks." Noah managed a shaky smile as he backed away. "Much obliged."

"It's not what you think, Pa," Beth said fifteen minutes later as she rode, perched behind her father on his horse, back toward Grand View. The going was slow, thanks to the deep, sometimes well over ten-foot-high drifts, but they retraced the search party's original trail, which helped immeasurably.

"And exactly what was I thinking," Conor asked, "considering Noah's my friend and a priest of God and you're my daughter?"

She gave a snort of disgust. "What anyone would think, seeing us half-dressed, even if we were each wrapped in a separate blanket. But you know Noah. You know he would never do anything purposely to compromise himself or a lady."

"Yeah, I know him very well. But I also know your feelings for him–feelings I'm willing to bet, despite the years, haven't changed all that much."

"And you think I'd seduce him?" Beth didn't know whether to be angry or hurt at her father's words. "That I'd purposely try to ruin him? And, even more to the point, if you think Noah would allow himself to be seduced, then you don't know him half as well as you think you do."

"Well, blast it all, Beth," Conor said, his voice going taut, "I'm sorry. I worried myself sick when I heard you and Noah were missing, so it was pretty disconcerting to find you two all wrapped up nice and cozy together."

Guilt flooded her. She was putting the blame on her father when she *had* been kissing Noah and had been the one to initiate the kiss.

"One way or another, none of this was Noah's fault. You have to believe that, Pa. He came out in the storm to find me, brought me to that house, and removed my clothes to warm me the quickest way he knew how, because I was unconscious and close to freezing to death." She rested her head on her father's back. "Saving my life meant more to him than some silly strictures or ideas of proper conduct. Perhaps it's the result of my medical training, but I do tend to look at things a bit differently than a lot of folks."

"I would've done the same thing in the same circumstances, no matter who it was." Conor sighed. "I guess I was just imagining the look of shock and guilt in both of your eyes when I first walked in then?"

Beth tightened her grip about her father's waist. "Just before you walked in, I'd finished telling him about some things that had happened to me back East. Noah was so kind, so gentle, so understanding, that this sudden surge of gratitude filled me. On an impulse, I kissed him—on the lips if you must know—and he kissed me back. That was all. Just a kiss. But when you surprised us . . . well, we realized what a compromising situation we seemed to be in. Hence, the shock and guilt."

"Can't say as how I blame Noah. He's got to have been tempted, lonely with Alice gone now these two years past, and you being such a lovely young woman. Still, there's going to be repercussions, what with Harlow seeing you two like that."

"Yes." Beth sighed. "There just might. Guess we'll have to deal with that as it comes." She hesitated. "Right now, though, I'm more worried about Noah and Millie. If he doesn't make it home in time . . ."

"He'll take it hard, and that's a fact. We'll have to do our best by him."

"Yes," she said, her thoughts already flitting far ahead to grim potentialities, "we will indeed."

☙

Beth found Noah kneeling beside Millie's bed, holding her lifeless hand in his, his head bowed, his body rigid with grief. For a long moment she stood in the doorway, watching, not knowing what to do. Then, squaring her shoulders, she walked in and hurried to him.

Sinking to her knees, Beth wrapped an arm around Noah's shoulders. He lifted his head and gazed at her. The sheer unmitigated agony she saw in his eyes tore at her heart.

With a soft, crooning sound, she pressed his head to her, cradling it on her breast. And for a long while they remained there, kneeling beside Millie, clasped in each other's arms.

☙

Millie's funeral was held four days later. Noah stumbled through the service as best he could, leaving the testimonials to others. Thanks to a good thaw after the storm, a grave was finally hacked out of the half-frozen earth in Grand View's forest cemetery.

184

As he stood at Millie's burial site, reciting prayers that left him dry and empty inside, Noah thought back to the first funeral he had presided at as the new assistant pastor. It had been fourteen years ago, and he, fresh from seminary, had come to aid his ailing uncle, Millie's husband. He had helped to bury Sally MacKay, Conor's first wife.

How many of Grand View's residents had he buried since then? Too many to count, it seemed. Too, too many, and the memory of them and how they had touched his life weighed especially heavy this cold February day.

Overhead, the huge ponderosa pines swayed in the wind, their branches scraping against each other to send an occasional spray of spent needles floating down onto the gathered crowd's heads. The sun was strong, the sky was a pure winter blue, and the little cemetery, with its headstones and wooden fencing around most graves, looked peaceful and tidy.

The souls buried beneath were peaceful, too; they had gone to their well-deserved reward. It was left to those who remained behind to slog on, mired in pain and loss, struggling to find some solace.

And answers. An answer for why, in saving Beth's life that night, he'd had to leave Millie to die without him. No time for tender farewells, for a final blessing. He felt cheated. And what had Millie thought, dying with her nephew once more out and away rather than there for her in her hour of greatest need?

But what choice had he? Noah asked himself as he turned and walked from her grave. What choice had he ever had, ever since he had given his life over to the Lord? He couldn't have saved Millie even if he had been there. It just hurt so badly to know she had died, and he had failed her in her last hours. If anyone deserved to die with her priest at her side, it was Millie. But then, Noah amended quickly, what had Millie really needed

185

from any man, when she'd had God with her in those final moments? Who, after all, could ever comfort her better than her beloved Lord and Savior?

He was glad that Millie had faith, even if he himself had found little comfort in his faith in a very long while. But no matter the sense of loss or desertion, he knew there was nothing else left for him if he turned forever from God. Without God, life was ultimately empty and pointless.

Noah smiled sadly. Hang on. Just hang on, he had told other people innumerable times. People who had experienced similar sorrows and dark nights of the heart. Even when we feel it least, he had assured them, the Lord is ever at our side. He has promised not to forsake us or leave us comfortless.

Hang on. . . . That's all that seems to be left for me, he thought, blinking back a sudden swell of tears. It wasn't enough, especially now without Millie, but it was all he had.

Due to the large gathering of mourners, the post-funeral reception was held in the town hall. The Ladies' Quilting Society and the Church Ladies' Social Club provided the food, which was, as always, eagerly consumed. Noah endured countless condolences and handshakes, plus offers of additional meals and aid in the days to come.

Finally, though, the ordeal was over. As much as he appreciated the heartfelt concern, Noah felt drained, unable to give anymore. After thanking all the women lingering about afterwards, he turned and headed for the door.

"Noah, wait up," Beth called out, hurrying to his side. Since the burial, she and Abby had spelled each other watching Emily at the rectory. Beth had come to the hall about ten minutes ago to help clean up.

Noah turned and forced a weary smile. "What is it, Beth? Is there something more I need to do?"

"All you need to do, Noah Starr," she said, eyeing him closely, "is head back home and get some rest. You look exhausted."

"No more so than you. You've been as busy as I these past few days."

"Well, I'll be back at the rectory soon enough. Don't you worry."

Her words plucked at a concern that had grown steadily within him in the past days. It was time he face it, call it by name, and deal with it once and for all.

"We need to talk, Beth. How soon will you be coming home?"

Her smile faded. "Another half hour should be enough to finish up here. Do you want to talk then?"

"Yes. That'd be fine. See you then."

With that, Noah turned and strode away, knowing if he had stayed an instant longer, he'd have lost heart and not uttered what must be said, much less done. But he must. The temptation to sin had grown too strong, and he had never been weaker. And this was one choice he still had the power to make.

Beth waited nervously at the kitchen table, stirring her cup of tea incessantly. Whatever did Noah wish to discuss? He had looked none too happy when he brought up the need for them to talk. Did it have to do with what had happened the day after the storm, or was it something else? Whatever it was, Beth had an unpleasant inkling she wasn't going to like it.

Abby returned from putting Emily down for her afternoon nap. She walked to the table and sat. "Guess I'd best be getting on. Your father's probably talked Jake Whitmore's ear off by now as it is."

"I'm sure the both of them are enjoying the chance for a visit." Beth grinned. "Sheriff Whitmore's always asking about Pa every time I see him."

"I suppose so. He, Noah, and your father have always been such close friends." Abby stood, then hesitated. "Are you sure you'll be all right? Noah's so grief stricken right now, I'm not certain how much help he'll be with the house or Emily. And you have your hands full enough with the clinic."

"I'll manage." Beth looked up at her. "Luanne's still coming to help every day. If I run into any problems, I'll figure something out."

Her stepmother hesitated. "Have you given any thought to leaving here?" she asked finally. "It was one thing for you to stay while Millie was alive. It's quite another for two unmarried adults of the opposite gender to be living in the same house."

Though Abby only put words to what she had agonized over the past several days, Beth filled with anger. "Yes, I've given it thought," she muttered tersely. "I'm not completely without social awareness, you know. But Noah and Emily need me right now. I can't desert them. And I won't."

"Noah's a priest, Beth. He cannot be involved in anything that hints of impropriety. And I've already heard rumors about what Harlow saw when he found you that morning. As time goes on, your staying here will only make matters worse."

Beth released an exasperated breath, threw back her head, and closed her eyes. "I'll talk to Noah. I'll do whatever he wants." She opened her eyes and met her step-mother's gaze. "But it'll be what *he* wants. Not what anyone else wants, no matter who they are. Noah's what matters to me, Abby. Noah and Emily."

"I know that, honey. And who knows? Maybe it'll all work out for the best for everyone. The Lord has His ways, after all."

"Just as long as the Lord sees fit to help Noah, I'll be satisfied."

"Funny thing. About the Lord helping someone, I mean. Whatever He does, it frequently seems to touch a whole lot more lives than just the one He specifically seems to be helping." Abby smiled. "Maybe that'll happen this time, too."

"Sure. I suppose that's as good a—"

Noah walked into the entry just then and saw Abby and Beth in the kitchen. "Hello," he said in greeting as he removed his coat and gloves. "Everything all right?"

Abby joined him in the entry. "Everything's fine. Emily's down for her nap, and I was just getting ready to leave." She removed her coat from the rack and donned it. "If you need anything, though, you know where to call."

He smiled. "I know. Thank you for all you've done for me, Abby. I couldn't have managed without the MacKays and the help of the good folk of Grand View."

Abby laid a hand on his arm. "We all love you, Noah. Never forget that."

"I won't."

She glanced over her shoulder at Beth. "Keep me posted, will you? If you or Noah need anything . . ."

Beth nodded. "I will."

"Good-bye, then."

They watched her depart, cross the street, and head down the boardwalk toward the sheriff's office. Then Noah turned to Beth. "Got any hot coffee?"

"Of course." She grinned. "I knew you'd be wanting some, so I made a fresh pot. It's ready."

As he took his seat at the table, Beth poured him a cup, then dumped her lukewarm tea and refilled the mug with coffee. After adding a generous serving of cream and a spoonful of sugar, Beth glanced up at Noah. He was studying her solemnly.

"Well, spit it out, will you?" she demanded, her anxiety rising the longer he looked. "Unless I've gone and grown an extra eye in the middle of my forehead, your staring is bordering on the impolite."

"I'm sorry." Noah sighed and glanced away briefly. "I was just thinking how much a part of this family you've become. And how much I'm going to miss you."

Her eyes narrowed. "And exactly why are you going to miss me, Noah? I've no plans to leave Grand View, or–"

"You can't stay here anymore, Beth. It's not . . . right. I won't compromise your reputation any more than I already have."

"My reputation?" Beth gave an incredulous laugh. "What reputation? You and I both know what I've done. I've no reputation left to protect."

"No one knows about that, and that's the way it should stay. It's no one's business but yours."

"Well, I don't care what other people think anyway," she countered hotly. "All I care about is not running out on my friends when they need me. If some folk are too blind and hard-hearted to see that, well, they're fools!"

"You're not running out on me, Beth." Noah laid his hand over hers. "You can come and visit as often as you'd like. Indeed, I'd be much obliged if you did come and see Emily. She's so young and doesn't understand what's happened."

Beneath his hand, her fingers curled, then clenched into a fist. "And what about you? Would you like to see me?"

Confusion clouded his eyes. "Of course I'd like to see you. Why would you ever doubt that?"

"Oh, I don't know." Beth relaxed her hand, then pulled it from beneath Noah's. "Maybe because, ever since we kissed that day, you've seemed rather uncomfortable being around me. Is it perhaps because you regret that kiss, Noah?"

Crimson crept slowly into his face. "It's not that, Beth. When we kissed . . . well, I enjoyed it very much."

"Then what's the problem?"

"That *is* the problem. That I enjoyed it very much, I mean."

Beth opened her mouth to reply, then snapped it shut again. She didn't know whether to be ecstatic or mad.

"It's a problem because you enjoyed kissing me," she said finally. "I don't understand."

"No, I don't suppose you would. You couldn't have known, after all, what's been going on in my heart all these months. And it was too shameful to share . . ." Noah sighed. "The simple truth is, though, I've lusted after you from the first day you came to the rectory and I realized what a lovely young woman you'd become. Lusted and fought a mighty battle to contain and eradicate such unholy feelings. But now . . . now it's just better if you don't live here anymore."

She stared at him, stunned. "You . . . you desire me? Me?"

He laughed, the sound harsh, raw. "Have you looked in a mirror lately? You're a beautiful woman, Beth. And I'm not the only man who thinks that. If you'd get your mind off your patients and the next medical treatment you're cooking up, you'd see how many men turn and look at you as you pass by."

"Well, I don't care what other men are doing." Beth found herself getting exasperated. "All I care is what you think about me. Tell me."

"No, you don't want to hear what I've been thinking." Noah shook his head. "Sometimes . . . sometimes it's hard enough for me to bear. You're a good woman, Beth. My good friend's daughter. I'm ashamed even to be telling you this, but I am, because I want you to understand why you must leave."

She wanted to tell him she loved him and that, if he but asked her, she'd stay with him forever. But Noah hadn't spoken of love. He'd spoken of lust. And it was painful to believe he could see her in only that way. She had thought they were friends.

Confusion filled her. Noah's revelation was too difficult to comprehend right now, especially with him so close. Gradually, though, a niggling fear came to Beth's mind. Was this all she'd ever arouse in any man—a carnal desire, but never love?

In the end, that had been the extent of Matthew's need for her. But Noah . . . She never would've imagined the extent of his caring was so shallow.

He had loved Alice. Beth was certain of that. It seemed that only his affection for her was so limited, so base.

She fought back tears, steeled her resolve, then met Noah's anguished gaze. "Fine," she said hoarsely, "have it your way. I'll leave today."

15

*Be of good courage, and he shall strengthen your heart,
all ye that hope in the Lord.*

Psalm 31:24

March came in like a lion and remained that way for most of the month, stalking about with fierce winds and more snow. Every morning required fresh shoveling, but by the next day, the snow had melted and the ground had transformed into a soggy, muddy mess.

Noah hardly noticed. He went about his daily routine of getting Emily up and feeding her before Luanne arrived for the day, then shoveling the front porch and walk before heading to his duties at the church. As often as he could manage it, he took an hour off for lunch to be with Emily, then worked straight through until supper. After eating with his daughter, he'd work until midnight or later on the church correspondence and book-keeping he brought home with him.

Most of the time, the relentless pace kept his mind occupied and his heart numb. He gave without thinking, slept little, and imagined he was dealing with his grief in the best way he could. Still, he continued to miss Millie deeply, and the ache in his heart every time he thought of Beth was like some gnawing pain slowly eating him alive.

There was nothing, however, that could be done for the empty void the two women had carved into his heart. Noah contented himself with the illusion all would be well if only he endured long enough.

One morning near the end of March, he woke with a high fever, body-wracking chills, and throbbing muscular aches. He dragged himself from bed, dressed, and retrieved Emily from her room. After almost losing his balance going down the stairs, thanks to his dizziness, he deposited Emily in her wheelchair and proceeded to put water on to boil for coffee.

A nice hot cup of coffee would do a lot to help him feel better, he told himself as he reheated some leftover biscuits from last night's meal, slathered them with butter, and sprinkled them with sugar and cinnamon for Emily's breakfast. The strong cup of coffee, however, only made things worse. Noah barely made it to the sink before vomiting what little was in his stomach. It was all he could do to stagger back to the table, where he sat and laid his head on his arms.

Luanne found him there when she came to work that morning. "Land sakes, Father Starr," she said, eyeing him with concern. "You look as near on death's door as any soul can get and still be alive. Why don't you head on up to bed? Once I get Emily cleaned and dressed, I'll put her in her crib and fetch one of the doctors to have a look at you."

"N-no." Noah couldn't take a chance it might be Beth who took the house call. After the painful way they had parted, he wasn't in any better condition to face her now than he had been in the past few weeks. "It's nothing more than a touch of the influenza that's been going around. I just need to sleep it off, that's all."

Luanne didn't look convinced. "Well, I can't say I'm so sure of that, but I suppose we can see how well you do today. I'll make you a nice pot of chicken soup. Then later you can see if you can keep some down."

Even the mention of Luanne's delicious chicken soup made Noah nauseous. It was all he could do to nod and hurry quickly away. Climbing the stairs and walking down the hall felt as if he were scaling Pikes Peak, but he finally made it back to bed. Noah collapsed there, promptly falling asleep.

The next day, Beth decided to take her lunch at Bledsoe's bakery. After suggestions from their regular patrons, the Bledsoes had set up several small dining tables in the ample space at the front of the bakery, covered them with white lace tablecloths, added decorative potted plants about the area, and posted elegant, handwritten menus offering freshly brewed coffee, various teas, pastries, and sandwiches. Bledsoe's Quality Baked Goods and Café the bakery was now called, and the small dining spot had been an immediate hit.

Despite the snowy and gloomy day, there was only one empty table left when Beth arrived. She took her seat, ordered hot jasmine tea, a roast beef sandwich, and a piece of apple strudel, then sat back to relax.

Cora Bledsoe soon delivered a steaming, flower-painted porcelain pot of tea. She didn't seem all that eager to return to her other duties, and, pulling out the other chair, she took a seat across from Beth.

"How have you been, honey?" Cora inquired. "You're always so busy, coming and going on house calls, I never find a chance to talk with you anymore." She cocked her head. "Is renting that room in the hotel working out for you okay? I'm sure it lacks the rectory's hominess, but everyone understands why you couldn't stay there anymore."

Beth was glad that her glance was lowered to her tea as she stirred in some sugar. For all her friendliness, Cora was a bit of a gossip. If Beth didn't miss her guess, the woman was digging for information.

"The hotel is quite adequate." Beth lifted her gaze. "I was most grateful to Mr. Samuels for agreeing to rent one of his rooms to me. And it shouldn't be for too much longer at any rate. Mamie Oatman thinks she'll have a vacancy in another couple of weeks."

"Oh my, yes," Cora agreed, leaning forward. "That'll be ever so much better, won't it? Still, you seemed so happy living at the rectory. I'm sorry all the unkind talk forced you to have to leave." She nodded emphatically and forged on. "We're not living in the Dark Ages anymore, after all. And anyone who'd doubt either you or Father Starr's integrity is the basest form of life . . ."

Though Beth was tempted to ask who was spreading the unkind talk, it wouldn't change anything. She knew where the rumors had originated, anyway, and that was with Harlow Peterson. To encourage further discussion, to react negatively, or to demand names, would only add tinder to the already smoldering fire.

"It's better this way." Beth paused to take a sip of her tea. Its warmth and fragrant flavor helped calm her. "Besides, my stay at the rectory was only temporary. My plan was always to take a room at Mamie's, just as soon as one came available."

"Yes, well, then I suppose it is all for the best." Cora glanced around, then leaned even closer and lowered her voice. "I just want you to know I never, not even for a single moment, believed anything improper happened between you and Father Starr that night of the storm. Helen Yates told me how frantic Father Starr was when he heard you might be caught out in it. It was so brave of him to risk himself to try and find you. But that's the kind of man he is, isn't he?"

"Yes, that's the kind of man he is." Beth made a show of checking her watch. "Will my sandwich and dessert be ready soon? I have a patient coming into the clinic in twenty minutes."

Cora Bledsoe rose. "Oh my, yes. Whatever was I thinking? I'll fetch them for you straightaway."

Beth watched her hurry off and was glad that particular topic of conversation was at an end. Though most people seemed to give little credence to the tales still filtering through town, there were always a few who seemed to revel in the scandal of a priest who might have acted in an immoral manner. It angered Beth that, for some, all of Noah's years of devoted, unstinting service could be so easily dismissed with the very first allegation of impropriety. It was unfair, not to mention unchristian, to treat Noah this way. Especially now, when he grieved so for Millie.

In the past month since Beth had moved out of the rectory, she had seen him in passing from time to time. There was no avoiding that; Grand View was too small a town not to run into Noah occasionally.

He hadn't looked well; his face had been gaunt, his features drawn, and shadows had been forming beneath his eyes. Though he had been cordial when he couldn't pretend not to see her, his smile had been perfunctory, never seeping any deeper than his lips. Beth couldn't help but wonder if he wasn't secretly relieved to be rid of her.

Cora delivered her food just then, bustling self-importantly across the café. "Sorry about keeping you so long talking," she said. "Hope you've enough time left to finish your lunch without rushing."

Beth picked up half her sandwich. "I'll be fine, Cora." She took a bite of the fresh roll and perfectly seasoned roast beef. "This is delicious," she said after chewing and swallowing. "Absolutely delicious."

"I'm happy you like it."

The front door opened, setting off the bell, and Cora and Beth looked to see who the newest customer was. Luanne Stout walked in, a worried expression on her face. When she saw Beth, however, relief filled her eyes.

"Oh, Dr. MacKay," the girl said, hurrying to Beth's table. "I hate to bother you at your meal, but Doc Childress is out somewhere, and I'm getting worried about Father Starr. He's been sick since yesterday with what appears to be the influenza, and he doesn't seem to be getting any better. Could you come and have a look at him?"

Beth set down her sandwich, wiped her mouth and hands with the fine cloth napkin Cora always provided, then rose. "Of course I'll come." She turned to Cora. "Could you wrap up my sandwich and strudel? I'll pick them up on the way back to the clinic."

"Sure, honey." Cora patted her on the arm. "And it's no charge, either. If I hadn't talked your ear off earlier, you'd have had time to eat."

"Really, it's all right," Beth said in protest. "I don't mind—"

Cora held up a hand. "I won't hear of it."

Giving up the battle, Beth grabbed her coat, threw it on, and picked up the medical bag she always carried with her. She turned to Luanne. "Let's head on out. I imagine you left Emily alone, to come find me?"

Luanne nodded. "Yes, ma'am. But she's down for her nap, so I thought it'd be all right to slip out just for a minute."

"Yes, but we should be getting back." With that, Beth led the way from the café.

She found Noah bathed in sweat, tossing and turning on his bed and mumbling incoherently. This wasn't going to be a short and sweet house call, Beth realized. Luckily, this afternoon's patients were all follow-up visits. She turned to Luanne.

"First, call the clinic and have Helen reschedule my afternoon appointments. Then bring me cold water—a big basin of it—and some cloths. We need to get his fever down."

As Luanne hurried back to the kitchen, Beth removed Noah's shirt, opened her medical bag, and extracted a thermometer and stethoscope. After slinging the stethoscope around her neck, she thrust the thermometer into his armpit and clamped his arm tightly against it. While she waited for his temperature, she did a quick examination.

Noah's skin was flushed, clammy, and hot to the touch. His pulse was rapid. His pupils were normal though, and when she lifted his lids to examine them, he stilled for a moment and focused on her.

"B-Beth?" he croaked, his voice hoarse. "Is that you, Beth?"

"Yes, Noah." She let his lids fall shut. "It's me. Are you having pain anywhere?"

"No pain," he mumbled, trying to open his eyes on his own. "Just hot. So hot."

She removed the thermometer and read it. One hundred one point eight degrees, which, for an axillary reading, meant it was really a degree higher. Beth laid the thermometer on the bedside table. "Well, you've good reason to feel hot. You've got a high fever."

Beth eased him over on his side, then stuck the end pieces of her stethoscope into her ears. "Take some deep breaths, Noah. I need to listen to your chest."

He managed to comply for several breaths, then dozed off again. It was enough to ascertain, though, that his lungs were as yet unaffected. Beth left him on his side and pulled a sheet up to cover him.

Luanne returned, a big porcelain basin full of water balanced in the crook of one arm, a stack of towels and washcloths in her other hand. "I called Helen. Everything's settled. And I didn't know how many cloths to bring, Dr. MacKay, so I brought a lot."

"You did fine, Luanne." Beth shot her an encouraging smile. "Just one thing more, and you can then see to Emily. I need a glass and a pitcher of water. Once I get Noah to wake up for a bit, I've got some medicine to give him."

The girl nodded. "I'll get that right away, ma'am."

Beth turned back to Noah. After uncovering him once more, she wet several small cloths with the cool water, wrung them out, and placed them over his chest and back. She used another cloth for the back of his neck and another for his forehead. For the next half hour, she constantly replaced fresh wet cloths for the ones that quickly warmed on his body.

Finally, after taking his temperature again, Beth was relieved to see Noah's temperature had dropped a degree. Now, if she could just get some aspirin into him . . .

Beth grasped Noah's shoulder and shook it gently. "Noah? Wake up. I need to—"

His lids fluttered open. "B-Beth?"

She grabbed the glass she had prepared with the aspirin powder added to some water, slid a hand under his neck, and lifted his head. "Here. Take this. It'll help you."

Noah opened his mouth, and Beth poured the solution down his throat. "That's good, Noah. Now take another drink. You need to get some fluids into you."

Noah did as he was told but finally turned his face away. "N-no more . . . water."

"Okay." Beth set the glass aside. "You drank enough for now. You can have more later."

"Yes . . . later." He closed his eyes, but his hand groped for hers and, finding it, held it tight. "Stay with me, Beth," he said. "Don't be angry . . . with me . . . anymore."

"Oh, Noah," she whispered, "I'm not angry with you. Far, far from it."

His eyes snapped opened. "I didn't send you away because I wanted to. I just wanted . . . to protect you."

She bit her lip and looked away. "It's all right, Noah. Just go to sleep. You need to sleep."

"It hurt, Beth. Hurt . . . not to have you here. I miss you. Miss you so badly . . ." His grip on her hand loosened, then fell away.

Beth swallowed hard and turned back to him. Noah lay there sleeping soundly, his skin a little less flushed. Tenderly, she brushed aside a lock of hair that clung damply to his forehead, then ran her finger lovingly down the side of his face.

"Oh, Noah, Noah," she whispered. "It hurt me so badly to have to leave. If you only knew how much it hurt . . ."

You're kindred souls, honey, and belong together.

In the dimly lit room, Beth could almost imagine Millie sitting there in the corner, speaking the words she had spoken that early January day, only weeks before her death. Strange that those words came back to Beth now. Perhaps they rose from the depths of her jumbled emotions, from seeing Noah so sick and hearing his admission of his continued need for her.

With a groan, Beth lowered her face into her hands. Perhaps they *were* kindred souls. All she knew was leaving him had all but ripped her heart asunder. And coming back to care for him had only torn it open again. She just wasn't whole anymore without him.

Kindred souls . . .

What else had Millie said to her that day? Something about not letting her fears keep her from the man of her heart, about her being the one who'd finally heal Noah's wound of losing Alice.

Beth threw back her head. Ah, if only she was that woman! If only Noah could find it within himself to love her! She'd give up everything that had ever mattered, if only she could have Noah. But she was too afraid. She didn't know what to do to win Noah's heart.

He just doesn't know the true depth of his feelings for you. Don't let your fears keep you from the man of your heart.

Beth looked down at Noah. Her heart swelled with the fiercest love, the wildest hope she had ever experienced. And, in that moment of silent consideration, she made up her mind. She determined to take a chance. She determined to risk what heretofore had been some crazy, girlhood dream.

Thanks to his strong constitution and good medical care, Noah soon recovered from his bout of influenza. He was taking home paperwork and seeing a few visitors two days later. By Sunday he was able to conduct a brief communion service, and he spent half a day in the church office on Monday.

After her first visit to the rectory that day Noah was so sick, Beth turned over his care to Doc Childress. For the time being, she decided, it was best to keep herself away from Noah. Once he was well again would be soon enough to confront him.

However, a little over a week and a half later, Beth could wait no longer. If she didn't speak to Noah now, she knew she'd lose the last of her courage. And what she planned on doing was one of the most terrifying things she had ever done in her life.

Beth left the hotel that night about half past seven and headed to the rectory. Pausing on the front porch, she squared her shoulders, inhaled a deep, fortifying breath, and knocked. Lord, she silently prayed as she waited for Noah to answer, help me in this. Right about now, I need all the strength You've got to spare.

A squirming towel-wrapped Emily in his arms, Noah opened the door. For a long, emotion-laden moment, they stood there, staring at each other, neither saying a thing.

"May I come in?" Beth asked finally. "I've a proposition that might interest you."

He arched a brow. "Indeed? Well, come on in, then."

She followed him into the kitchen. Noah unwrapped Emily from her towel and placed her back in her bathtub. Emily splashed happily for a minute or so, then lifted her chubby, water-slick arms to Beth.

"Bef! Bef!" the little girl cried.

Beth knelt beside the tub, took one of the toddler's hands, and pressed it to her lips.

"How have you been, sweetheart? I've missed you."

Emily giggled, patted Beth's face until it was wet, then resumed her splashing in the tub. Beth knelt there for a few minutes more, then stood.

"She's missed you, too," Noah said as he began drying the dishes he had just finished washing. "Not a day goes by Emily doesn't speak your name."

"Well, I think I've come up with the perfect solution to that problem." Beth walked to the table, took a seat, then gestured to the chair opposite her. "Could you leave the dishes for just a moment and sit down?"

"So, this proposition of yours is so earth-shattering I need to be sitting, do I?" he asked with a chuckle as he laid aside his dishcloth and ambled over to the table.

"I suppose that depends on how many women have ever proposed to you in your life," she replied evenly, though her heart seemed to have tripled its rate. "And how many would that be, Noah?"

He went very still. He eyed her warily.

"Forgive me if I've misunderstood what you just said," he croaked out at last, "but did you just propose marriage to me?"

Beth gripped her hands so tightly on the table that they hurt. Be right about this, Millie, she thought. Oh, please, please, be right!

Then she forced herself to nod her assent. "Yes, I did. Will you marry me?"

16

Now ye are clean through the word which I have spoken unto you.

John 15:3

Beth watched the emotions play across Noah's face. Shock, then a brief flash of what she thought might be joy, and, finally, rejection. Her heart sank. He didn't want her for his wife.

"Beth," Noah began, shaking his head, "it wouldn't work. You deserve better than me. You'd see that someday and regret your hasty decision."

"This may come as a surprise to you, Noah Starr," she said between gritted teeth, suddenly so embarrassed she wanted to leap up and run out of the room, "but I've been thinking about this, in some form or another, since before Millie died. In fact, she was the one who brought up the subject to me. Whether you agree or not, Millie seemed to think there was something special growing between us."

"There *was* something special between us," he said, a fierce certainty glowing in his eyes. "A deep friendship, a sense of kinship even. When I talked with you, I always got the feeling you understood me, that you cared. And that was a very precious gift to me, Beth. But a marriage?" He sighed. "Well, it just wouldn't be fair to you."

"And exactly why wouldn't marrying you be fair to me? Come on, Noah. Tell me why."

He shrugged and looked away. "Why else? For one thing, I'm thirteen years older than you. And then there's the fact I don't know if I'm capable of ever loving you like you deserve to be loved. It just hurt too much, losing Alice. And to top it off, I can't be depended on to be there when you need me. My first calling must always be in the service of the Lord. Any wife and children would always come second."

"Kind of like me and my medical practice," she muttered with an edge of sarcasm. "Still, I think we must all find some kind of balance in our lives. And you must do that just as I must, to have a full and satisfying life."

"It's too late for me, Beth."

"Hogwash! I say, instead, you're acting like a coward. You'd rather run away from your needs and emotions than stay and face them. But how can you ever work things out if you keep running away? And what of all the potential happiness you deny yourself in the doing?"

"I was thinking more of all the potential pain I avoid instead," he replied dryly. "I don't think I'm cut out to be a good husband or a father." He gestured to Emily, who was gazing adoringly up at him. "Look at that little girl. For all her handicaps, she's such a happy, unselfish, generous child. Yet most times when I look at her, all I see are her limitations. All I see is my guilt in not being there for Alice."

"Do you seriously think you could've prevented Alice's childbirth difficulties? Do you, Noah?"

He glanced down and shook his head. "Maybe not. But I just can't get over my sense of failure. I just can't—"

"Can't forgive yourself?" Beth supplied for him. "Even though, with your help, I'm finally coming to forgive myself with *all* my failings? And even though God has forgiven you long ago, if there was truly anything really *to* forgive?"

"Yes, I suppose you're right." Noah met her gaze. "I still can't forgive myself."

"But you didn't sin. You just erred in your well-meant intention to try to be everything to everyone at all times." She smiled sadly. "That's a pretty heavy load for anyone— save God—to bear for long. And it's pretty arrogant and prideful, too. As prideful as refusing to forgive yourself."

For a long moment, Noah just stared at her. "You're right," he admitted at last. "I *am* arrogant and prideful if I imagine I'm above forgiveness. Funny thing. I guess I never imagined myself above sin, just above forgiveness." He reached for her hand. "Do you see what I mean, Beth? Among all the other things I treasure in you, I treasure how you can cut straight to the heart of things for me."

"But you don't treasure me enough to want to marry me."

"Ah, Beth, Beth." He exhaled a deep, mournful breath. "It's not like that. I just feel so . . . so unworthy of you."

"Unworthy?" She gave a disbelieving laugh. "Do you know, since that day when I was fourteen and you saved me from that rattler, I fell hopelessly in love with you? That when you wed Alice, you broke my heart? Up until then, I was even willing to forego medical school to be your wife. That's how much I loved you."

"But that was a schoolgirl crush. You're a grown woman now."

Beth began to tremble with the rising intensity of her emotions. If she told Noah of her love for him now, and he rejected it . . . But what other choice was there? In some deep, secret part of her, Beth knew this was the only chance she'd ever have. Indeed, her only chance to find the courage to dare.

"Yes," she said quietly but with deep feeling, "I'm a grown woman now. And I love you now with all the needs and emotions of a grown woman. I see you for the man you are, Noah Starr. I see your weaknesses as well as strengths, your courage, goodness, and your fears. And as your strengths draw me, your failings don't turn me away. You're human, and I love your humanness. I love you."

Noah covered her hand with his. "If you knew . . . if you knew how much I've desired you . . . Well, it frightens me, Beth. Such passion . . . I never felt that with Alice, leastwise never as strongly, as gut-twistingly as I feel it for you. There are times, I must confess, when I can't see past it to the person you are."

"Do you think it's sinful, the feelings you have for me?"

Noah looked up, his eyes twin pools of misery. "I don't know. I suppose not if we were man and wife." His brow furrowed. "Maybe it's more that I fear my need for you would consume me, that it might eventually become more powerful than my need for God. And I can't let that happen."

"I'd never ask or want that of you. You know that."

Beth could feel her hope dying, withering away in the realization she could never ask such a sacrifice from him. God was such a vital part of who Noah Starr was. It'd destroy him to lose that very essence of his being.

Ever so gently, Beth pulled her hand free of his clasp. "I know what I want, and I want you. You and Emily. But I don't see my love for the two of you as an either-or situation—God's love versus human love. In fact, believe it or not, I see you and Emily as a gift from a loving God. A gift I want to cherish all my days until I'm finally called home to heaven."

Beth shoved back her chair and stood. "If you can't see me that way, if you truly believe you'd compromise your love and service to the Lord if you wed me, then I don't want you to. I'd never, ever, ask such a thing of you.

"So, think on what we've said here tonight, Noah. Search your heart. And then tell me what's in it. One way or another, I'll accept it. It won't change what I feel for you, but I'll accept it."

After Beth left that evening Noah lay in bed, praying long into the night. Despite Beth's words to the contrary, he still found it difficult to believe she loved him. He beseeched the Lord to make clear His will for them. Could it be, was it possible, God truly meant for them to be together? At the merest consideration of the prospect, Noah's mind roiled crazily, even as his body ached at the thought of taking Beth as his wife.

Ah, how he needed someone to confide in at such a time as this! But Millie, his dearest confidante and friend, was gone. And Beth, as much as he respected her insights and advice, was hardly the person to help him now.

There was Conor, though. Noah smiled at the irony. Conor, who was one of the wisest men he knew, was Beth's father. How could he possibly go to him, knowing in what a difficult position it would place his friend?

Yet who knew both him and Beth better than Conor MacKay? And who loved them more and would do his utmost to help them traverse this difficult path in the best way, the only way the Lord wished for them to go?

Noah turned on his side, adjusted the pillow more firmly beneath his head, and closed his eyes. A strong sense of peace filled him. First thing tomorrow, he'd pay Culdee Creek's owner a visit. If any man knew the Lord, it was Conor MacKay.

The next morning after Luanne arrived, Noah saddled up his horse and headed out to Culdee Creek. It was a brisk but sunny March day, the snow was all but melted, and sprigs of bright new grass were poking up their heads all over the place. It was one of those invigorating, great-to-be-alive kind of days. Spring was obviously on its way.

Conor hadn't yet headed out to do any range work, so when Noah arrived, Abby led him to the study, where Conor was bent over what appeared to be the ranch accounts.

Conor looked up in surprise. "Well, well, and what brings you all the way out to Culdee Creek so early in the day?" he asked, standing.

As Noah accepted his friend's outstretched hand, he noted Abby discreetly pulling the door closed. "I've got a problem. A big problem, and I thought you might be the man to help me with it."

Conor indicated the armchair in the corner. "I'll do what I can. You know that." He pulled his desk chair close and sat.

Noah took his seat. Here goes, he thought.

"Let me get right to the point. Beth proposed to me last night."

Culdee Creek's owner eyed him for several seconds, then gave a snort of disbelief. "Well, I'll be . . ." He chuckled. "I always knew my daughter had a lot of guts, but that surprises even me." He cocked his head, a look of interest in his eyes. "What did you say to her? Once you picked yourself up off the floor, I mean?"

"I was so confused and scared, I told her I'd have to think on it." Noah smiled ruefully. "Or, rather, once it became evident to Beth I didn't really know *what* to think, she told me it was up to me. She said she knew how she felt about me. Now it was up to me to decide how I felt about her."

Conor scratched his jaw. "Well, that doesn't surprise me. Abby and I have been watching your relationship develop for a while now. And I've always known how Beth felt about you. Question is, how do you feel about her?"

"That's the problem, Conor." Noah sighed. "My feelings for her are all in a jumble. I respect and like her. I care for her. We get along so well, and she's never been afraid to tell me when she thinks I've gone astray. But do I love her? I don't know."

"Or, rather, are you just afraid of letting yourself love again?" his friend asked quietly. "Ever since Alice died, I've seen how you pull into your shell any time a woman seems interested in you."

So his avoidance of romantic involvements had been obvious. Noah smiled sardonically.

"I guess I'm just afraid of disappointing or hurting anyone again. And I'm even more afraid of how Beth makes me feel and that I'll end up putting her above God."

Conor gave a disgusted snort. "Appears more like you might be using God as some shield to hide behind, thinking to protect yourself from the pain that sometimes comes with risking your heart. Just be careful,

Noah. Don't use the Lord as an excuse not to get out there and live the life He truly wants you to live."

His friend's observation struck closer to home than Noah cared to admit. Frustration filled him, and he buried his face in his hands.

"I don't want to run from life, Conor. If only I could be sure this was the right thing for me to do. It's not that I don't want Beth. It's just that I'm so afraid of failing her, of disappointing her."

"It's impossible to know what life holds for us," Conor said softly. "All any of us can do is trust in the Lord, listen to His call, and then follow, doing the best we can do. As you always have, Noah, whether you can see that now or not. That's why Alice and Millie loved you to their dying day. And that's why, if you can find the courage to let yourself love my daughter, you'll have my blessing on your marriage to her."

Noah looked up. A weight seemed to fall from his shoulders, replaced by a sweet tranquility. If he had the courage . . .

He smiled. "Thank you, Conor. Once again, you've helped me more than you might ever know."

Two days later as Beth was finishing the notes on her last patient for the day, Helen stuck her head in the door.

"There's one more patient," she said. "He just walked in and insists he's got to see you right away."

Struggling to hide her exasperation after a particularly trying and busy day, Beth looked up. "And what exactly did he say his complaint was, that it can't wait until tomorrow?"

Helen smiled mysteriously. "He said to tell you it has to do with his heart, and it'll surely break if he has to wait a moment more to see you."

"What?" Beth stared at Helen in amazement. "That's the craziest—"

The door swung open. Noah stood there, a broad smile on his face. Beth's shocked glance moved from him to Helen.

"Just relaying exactly what the patient told me, Dr. MacKay," the older woman said before hurrying away.

Noah gestured to the office before him. "May I come in?" He pointed to his chest. "There's this problem with my heart, you know. A problem only a certain lady doctor can cure by giving me another chance."

"And how exactly do you plan to make amends?" she asked, her pulse quickening.

"Well, for starters," Noah said, walking into the office and closing the door behind him, "by taking you up on your offer to marry me. If you'll still have me, that is, after the fool I've been."

Beth rose, came around her desk, and walked up to stand before him. "Yes, I guess I'll still have you." She smiled, her heart overflowing with joy. "Yes, I think I will indeed."

"Good. Then it's settled." And with that, Noah took her into his arms and kissed her.

Two months later, the day before their wedding, Beth frantically tried to see the patients she had scheduled that morning so she could take the rest of the afternoon off to finish up some last-minute wedding details. As things always happen, however, just as soon as Doc left on a house call, Cora Bledsoe walked in with a broken toe from dropping a big jar of spiced apples on her foot.

213

Then just as Cora finally hobbled away on crutches, Nola Teachout stopped by to discuss some personal female problems.

It was almost four in the afternoon before Beth was finally able to leave the clinic for the day. Her mind reeled with the myriad tasks still before her. First thing, though, she must pay a visit to the post office. The complete set of the *Men of the Bible* series she had ordered for Noah had arrived, and she wanted to give it to him tonight as an early wedding present. Then she needed to pick up some scented bath soaps and a new bottle of cologne to take with her on their honeymoon. Though such fancy indulgences weren't her usual habit, Beth wanted to do everything she could—

From behind her, an arm snaked about her middle, jerking her backward. Startled from her thoughts, Beth gasped, then swung around, her medical bag held high to defend herself.

"Hold up there, Elizabeth. Hold up, I say," a tall, chestnut-haired young man cried, instantly releasing her and backing away. "I meant ye no harm. Truly I didn't."

Beth gaped up at him for a moment, hardly believing her eyes. Then with a most unprofessional squeal, she dropped her bag and flung herself into the man's arms.

"Ian! Oh, Ian. I can't believe it's you!"

Ian Sutherland grinned down at her. "Now, that's a far better welcome than being brained with that deadly looking bag." His arms tightened around her and he pulled her close. "A wee kiss would be even more welcoming, though."

She laughed, stood on tiptoe, and planted a quick kiss on his cheek. "Now," Beth said, leaning back to admire how fine and handsome her childhood friend had become in the years since they had last parted, "tell me everything. When did you get in? Claire never men-

214

tioned a thing about you coming back to Culdee Creek for a visit. And how could you spare the time to leave your farm or, for that matter, that bonnie lassie you claim to be so fond of?"

"Well, for starters, I just got off the train from Denver fifteen minutes ago, so ye're the first person I sought out. If ye'd been paying closer attention, ye would've heard me calling yer name a long ways back. And I didn't tell Claire I was coming. After getting your letters of late, I just decided to come.

"As for the bonnie lassie"—Ian paused to draw in a breath—"she claimed she grew weary of waiting on me to make up my mind and upped and wed another." His mouth twisted wryly. "So much for undying love and devotion. Understandably, I was so verra crushed and heartbroken I decided a change was long overdue. I sold the farm. Most likely I'll eventually return to Culdee and the Highlands, but in the interim I decided a wee adventure or two was in order."

Beth shook her head and sighed. "I must admit I was surprised you stayed with the farm as long as you did. I never took you for a man ready to settle down yet."

He grabbed her hand. "I'd settle down with the likes of ye in a heartbeat, lass. Ye've only just to ask."

"Oh, Ian," she said with a laugh, "you're still the charmer as always."

His expression grew solemn. "I'm not saying this to be the charmer. I've always loved ye, lass. Ye know that."

"And I've always loved you. But as a dear, dear friend, as my second brother."

"Yer feelings for me used to go a lot deeper than that, Elizabeth."

Beth squeezed his hand and smiled. "That was a long time ago, Ian. And we were so very young."

A sudden thought assailed her. If Ian hadn't written Claire of late, and he hadn't yet been out to the ranch, he couldn't possibly know about her plans to marry Noah tomorrow. In all the excitement, Beth had forgotten to write and tell him. This was no place, however, out on the boardwalk in the middle of town, to tell him.

"Come along." She tugged on his hand. "I just have a few errands to run, and then we can get something to eat. The hotel where I stay has a small dining area, and they'll be serving supper soon. Surely you're famished after that long train trip. We'll go there and talk some more."

"Aye, I am famished. Lead on, lass," Ian said. "I left my bag at the train depot, and it should be fine there for a time. Besides, in the years I've been gone from here, Grand View has grown. I'm not so certain I can find my way about the place anymore."

Beth grinned and quickened her pace. "Oh, but you will soon enough, my friend. You will soon enough."

After a satisfying meal of beefsteak, mashed potatoes, mixed vegetables, and a rich custard drizzled with caramel sauce and topped with whipped cream, Beth smiled across the table at her dinner companion. "There's something I need to tell you, Ian," she said. "Something very, very important to me that I hope you'll understand and be happy about."

He glanced up from his cup of coffee. "Aye, lass, and what would that be?"

Beth paused for a steadying breath to help calm her. "I'm getting married tomorrow. To Noah Starr."

Ian's mouth tightened. He stared at her for so long, Beth began to wonder if she shouldn't say something more. Then, at long last, he shoved his cup of coffee aside and leaned back in his chair.

"I thought ye'd gotten over that daft, girlish affair a long while ago. Noah's a fine man and all, but he's far too old for ye. And then, I never saw ye as the kind of woman cut out for the life of bein' a preacher's wife."

Irritation flared in Beth. Perhaps this news was a surprise for Ian, but he could've chosen his words with greater care. A daft, girlish affair indeed!

"Well, contrary to your assumptions, my feelings for Noah are far more than the simple, childish love that you seem to think they are. And Pa, when he married Abby, was nearly as old as Noah is now, and Abby was quite close to my age. So, there's hardly any difference between the span of years between Noah and me, and Pa and Abby."

Ian scowled. "Maybe so, but ye've yet to address the issue of yer suitability to be a parson's wife. I know ye, Elizabeth. Ye're far too independent and freethinking to settle for all the close watching ye'll be getting once ye wed Noah Starr."

His observation stung, mainly because she knew he was right. It was no one's business how she lived her life, but Beth knew she was unrealistic to imagine it'd be otherwise as Noah's wife. And though it didn't matter to her what others thought about her, she didn't ever want to harm Noah in any way.

"All newlyweds need to make adjustments," she retorted. "And it's not as if Noah isn't well aware of my opinions on things. That's one of the reasons I love him so. He's kind, generous, and loves me just as I am."

Ian gave a disbelieving snort. "Well, mark my words, lass. That'll soon change once ye're wed. Noah Starr can't afford any hint of scandal or impropriety."

"As I said before," Beth muttered. "We'll work things out."

Ian cocked his head, studying her quizzically. "So, ye've gone and decided to give up yer medical practice,

217

have ye, and devote yer life in the service of the Lord? Funny, but I never took ye for such a deeply religious person."

Beth glared at him. Leave it to Ian to speak his mind, whether one cared to hear it or not. But he was right. Even as a girl, she had been dutiful but never fervent in her religious devotion. And then when she had gone away to medical school . . .

Nonetheless, the Lord had begun to touch her life, through Millie and Noah, through her patients, and through the events that had transpired since she had returned to Grand View. Was she truly a spiritual person, though?

No, she couldn't in truth say she was, but at least now she felt more open to the Lord and His workings in her life. Once again, she felt loved and accepted by Him. And she was willing, no, eager, to learn, to trust, and to obey.

It was a good start. Even Beth saw that as the truth it was.

"I never said I intended on giving up being a doctor just because I'm marrying Noah," Beth said at last. "And perhaps I'm not as deeply religious as I should be, but at least I now care again enough to try. That's a start, to be sure. With Noah and the Lord's help, I intend to keep on trying, day in and day out, for the rest of my life."

She reached across the table, offering her hand to Ian. "Please be happy for me, Ian. Please give me your blessing on this. It'd make my wedding tomorrow that much better if I knew you were happy for me."

He eyed her dubiously for a moment, then sighed and took her hand. "More than aught, Elizabeth, I've always wished for yer happiness. And if marrying Noah is what ye truly need, then I'm happy for ye."

He smiled wryly. "To be sure, though, two lasses standing me up in less than a year is hard on my pride. Verra, verra hard indeed."

On June 7, Beth and Noah were married. Thanks to the generosity of the congregation, which took up a collection, they were able to have a few days away honeymooning in Colorado Springs at the Broadmoor Hotel and Casino. After a late-morning wedding and a reception that lasted until a bit past noon, Beth and Noah departed in a buggy for the Springs. They arrived at the Broadmoor at about seven and checked into their room, which was luxuriously furnished with a big bed with a huge, dark-walnut headboard, an ample wardrobe, a sitting area with a table and two overstuffed chairs, and a fine Turkish rug. They freshened up and headed down to the elegant dining room for a sumptuous supper.

After dancing to the orchestra for an hour or so, Beth decided it was time to retire. Noah, once again surprised but secretly pleased at his unabashedly forthright wife, readily agreed. While he reclined in one of the plush chairs in their suite, Beth, her nightgown in hand, disappeared into the bathroom with its full accoutrements of sink, flush toilet, and claw-foot bathtub.

After a time, however, Noah began to wonder what was taking his new wife so long. Had she suddenly had an attack of shyness? Or, even worse, regretted marrying him or developed a sudden fear of the marriage bed?

Finally, Noah went to the bathroom door and knocked. "Beth? Are you all right in there?"

"Y-yes," came the muffled reply. "I . . . oh, Noah!" The door opened and Beth stood there in her lace-trimmed nightgown, her eyes red, tears streaming down her cheeks.

Dismay filled him. Noah pulled her into his arms.

"Whatever is the matter, sweetheart? Was it something I said or did? If so, I'm sorry. I'm so very sorry. Just tell me, and I'll make it up to you."

"I-it's not y-you," she sobbed, laying her head on his chest. "It's m-me. Me!"

"You? Whatever have you done?"

"I-I know it's silly of me to dwell on this so, but I always . . . always dreamed of this night with you. How it'd be so special because you were my only love, and I'd saved myself for you. It—my innocence—seemed like such a wonderful gift to give to the man I loved. But it's too late. I've squandered it. I'm sorry, Noah. I'm so s-sorry."

He held her close as she wept as if her heart would break. A bewildered sorrow filled him. What could he possibly say to ease her pain?

Her innocence would have indeed been a wondrous gift, one he would've honored and cherished forever. But there was nothing to be done for what had been given away. What mattered now was healing, once and for all, the grievous wound tormenting Beth's soul.

"Your sin was long ago forgiven, sweet one," he said, lifting her face to kiss her tenderly on the forehead. "You must put it behind you now, and not bring it into our marriage. As for me, I'm so happy to have you as my wife and so excited at the prospect of our life together, my heart is too full to dwell on what is past. I love you, Beth, just as you are."

She gazed up at him in joyous wonderment. "Do you know that's the first time you've told me you loved me?"

He realized she was right. "I'm sorry it took me so long to say the words. That must have hurt you."

"I knew you loved me. I was willing to wait until you recognized it and felt you could say it."

At the consideration of the gift she had so willingly offered, in trusting him, in giving him the time he needed, a great love swelled in Noah. "It's hard to give yourself to love again," he said softly, "once you've been hurt in the loving. Yet, strangely enough, in that loving and loss, the experience stretches you, opens you wider to even more love, if only you find the courage."

Lifting a finger, Noah gently wiped away her tears. "Among all the other wonderful things you've done for me, sweetheart, you've helped me overcome that fear. You, being the woman you are, overwhelmed my defenses, made it so I finally saw I lost so much more hiding behind them than I ever risked daring to love again. I'll never forget that, Beth.

"And," he added, slipping an arm beneath her legs and lifting her up close to him, "more than anything else you might have wished to give me, I think that's the best wedding present I could've ever had."

17

There are diversities of gifts, but the same Spirit.
1 Corinthians 12:4

"You know," Noah said the next morning as they luxuriated in the big, elegant hotel bed, "I must confess to a tiny twinge of jealousy the evening before our wedding, when I left the rectory to visit you at the hotel and found you chatting away with Ian Sutherland in the dining room. I almost imagined he'd returned home just in the nick of time to rescue the fair maiden from the dragon."

"And you being the dragon, of course," Beth offered from her warm, comfortable haven on her husband's chest. "Hmmm, I hadn't seen it quite that way, but now that you mention it . . ."

Are all males so possessive when it comes to their women? she wondered. It certainly seemed so, if a man as kind and generous as Noah could experience such feelings. Though she had no intention of exploiting his possessiveness, a part of her was pleased at the discovery.

Noah chuckled. "Well, be that as it may, it's too late now for any last-minute rescuing. After last night, I mean."

Beth levered herself up to look into his eyes. "Pretty sure of yourself, aren't you?"

He shrugged, but a smile continued to play about his well-molded mouth. "No, just sure of how happy you've made me. And of my love for you."

She considered that for a moment, then nodded. "Well, in that case, I think you deserve another kiss. But only because you've the most beautiful lips, and I don't think I'll ever, even in another fifty or so years, get tired of kissing them."

As she spoke, Beth lowered her head, and Noah, apparently just as enamoured of kissing her, gently clasped the back of her neck and held her mouth to his, working a tantalizing magic that only made Beth hungry for more. Finally, though, she pulled away. If they kept at this much longer, they'd end up spending the whole day in bed.

"So," she said, "we've got today and tomorrow to sightsee, eat ourselves silly, and just enjoy being together. What are you interested in doing?"

He studied her from beneath half-lowered lids. "Besides staying in bed all day with my beautiful wife, you mean?"

Beth rolled her eyes. "Yes, besides that. How about a steam locomotive ride up to the top of Pikes Peak? Believe it or not, in all the years I've lived in the area, I've never been up to Pikes Peak."

Interest flared in Noah's eyes. "Well, I've never been to the top, either. Let's do it!"

Excited now, Beth grabbed the complimentary information sheet she had taken from the main desk.

"Hmmm, let's see . . . Seems the steam locomotive has been making the ascent since the 30th of June, 1891, when the first run was made carrying a church choir from Denver. An auspicious beginning, I'd say, if ever there was one."

"What time's the next run?"

"In two hours, it seems."

"Then we've got just enough time to enjoy this remarkable bathroom and its big tub before heading on out. Care to join me?"

"I'd love to." Beth hesitated a moment. Maybe it didn't need saying, but she was going to nonetheless. "Just one thing, Noah."

He arched a brow. "And what's that, sweetheart?"

"You don't ever have to be jealous again. You're the only man of my heart, and always will be."

"I know, Beth." An ardent look burned in his eyes. "It might have taken me a while to see that, much less accept it, but I do finally know."

It was great to be home. Home at the rectory. Until Noah carried her across the threshold two days later and set her down in the entry, Beth didn't realize how much she had missed the place, and how right it felt to be back once more.

She stood there, savoring the familiar scent of beeswax-rubbed furniture, fresh-baked bread, and sun-warmed wood, until Abby, who had volunteered to stay at the rectory and care for Emily in their absence, happened down the stairs. With a smile of welcome, she hurried over.

"So, how was your honeymoon?" she asked. "Did you two enjoy yourselves?"

Beth glanced up at Noah. "Oh, yes. We had a wonderful time. Didn't we, Noah?"

"Yes, a wonderful time indeed," he replied, looking lovingly at his wife before turning to his new mother-in-law. "Beth insisted on seeing all the usual tourist sights, though, and plumb wore me out. I told her I needed to come home and get back to work, just to get some rest."

Abby laughed. "Well, what matters is you enjoyed each other's company."

"Hardly a problem. We had most of that worked out long before we married." Noah paused to look around. "Where's my daughter? How did she do with us gone?"

"Emily was a bit fussy the first day. She settled down nicely, though, what with all the visitors when Conor, Evan, and Claire came to help move Beth's things over from the hotel. And she especially enjoyed playing with Erin and Sean."

"After all that company and excitement," Beth said, "Emily's going to find our homecoming positively tame."

"She's just been put down for her afternoon nap. You'll at least have time to relax a while before she wakes. In the meanwhile, I can call your father to come to town and fetch me. Knowing that brood of mine at home, I'll bet the laundry's piling up as fast as the dirty—"

The sound of footsteps on the front porch drew Abby up short. She looked from Beth to Noah.

"Were you expecting someone? I certainly wasn't."

A sharp rap came at the door. Noah walked the few feet across the entry to answer it. Mary Sue Peterson stood there.

"May I come in, Father Starr?" she asked, her voice wobbling. "I . . . I need to speak with you."

Abby and Beth sat at the table, toying with their cups of tea. Neither spoke much, well aware Noah and Mary Sue were just down the hall in his study. Finally, though, Conor arrived. After a bit more small talk, Abby left with her husband.

Beth carried her and Noah's bags up to the bedroom they'd now share, then checked on Emily. She was still sound asleep, curled on her side, her light blond hair matted damply to her face, her long lashes brushing the rounded swell of her rosy cheeks.

In slumber, Emily looked like any other child, healthy, normal, full of limitless potential. A lump formed in Beth's throat. Here she was, a doctor, and she couldn't give her husband what he wished for most—a cure for his daughter's terrible malady. All she could do was be there for him and for Emily. All she could do was help them both live out the lives that had been given them.

That's all anyone could do, Beth mused. Accept their gifts and limitations, bring them to their greatest fruition, then joyfully offer them back to the God who had first given them. It was much like the servants in Matthew who had been given the extra talents. Some had done more with the talents than others, and when the master returned, he found great pleasure in the servants who had invested wisely. But he turned his back on the foolish ones who, through fear and ignorance, had not only failed to increase their gifts but had even hidden them away.

That was the greatest tragedy. Not what one was given, however little it might be, but failing to see its glory and redemptive promise. As it was with Emily, whose crippling ailment seemed like such a mean gift, but who was nonetheless a happy child, bursting with a God-given potential all but hidden from most eyes.

With a tear-filled gaze, Beth turned and tiptoed from the room. What a blessing this beautiful child was, a blessing that touched all their lives. In her own simple way, Emily had so very much still to teach them.

Emily, God's gift to her, and now her very own little daughter.

ॐ

A troubled look on his face, Noah awaited her in the kitchen. Beth walked up to him.

"What's wrong? Has Mary Sue left?"

He shook his head. "No. She's on the verge of hysteria. I came to get you."

"Is it Harlow again? Is he beating her?"

"Yes. Just nowadays he takes greater care not to leave any marks where they can be seen easily. And she's afraid to go home."

Anger swelled in Beth. "Then she shouldn't. Will her parents take her in?"

"I hadn't thought to ask her that." Noah sighed. "I just hate for them to separate. How can they possibly find some–"

"They need to separate, Noah," Beth ground out the words, "because if they don't, Mary Sue might not live long enough for them to reconcile. Not that I hold out much hope of that happening at any rate. If he won't admit his fault and try to remedy it . . ."

"I'm going to go see Harlow right now and talk with him. This has got to stop. Here and now."

She grabbed him by the arm. "Be careful. Perhaps it'd be a good idea to have Jake Whitmore with you. When his back's up against the wall, I'll bet Harlow's a pretty dangerous man."

227

"Bringing Sheriff Whitmore along would only make things worse," Noah said. "It'd cause talk at the bank, and that might set Harlow off for sure. And you forget. I'm capable of defending myself."

"Sure, if it came to blows, I'm certain you would be, what with all your boxing experience. But what if he drew a gun on you, Noah? Fists aren't a lot of help against a gun."

He chuckled, pulled her to him, and kissed her on the cheek. "Harlow's not that irrational. He's just a very angry, confused man." Noah released her. "Now, why don't you go ahead and see what you can do to calm Mary Sue down, while I pay Harlow a visit and try to get him to come back to the rectory with me? They need to talk, and this is the best place to do it."

"Fine," Beth muttered, still not convinced she cared all that much for his plan. "I'll go see Mary Sue. All I can say, though, is this is a really poor way to spend our first day at home."

"The day's not over, sweetheart. But in the meanwhile, this is the work the Lord's given us to do, isn't it?"

"Yes, I suppose it is," Beth agreed grudgingly before turning and heading toward Noah's study.

When Beth entered the room, Mary Sue took one look at her, twisted her tear-streaked face into a mutinous glare, and stated flatly, "I'm not going back to him. It's over, Beth. It's over."

"Okay." Beth walked to the other armchair placed before the window and sat. "Did you really think I'd try to talk you out of leaving Harlow?"

Mary Sue looked out the window. "Well, Noah all but did. Sometimes I wonder whose side he's on."

"He's on God's side, Mary Sue. To that end, Noah tries to honor God's laws, one of which is upholding the sanctity of marriage vows."

"Which, of course," the other woman said bitterly, "is far more important than my physical well-being or my life."

"You know better than that." Beth leaned forward and laid a hand on Mary Sue's knee. "Noah cares for you. But he also cares for Harlow and wants to do all he can to save your marriage—if it truly can be saved. That's why he left, to go talk with Harlow again."

"Harlow won't listen. He's started telling everyone it's all my fault. That I'm inflicting all my injuries on myself because I'm imbalanced, crazy even." She grabbed Beth's hand. "But I'm not crazy, Beth. You believe me, don't you? No matter what, you'll stand by me against Harlow?"

And what if Noah ended up standing with Harlow? What would she do then? Whose side would she have to be on?

The answer came easily. She must stand with her patient or forfeit the right to call herself a doctor. And in her heart of hearts, Beth knew Mary Sue was telling the truth.

"I believe you," she replied finally. "And I'll stand by you. That doesn't mean, however, I won't support Noah in his efforts to effect a reconciliation between you and your husband. I'll just see to it that, in the doing, your safety is paramount."

"And for how long will you support Noah?"

"For as long as necessary," Beth replied. She sighed, withdrew her hand, and leaned back. "Until you either see fit to return to your husband or leave him once and for all."

"Mr. Peterson can't see you, Reverend Starr," the bank teller said after returning from her trip down the hall.

"He's very busy right now with an important account, and—"

"What I've got to say to Mr. Peterson is more important than some paperwork. Thank you very much, though, for your time and effort."

With that, Noah stepped around the teller and headed in the direction she had just come. The woman gasped in dismay, then seemed to think better of trying to stop him. Which was all for the best, he thought. He really didn't want to make a scene any more than she seemed to.

Harlow's door was unlocked, and after a quick knock on it, Noah walked in, shutting it firmly behind him. The banker glanced up. At the sight of his pastor standing there, he scowled.

"Blast it all! I told Dottie I wasn't to be disturbed. That girl's going to lose her job for sure if she keeps up this kind of behavior!"

"Dottie's not at fault, Harlow." Noah pulled up a chair and sat before the banker's big desk. "She tried to stop me. I just didn't want to be stopped, that's all."

Harlow grunted. "You're getting to be rather pushy these days. Can't say as how I find that particularly pleasing in a man of God."

"Well, that makes two of us who aren't particularly pleased then." Noah locked gazes with the man across the desk. "This problem between you and Mary Sue has got to stop. Now. Today."

Harlow eyed him narrowly. "And who are you to tell me what I can or can't do in the privacy of my own home?"

"I'm your pastor, Harlow. Do you think I could in good conscience allow this to continue, now that I know what you're doing? Do you?"

"Blast it! I'm not doing anything!" Harlow stood and leaned forward on his desk. "It's all Mary Sue's doing.

She's sick in the head. She's harming herself, then trying to pin the blame on me."

"And why would she do that? It doesn't make sense."

"Well"–Harlow lowered his bulk back into his chair–
"that's why they call crazy people crazy, don't they? And
with Mary Sue, there's no telling what got into her head."
He shrugged. "Maybe she thinks I'm seeing another
woman. Or maybe she's just mad because I can't afford
to give her everything her greedy little heart desires."
He threw up his hands. "How should I know? Ask your
wife. She's the expert on sick people, isn't she?"

"Beth doesn't think Mary Sue's crazy," Noah said quietly. "She does think, however, that Mary Sue should
leave you."

Slowly, crimson suffused the banker's face. "I'd never
allow it. Mary Sue's mine. No matter how bad it gets, I'll
never let her go."

Even if it gets so bad you end up permanently maiming
or even killing her? Noah asked silently. He decided
against putting voice to his thoughts, however. Harlow
Peterson wasn't a man to be won over with accusations.

"Well, if you feel that way," he said instead, "then
there's still hope things can be worked out. Say you'll
start coming back to the rectory to talk this out, Harlow.
If you don't try to meet Mary Sue halfway, I don't know
what else can be done to save your marriage."

"How about just staying out of it and letting us work
this through by ourselves?"

Noah shook his head. "It's well past time for that, and
you know it."

Harlow slammed his fist down so hard on his desk it
made Noah jump. "Blast it! A wife's supposed to be obe-
dient unto her husband. If Mary Sue would just do that
and quit acting so crazy, none of our problems would've
ever come to this. That's what the Bible says, and you
know it."

"The Bible also counsels husbands to love their wives as Christ loved the Church. Beating Mary Sue into submission isn't love. Not in the Bible, and not in my mind, either."

"Well, you're hardly the one to cast aspersions, are you?" Harlow demanded with a sneer. "You only think you covered up that scandal surrounding you and Doctor MacKay by marrying her. There are still folks who continue to question your morals and your fitness to remain as the Episcopal church's pastor." He smiled maliciously. "I'm surprised you haven't yet received a letter from your bishop regarding those concerns."

Noah was grateful he had kept his temper for as long as he had, but he could finally feel his anger rising. He shouldn't be surprised, though, that the conversation had taken this ugly turn. Harlow Peterson had always struck him as a man who would fight dirty when his back was against the wall. But Noah also knew Harlow was afraid—afraid of a lot of things. What he needed most right now was compassion and support, not anger.

"If that happens, I'll deal with it when the time comes," Noah said, struggling to keep his voice calm, his words kind. "In the meanwhile, what matters is you and Mary Sue. I want to help the both of you. To do that, though, I've got to get you two to talk, to begin working to solve your problems."

"You mean *my* problems, don't you?"

"I never said some of the fault doesn't also lie with Mary Sue. Right now, though, you and I are talking. All I can do is deal with you. But if you promise to come to the rectory and meet regularly for a while, I think—"

Harlow shoved back his chair so hard it crashed into the wall behind him; then he strode around the desk to where Noah sat.

Noah rose to his feet and stood there, refusing to be intimidated. For a fleeting instant as Harlow bore down

232

on him, his face purpling with anger and his fists clenched, Noah feared he might have to defend himself. Then the other man slid to a halt before him.

"You don't know when to quit, do you?" the banker demanded, glaring down at Noah. "Well, I've had about all I can take. Get out of my office. You're not going to believe me no matter what I say, and if I have to listen to you another minute, I'm afraid I'll forget who you are and hit you."

"Just like you hit Mary Sue," Noah asked softly, "whenever she doesn't see things your way? Is that how it is, Harlow?"

The blood drained from the man's face. His mouth opened, moved, but no sound issued forth. He just stood there, staring, until Noah decided it was probably past time to make an exit. If he was lucky, maybe he had gotten through with that last, brutally painful remark. He could only hope so—for all their sakes.

Either way, nothing more could be done today.

18

I have chosen thee in the furnace of affliction.
Isaiah 48:10

That night at half past ten, an insistent pounding came from the front door. It woke both Beth and Noah, who had retired only a half hour earlier. Noah was the first to slip from bed and begin dressing.

When Beth made a move to get out of bed, Noah stopped her. "No sense in both of us getting up. If it's one of your patients, I'll come fetch you."

Gratefully, Beth slid back beneath the covers. Even in June, the nights could be chilly. Thanks to Noah's recent presence, though, the bed was still cozy and warm.

"I guess it *could* be someone needing your pastoral assistance as easily as it could be a patient," she said. "It's just going to take some getting used to, having a husband who can just as likely be called out at night as I am."

As he buttoned his shirt and tucked it into his trousers, Noah grinned. "Well, considering it's only your first night home as a pastor's wife, I suppose I can forgive your mistake. Just don't let it happen again."

Beth stuck out her tongue at him. "So not only are you very sure of yourself, but now you're already starting to lay down the law. What comes next? Me being at your beck and call?"

He appeared to consider that for a moment, then nodded. "Sounds like a fine plan. And when exactly were you thinking to begin?"

She made a rude sound and sent a pillow sailing toward his head.

With a laugh, Noah dodged it, then headed toward the door. Beth snuggled down beneath the covers and, for a time, waited on Noah. From below, the sound of men's voices rose, their conversation indistinct. Clearly, though, one voice was calm and one was agitated and apparently pleading with the other.

As the conversation dragged on, curiosity finally got the best of Beth. She climbed from bed and tiptoed to the window. From there, the voices came more clearly now, and one of them was Harlow Peterson's.

Beth ran over and began to dress. There was only one reason he could be here at this hour. Earlier that evening she had convinced Noah again to allow Mary Sue to stay at the rectory after the woman had admitted her parents refused to involve themselves in her marital disputes. Harlow was surely here now, demanding his wife return home with him.

Beth found Mary Sue standing near the bottom of the stairs, out of sight, but close enough to hear what the two men were discussing. Beth walked over and took her hand.

"Don't worry," she whispered, leaning close. "Harlow won't get by unless Noah lets him." She gave Mary Sue's hand a quick squeeze, then released it.

"Let me in, Father Starr," Harlow was saying. "Please, let me in to talk with Mary Sue. I've already told you. I've done wrong by her. I admit that, and I repent of it most sincerely. So please, just let me in."

"Harlow," Beth heard Noah say in that low, soothing tone of his, "not tonight. It's too late. The women are asleep, and so's my daughter. Come back tomorrow, and we'll all talk. I promise."

"B-but you d-don't understand." The banker's voice became shaky. "I can't bear for my Mary Sue to leave me. I swear. I-I don't know what I'll do if she leaves me. I love her. I love her s-so much!"

"She hasn't left you, Harlow. She's just spending the night somewhere else. She'll be gratified, though, to know how you feel about her. I'm glad you came, that you had a change of heart, but you really need to head on home. It's just too—"

"No. P-please!"

Even from their hiding place, Beth could tell Harlow had begun to weep. Beside her, Mary Sue inhaled a ragged breath.

"Harlow," she whispered. "Oh, my poor, poor boy."

She took a step forward. Beth grabbed her arm.

"Don't, Mary Sue. Noah's right. This can wait until the morning."

Mary Sue hesitated. Then, as her husband's sobs grew louder and even more intense, she shook her head.

"He needs me, Beth. I can't let him leave like this. At least let me speak to him."

Maybe seeing his wife would ease enough of Harlow Peterson's anguish to convince him to go home for the night. Beth certainly hoped so. One thing for certain, though. Mary Sue needed to stay here. Even if Harlow

236

was finally beginning to face his part in this sorry mess, he still had a long way to go in understanding and controlling his volatile temper.

"Fine," Beth said at last. "Go to him. Reassure him of your love, then send him on his way. In the meanwhile, you two need to stay apart until we can get some things worked out."

Mary Sue nodded. "Of course. I just can't bear to hear him crying, that's all."

Beth motioned for Mary Sue to go ahead of her. She stepped out immediately, hurrying into the entry to stand beside Noah. Beth followed in her wake.

As soon as Harlow caught sight of his wife, he shoved past Noah, threw himself at her feet, and flung his arms about her legs. "Oh, beloved. My beloved!" He began crying once more. "I'm sorry. So very, very sorry. Can you forgive me? Can you?"

With a soft, crooning sound, Mary Sue bent and cradled his head against her. "I love you, too, sweetheart. I've always loved you. I just didn't know what to do anymore, and you scared me so."

"I-I know," he said, sobbing. "I know. I was wrong. I was so wr-wrong! Just say you'll forgive me and come home, or I don't know what I'll do."

"Hush, hush, my love." Mary Sue began to weep as well. "I can't bear to see you like this. I just can't bear it."

"Th-then say you'll c-come home with me. Say it, Mary Sue. Say it!"

She lifted her gaze and met Beth's. In it, Beth saw the growing doubt, the change in her resolve.

"No," Beth mouthed. "Don't do it. Wait."

Mary Sue closed her eyes. When she opened them again, she looked to Noah. "What should I do?" she asked softly.

Beth watched the emotions play across her husband's face. She saw him glance down at the sobbing Harlow, then up to gaze into Mary Sue's pleading eyes. He hesitated. Then, as if he had made up his mind at last, Noah gave a curt nod.

"If you think you'll be safe, go home with him, Mary Sue. This may well be a significant breakthrough for Harlow. I'm hopeful now that your marriage might be saved."

"No!" Beth grasped her husband's arm, squeezing it tightly. "No. Mary Sue mustn't go home tonight, or for many nights to come. Harlow might be repentant right now, but the real proof lies in his willingness to face his problems and begin to work through them. And that's not all going to happen tonight."

Noah turned to her and laid a hand over the one she had placed on his arm. "It'll be all right. I agree. Harlow and Mary Sue have a lot of work ahead of them, but I think he's turned a corner tonight. And they need to begin their marital healing at home, as much as they need to with the Lord, with my assistance. Keeping them apart will only slow, if not damage, that process." He smiled. "I feel it in my heart, Beth. This is God's will."

She stared up at him, stunned. Was Noah blind? Nothing of any great significance had been accomplished tonight. Indeed, she'd bet this was the usual sequel after all Harlow and Mary Sue's fights. He begging forgiveness, she magnanimously granting it, and then another period of quiet and loving union. Until the next time, and the next, and the next.

But how could Beth go against her husband, especially now, in front of others, questioning his judgment as a man of God? It wasn't fair. They had only been married three days, and already she had slammed right up against the reality of the lot of a preacher's wife.

What had Ian said that night they'd eaten in the hotel? *I never saw ye as the kind of woman cut out for the life of bein' a preacher's wife. Ye're far too independent and freethinking. . . .*

But this wasn't being independent and freethinking. This was something entirely different. This was sound medical judgment, common sense, even. Still, Noah was far more experienced in these kinds of matters than she was. She had been out of medical school now barely two years, while Noah had been a priest almost fourteen.

Beth chewed on her lip. She looked from Noah to Mary Sue to Harlow, who had finally stopped crying and was gazing now at his wife with eager, imploring eyes.

Her glance snagged with his. Yes, the repentance was there, she realized, but something was lacking. Was it, perhaps, a soul-deep understanding of what was necessary for real and lasting change, or even a true commitment to that change?

Beth couldn't quite put her finger on it, but she knew what she felt, and trusted those instincts. "It may be God's will that a man and wife cleave to each other, but I don't think it's His will that one of them rush unnecessarily back into danger in the process. The Bible says blessed is he who waiteth, and it won't do Harlow any harm to wait to have his wife back with him." She shook her head with vehemence. "I'm sorry, Noah, but as Mary Sue's doctor, I must advise against her going home with her husband tonight. Everyone's been far too easy on Harlow. I think he needs to earn the right to have his wife back. And that earning will come with his faithful attendance at his talks with you."

Noah eyed her, and to any other person he probably looked composed. But Beth knew him. She caught the tightening of his mouth, the glint of disappointment in his eyes. It hurt, knowing what she had said had wounded him. But it needed to be said.

"In the end," Noah replied, still looking at Beth, "it doesn't matter what either of us think. The decision is ultimately up to Mary Sue. Neither of us can keep her here against her will." He turned from Beth and toward Mary Sue. "What do you want to do, Mary Sue? Stay or go? Either way, I'm betting Harlow will come back here tomorrow."

Mary Sue's eyes filled with tears. She looked down at her husband. "Harlow, I don't know. Maybe it's best if I stay, at least for tonight. There's always tomorrow . . ."

The banker climbed to his feet, engulfed her in his arms, and pulled her to him. "Yes, beloved, there's always tomorrow. But I need you home tonight. Now that we've finally admitted our problem, there's no reason to remain apart. And Noah's right. We're both coming back here tomorrow and every day after that, for as long as we need to. I swear it!"

He began to kiss her ever so tenderly. First on the hair, then forehead, then cheeks, nose, and finally the mouth. Beth could see Mary Sue melt against him, her resistance and good sense evaporating in the intensity of his assault. She wanted to scream at Mary Sue, beg her not to give in, but knew it was over. If she and Noah had stood united, the odds were strong they would've prevailed in convincing her to stay. But now all Beth had left was prayer.

Prayer that God would be merciful to Mary Sue. That Harlow had truly moved from violence to repentance. And that, at long last, he truly meant what he had said and was willing to work through his problems.

Yes, all that was left now was prayer. The sad thing was, Beth was in no mood for praying.

She shot Noah one final, furious look, then turned and stalked away.

ح

Noah returned to their bedroom a half hour later. As quietly as he could, he undressed in the dark and climbed into bed. It soon became evident, however, that Beth wasn't asleep.

He lay there for a time, listening to her breathing, feeling the anger and tension radiating from her like the warmth from a cast-iron cookstove. Noah couldn't say he was all that happy with Beth, either. As his wife, if not as a friend, he expected her to support him in his pastoral duties and decisions. Obviously, though, he had presumed too much.

Lord, Noah prayed, grant me the patience, wisdom, and humility to solve this problem. Help me to help her understand, and help her to help me do the same.

"I know you're awake, Beth," Noah said finally. "And I'm willing to guess neither of us is going to get much sleep unless we talk this out."

"So you think there's something to talk about?" she asked from her position turned on her side away from him. "It's not already immutably written in stone that the pastor's wife should be seen but never heard?"

He sighed. "Beth, we had a difference of opinion tonight. I acted as I saw fit, as did you. We do need, though, to work out a few ground rules."

She turned over, shoved her pillows up, then pushed herself to a sitting position. "And why do I get the feeling these rules will all flow in one direction—mine?"

"That's not fair." Noah tried to quash his irritation. "I just don't think you understand how delicate matters like Harlow and Mary Sue's can get. And if you recall, this time both of them came to me as their pastor, not to you as their doctor."

"So the rule is, the person they come to has total jurisdiction. Is that it?"

"Well, if not, how should we approach similar problems in the future?"

She turned to him. "I think personal safety must always be paramount, even above some biblical admonition that marriage is indissoluble. Other than that, I can't see much else that might be a source of conflict between us. Oh, yes, and I don't particularly appreciate it when you bring in God as your ally, either. It's kind of hard to go up against Him."

"Well, I did feel that way, that it was the Lord's will that the Petersons reconcile."

"No," she said tautly, "you claimed it was God's will they go home together tonight, or it'd slow the recovery of, if not damage, their marriage. And you were quite firm, even a bit patronizing about it all, too. You put me in the position of having to make a choice for you and God, or Mary Sue."

"Frequently, things do come down to that."

"But not, I reiterate, when it comes to personal safety."

Frustration filled him. They weren't getting anywhere; they were just talking in circles.

"Beth, I didn't—"

"You undermined me as a doctor, Noah," his wife said. "And I'm sorry, but I still feel you were wrong in what you did tonight. As sacred as wedding vows are to God, no harm to that tottering mockery of a marriage would've been done if Harlow and Mary Sue had spent some time apart while they endeavored to work through their problems. Each time they fight, Harlow hurts her worse. He may kill her. How can you be so sure that won't happen the next time they fight?"

"No one can know the future. All I can do is go on what I feel. And I felt Harlow's true repentance this evening."

Beth gave a snort of disgust. "Well, repentance isn't a whole lot of help without a plan for not sinning again, is it? Do you seriously think Harlow Peterson as yet has

242

any inkling how to control his temper, much less know why he even gets that way? Do you, Noah?"

For the first time that evening, a twinge of uncertainty pierced him. Was Beth right? Had he been so caught up in the rightness of his outlook that he had failed to see the human needs and failings feeding into this tragedy waiting to happen?

Harlow hadn't come to the rectory tonight because he had sinned against God and had repented of it. He had come solely because he repented of anything that kept him from his wife. Indeed, he had appeared almost on the verge of hysteria because he so desperately wanted Mary Sue with him. Harlow would've said anything to achieve that end. Anything.

Noah groaned and shook his head. "No, you're right. As yet, Harlow's repentance doesn't go very deep. And though I truly believe he loves his wife, right now it's a flawed, dangerous love." He banged his head back against the headboard. "But what could I do, Beth? Mary Sue wanted to go home with her husband."

"She's as confused as Harlow is, if in a different way. Her love is just as flawed and dangerous, if not for Harlow, then most certainly for herself. But I think if we'd stood together, she would've decided against going home with Harlow tonight. But we didn't, Noah. We didn't."

Guilt filled him. "I'm so sorry. I was a fool and in my foolishness, I failed not only you but also Mary Sue." He turned and took her hand. "How can I make it up to you?"

"You don't need to do anything, Noah, but just listen the few times I might protest or question one of your decisions. That's all. I don't want to interfere in your pastoral assessments. But sometimes I just don't think things are as black and white as you may want them to be."

"I know you might find this hard to believe, considering what transpired this evening, but I value that in you. Your counsel, your insights. For a young woman, you've got a very mature head on your shoulders." He grinned and squeezed her hand. "I married you for a whole lot more than your stunning beauty, you know."

Beth squeezed his hand in turn. "Well, that may be," she said with a chuckle, "but I did marry you solely for your looks. Just so we get that matter cleared up once and for all."

Noah laughed, relieved they had overcome their first marital spat so successfully. He silently lifted a quick, fervent prayer of gratitude. Thank You, Lord. Thank You.

"Do you think," he asked, his thoughts turning back to the Petersons' problems, "any good would be served trying to bring Mary Sue back here tonight? If you're really that concerned about her safety . . ."

She considered that for a moment, then shook her head. "No. I think it'd only make matters worse, leastwise tonight. They're both so exhausted by now, they'll probably just go to bed. Tomorrow, though, when they come for their visit, it might be worth some serious consideration. Having them physically separate for a while, I mean."

"Okay." Noah scooted down in bed and pulled up the covers. "You've just got me really worrying about Mary Sue now, that's all. If she should come to any harm . . ."

"I know. I feel the same way." Beth snuggled down beside him. "I think, though, that we're safe for tonight."

From out of a deep, dreamless sleep, an incessant pounding and the sound of voices permeated Noah's unconscious. He muttered something, then turned over and covered his head with his pillow. Silence reigned once more, and he drifted back into somnolence.

Then a hand grasped his shoulder, roughly shaking him awake.

"Noah, wake up. There are people at the door, and one of them sounds like Jake Whitmore. Wake up!"

Downstairs, the telephone rang. With a moan, Noah dragged himself from his slumber. He felt exhausted, weighed down, and dull-witted. Flinging back the covers, he shoved himself upright, then sat on the edge of the bed.

"Who in the world needs me at this hour?" he asked thickly, glancing at the bedside clock.

Four fifteen. He had finally drifted off to sleep around midnight; he had barely managed four hours of sleep.

"I told you," Beth said from across the room, where she was hurriedly flinging on her clothes. "I think Jake Whitmore's outside. And the telephone's still clanging away downstairs. Get dressed. I'll let Jake in, then answer the phone."

He stood and groggily groped around for his own clothes. "You're surprisingly perky for this hour of the morning."

"Comes from my internship days. We slept in the hospital. When the nurses came to fetch us, we learned to wake up and clear our minds in minutes. Life and death situations work wonders for that." She walked to the door and opened it. "Now hurry up and finish dressing. And don't you dare lay back down on that bed for even an instant."

Obediently, Noah did as directed. By the time he headed down the stairs, Jake Whitmore and one of his deputies had been let in and were awaiting him in the entry. He heard Beth on the telephone in the kitchen. From the snatches of conversation, Noah could tell she was talking to Doc Childress about someone.

He walked up to the sheriff. "Sorry to be so long in getting down here. I got to bed late and was more tired than I realized."

"Well, I'm just as sorry to have to get you out of bed," Jake said, "but we've had a shooting. Harlow Peterson is dead."

Any lingering drowsiness disappeared. Noah's heart gave a great lurch.

"What? What did you say?"

"Harlow Peterson's been killed. I thought you, being his pastor and all, would like to go to the house and do some praying over him."

"H-how?" The words stuck in his painfully dry throat. "I just saw him about five hours ago. How did it happen?"

Jake Whitmore shrugged. "What brought on the killing has yet to be determined. All we know right now is it was with one of his guns. And, even stranger than that, it was his wife who did the shooting."

19

Rejoice not, that the spirits are subject unto you; but rather rejoice, because your names are written in heaven.
Luke 10:20

By the time Beth and Noah reached the Petersons' house, a small crowd had already begun to gather. Funny how bad news always seems to travel faster than good, Beth observed grimly, following the sheriff as he pushed his way through the people. She soon found Harlow lying on the living room floor, his lifeless body covered with a blanket. Another one of Jake Whitmore's deputies stood nearby.

Across the room on the sofa, Doc was applying a bandage to a battered and stunned Mary Sue. Beth headed immediately for them.

"Need help with anything?"

At the sound of Beth's voice, Mary Sue looked up. "Beth. Oh, Beth, what have I done? What have I d-done?"

Her head dropped like a flower wilting on the vine, and she began to sob. Though her arms hung limply at her sides, her thin body trembled with the force of her weeping.

Beth exchanged glances with Doc. He finished tying off the bandage on Mary Sue's arm, then rose.

"She still has a few cuts and bruises that need tending," he said, "but I think right now she needs your comforting far more than your doctoring."

With a nod, Beth took the place he had just vacated. She wrapped an arm about Mary Sue's shoulder and pulled her close. Mary Sue came willingly to her, clutching Beth as if she feared she'd be taken from her.

"I-I couldn't h-help it," she said between hiccupping breaths. "It . . . it was all an act, Harlow's remorse. He only m-meant to get me back home and teach me a lesson. He said he was going to b-beat some obedience into me . . . once and for all. And then . . . and then he began to do just that." Mary Sue lifted her tear-stained face to look at Beth. "I thought he was going to kill me for sure this time. Then . . . then I remembered the gun Harlow kept in that drawer over there." She pointed to the antique mahogany lowboy placed against the wall near the door.

"And then what did you do?" Beth asked softly.

Mary Sue sighed and wiped the tears away. "What else *could* I do? Somehow, I made it to the gun, pulled it out, and pointed it at Harlow. It didn't stop him though, the gun's threat, I mean. He just laughed and kept on coming."

Over Mary Sue's head, Beth's gaze met Noah's. He stood there beside Harlow's body, watching them and listening. His face was drawn, the flesh stretched tautly across his bones. His eyes burned with anguish—and the brutal realization of the part he had played in this horrific tragedy.

Her heart went out to him. In the days and weeks to come, she knew there'd be more than Mary Sue who'd need her counsel and comfort. Mary Sue had killed to protect herself. Noah, however, had judged wrongly, and someone had lost his life because of it. It had been an honest mistake, but Beth sensed her husband would take on the full blame nonetheless.

This wasn't the time, however, to deal with that. For the present, Mary Sue's needs must take precedent.

Beth turned back to her. "You had no choice," she said, stroking the tangled hair from Mary Sue's ravaged face. "Harlow might've killed you."

"He said he was tired of me embarrassing him. He said if I ever tried to leave him again, he'd kill me." She grabbed Beth and stared up at her. "But I didn't think he intended to wait until next time. The look on his face . . ." She shuddered. "It wasn't the face of my husband, but someone else. Someone so consumed by rage he seemed almost insane."

"You must have been terrified."

"I was, Beth. I wished, oh, how I wished I'd stayed at the rectory rather than gone home." Once more, Mary Sue hugged her close. "You tried to warn me, but I wouldn't listen. I'm so sorry I didn't."

"You did the best you could. You loved Harlow, and he seemed so distraught. You were just trying to be a good wife."

"A good wife?" Mary Sue gave a shrill laugh. "What kind of a wife kills her own husband? Answer me that, Beth."

"More to the point," Beth demanded with a sour edge to her voice, "what kind of a husband beats his wife over and over? Answer me that, Mary Sue."

"He . . . he was sick, hurting. And he was so afraid of losing me."

"That's no excuse." Beth opened her mouth to say more, then realized Noah was still standing there waiting to pray over Harlow, and Jake was waiting to take the body away.

Beth looked to the sheriff. "Do you need to question Mary Sue further just now? She hasn't had any sleep, and she's exhausted."

Jake scratched his jaw. "No, I reckon not. This is kind of touchy, though. I have to hold her on charges of murder, leastwise until we can get a judge out here to consider her case."

"Are you telling me you intend on jailing Mary Sue? Why, I've never heard of such an outrageous—"

Noah stepped over to Jake. "Considering the circumstances surrounding this unfortunate incident and the fact Mary Sue's not likely to run, couldn't an exception be made? We'd like to take her back with us to the rectory. She's stayed with us there before."

The sheriff appeared to consider Noah's request, then shook his head. "I'd like to, Noah. Really, I would. But the law applies equally to women as to men. Until I get a judge even to rule on whether she can be released on bail, I need to lock her up." He turned to Mary Sue. "I'm real sorry, ma'am. Hopefully it'll only be for a few days at most. The chances are good, considering the circumstances, the judge will let you out on bail pending your trial. In the meanwhile, though . . ."

Mary Sue dragged in a deep, shaky breath, gave Beth one final squeeze, then pulled away. Squaring her shoulders, she met Jake's sympathetic gaze.

"It's all right, Sheriff. You're only doing your job." She smiled bitterly. "And, after all, Harlow was one of Grand View's most prominent citizens. Some folk are sure to talk if you don't follow the law in every way." She stood and glanced at Beth. "Thank you for all your help and support. I don't know what I would've done without it."

"I'll continue to support you, Mary Sue." Beth gazed up at her with a fierce resolve. "Just don't forget. You've got some other very prominent citizens on your side."

Mary Sue smiled through a glimmer of tears. "Yes," she said, turning from Beth to Doc, "I know and thank God for that."

❦

By the time they returned to the rectory, the sun was rising. Beth watched it ascend over the eastern horizon, a warm, glowing orb in a soft lavender-blue sky. Even on such a morn, when death was fresh in the air and a woman's life teetered on the brink of ruination, the sun rose, the world turned on its axis, and life went on as it always did, safe in the hands of God.

There was comfort in that. Even in the worst of times, God watched and cared and loved. And there was always forgiveness and mercy to be had—even for Harlow, even for Mary Sue.

Beth glanced at her husband as they walked along. She wanted to speak to him, to tell him of that mercy and forgiveness, and that it applied to him just as much as it applied to Harlow, Mary Sue, and all the rest of them. But the look on his face—a dark, congested expression that didn't welcome conversation—gave Beth pause.

More than anything right now, she wished dearly for years of marriage with him. Years in which to get to know him, his moods, his fears, and what to say to help him in those dark times. In a time like today.

No words came, however. No inspiration from above, and, finally, they arrived home. After sending home Helen Yates, who had come to watch Emily, Beth hurried to the stove, took up the coffeepot, and soon had it full of water and fresh grounds. By the time she was

251

ready to place the pot back on the cookstove, Noah had the fire going.

"Would you like some breakfast, or will a nice cup of coffee be enough this morning?" she asked as she put the pot back on the stove.

He shook his head. "Right now, my stomach couldn't handle either. I'll go get Emily up and dressed, then bring her downstairs before I head to the church. I've got a lot of work piling up there."

"Noah, it's barely 6:00 A.M.," Beth said, her concern for him growing. "Emily never gets up before seven. If you don't want any food or coffee, fine." She walked to the table and sat. "I need some coffee badly, and I'd like to spend a few minutes with you." She indicated the chair across from hers. "Just sit and unwind a bit, okay?"

He studied her for a long while, his gaze sad, considering. "I appreciate what you're trying to do, Beth," he said finally. "Really, I do. But I'm just not ready to talk about this. Right now my heart's so ripped apart, I can barely think, much less sort anything out. I need some time . . . to be alone, to pray."

"I understand, Noah." Beth folded her hands on the table. "I just want you to know I'm here when you finally do want to talk. Because we do need to talk. This is too big a burden for you to carry alone."

"It's mine to bear if it's my fault," he muttered, "which it is."

"Noah, that's not true, and you—"

He held up a hand. "Not now, Beth. I'm sorry, but not now."

Before she could even formulate a reply, he turned and stalked from the kitchen, across the entry, and out the front door.

By some special grace of God, Noah managed to get through Harlow Peterson's funeral. He had thought Millie's service had been difficult, but even in his grief at her passing, he had still felt connected to God. Now, though, Noah lived in total darkness. His prayers were dry as dust. His joy had shriveled. Surely the Lord had forsaken him.

But what else did he deserve? In his pride and arrogance, he had thought he knew the Lord's will, when it had always been but his own. He had imagined himself above most men in his wisdom and ability to discern the proper course people's lives should take even if, for a time before Beth had come back into his life, he had begun to doubt himself. And he had been so very, very wrong.

Was Harlow's death the thing that caused him to see the truth for the first time? Noah greatly feared it was so. He knew too well of the lies people could tell themselves in the name of God. Lies that blinded the eyes as they wreaked havoc on the hopes and dreams of others. Lies that possessed not a bit of true, Christ-centered charity but only self-love and self-righteousness.

No wonder the Lord had finally forsaken him and his ministry. God had waited on him for years now, hoping His servant would learn to walk the one true path in humility and love. But instead he had persevered in his ignorance. He was worse than a weak, ineffectual pastor. He was a threat to all the good, trusting folk who called him Father.

Had he ever really even been called to the priesthood? Had he instead, in the depths of his pride, imagined the call? Perhaps it was best to admit his mistake now, before he did more damage. Before he was the cause of even greater tragedy.

As the days passed, it became increasingly difficult for Noah to set foot in church or even to go to his office there. He felt like a hypocrite, unworthy and mired in despair.

Beth, being the perceptive woman that she was, was bound to notice and eventually speak her mind. And one evening after supper was finished and Emily had been put to bed for the night, Beth broached the topic they had both danced around for over a week.

"You're eating your heart out," she said, glancing up at him from the dishpan full of sudsy water and dirty plates and silverware. "I've held my tongue as long as I can, but I can't stand by and watch you suffer any longer. You need to make peace with what happened to Harlow."

"This goes much deeper than my part in Harlow's death," Noah said, well aware there was an edge to his voice. In an odd sort of way, he was almost relieved she had finally broached the subject. Yet in another, more perverse way, he was angry, too. It seemed almost as if putting the pain to words was to make light of it.

He accepted a soapy glass from her, rinsed it clean, then put it in the rack to dry. "I showed a profound lack of judgment in how I advised them. A lack of sensitivity, of love, and just plain common sense. My pride blinded me, Beth, and that's a fatal flaw in a priest."

"Pride's just as fatal a flaw in a physician. But, some-times—most times, if the truth be told—it's the mistakes that make us better. Better doctors, better priests, better human beings. If, of course, we find the humility in the midst of our overweening self-importance to learn and amend our lives." She smiled wryly. "Sad, isn't it, that the only way we seem to learn true humility is in the realization of how very weak and ineffectual we fre-quently are? But we need those empty places humility fashions, swept clean of our conceit, if we're to have any hope of God using them and entering through them and into us more fully."

Beth's statement filled Noah with awe. "And when exactly did you gain such deep insights into the nature of God and suffering?"

Beth shrugged. "I don't know. Maybe it was from something my parents said, or perhaps you shared it one Sunday in one of your mesmerizing sermons. One way or another, it touched me deeply, that truth, and I've thought about it many a time. I do believe it, you know."

Over the years, Noah had given many homilies addressing the topic of suffering and its wondrous redemptive value. Indeed, he had presented one just recently at Millie's funeral. The realization comforted him. Perhaps, just perhaps, he had managed, after all, to have been of some use to someone. But it wasn't enough.

"I've been giving serious thought to leaving the priest-hood," Noah said. "How would you feel about that, about me, if I did?"

Beth finished the last dish and handed it to him. Then, as he rinsed and stacked it with the others, she emptied the dishpan, rinsed it, and set it on its side. Only then did she turn to him.

"How would I feel about you?" she asked. "I'd love you no matter what. But that said, I think leaving the priesthood would be the biggest mistake of your life and a denial of your divine call. If any man was meant to be a priest, it's you, Noah Starr. I can well guess, though, why all this has led to such terrible self-doubts. You wouldn't be the man you are if such a loss didn't affect you so deeply."

"I feel . . . I feel like I've failed everyone. Harlow, Mary Sue, and even you." Noah looked down. "I just . . . I'm just so tired, Beth."

She closed the few feet separating them, taking him into her arms. "I know," she said softly. "I know. But if in this time of pain you feel too weary and confused to bear the yoke the Lord has placed on you, then let me help you carry it. Your sorrow is mine. Let me and all the others who love you share this load. But never, ever doubt what you were always meant to be in the service of the Lord. Never!"

He leaned against her, his arms slipping around to pull her close. It felt so good to hold Beth, to feel her love and concern and know her support. Even now, when it seemed as if the Lord was so very far away, Noah knew that He was as close as the woman he held in his arms. Even now, God's loving promise that He'd never forsake his children was apparent.

"Then help me, Beth," he whispered hoarsely. "Help me find a way out of this."

She kissed him on the forehead. "How about starting with Mary Sue? She's been free from jail for over half a week now, waiting and worrying on her trial, and you haven't been to see her once. Perhaps if you talked with her, asked for her forgiveness . . . Harlow's not the only victim. She was harmed by what happened that night, too. Perhaps that's where you need to start to begin your healing."

Beth had voiced what had been in his heart since that horrible night. But he felt so ashamed, so afraid. Afraid of what Mary Sue would say, afraid that she wouldn't forgive him.

"You're right, of course," he said, pulling back from her, but not meeting the piercing scrutiny of her gaze. "I'm not setting a very good example, am I, in not asking her forgiveness?"

"I couldn't care less about the example you should set as a pastor right now. What matters to me is you as a man and that you come back to the Lord."

Noah glanced up sharply. Was it that apparent that he wavered so erratically in his faith right now? The realization shamed him anew.

Beth must have noted the color that flooded his face. "It's all right, you know. It's human to lose hope, to question, to rail against the unfairness of it all. God understands. His own Son experienced the same painful emotions. In the end, though, all that matters is that you continue to love the Lord through it all and trust in Him. Trust that it'll all work out for the best."

Noah leaned against the wall behind him and rested his head. He closed his eyes. "Why, Beth? Why would God let a man die just to teach me some lesson I need to learn?" He banged his head against the wall. "I know, I know. I've offered the same answers to others many a time, but I see now I never really understood it. Not really."

He opened his eyes to meet her gaze, his mouth twisting bitterly. "All this time, all I had to give were lame, shallow answers. I was such a hypocrite."

"No, you weren't a hypocrite." She took his hand. "You gave from the wellspring of your own knowledge and belief. You gave from the heart. Sometimes just because you don't fully understand something doesn't mean it isn't still the truth. It just means you've got more to learn."

"Well, that much is certainly true," Noah said with a harsh laugh. "I still have a *lot* to learn."

Beth squeezed his hand. "Go talk with my father. He's so much wiser than I. He'll help you, if any man can. And make your peace with Mary Sue, whether she can forgive you or not."

"I'm not supposed to be the one who asks for the help." He shook his head, feeling foolish. "I'm the one who dispenses it."

"And if that isn't pride speaking, I don't know what is. You're our pastor, Noah, not the Almighty. You're as human as the rest of us and will be to your dying day." Beth smiled. "But that's also what makes you our finest example and inspiration. In you, we see living proof the Lord spares no one in allowing life to take its course. But we also see the glorious power of His love manifested in you in how you live for Him no matter life's trials and tribulations. In how you persevere, overcome, and never long lose the joy."

20

He that overcometh shall inherit all things.
                                    Revelation 21:7

"No, Reverend Starr, I'm sorry. I can't find it in my heart to forgive you."

Noah dragged in a long, deep breath, glanced down at the hat he held between his knees, then looked up to meet Mary Sue Peterson's cool gaze. "Why? If you don't mind telling me, why can't you forgive me?"

She eyed him for a long moment, then sighed. "Perhaps it's a failing in me, but I can't come to terms with the thought that you seemed to care more for God's law than for God's children. And me, in particular, as one of those children." She shook her head. "I thought you were a godly man, but now . . . now I no longer know what to think."

A sharp pain lanced through Noah, stabbing clear to his heart. *You seemed to care more for God's law than for God's children . . . I thought you were a godly man . . .*

"Do you still love and serve the Lord?" Noah asked, struggling to contain his anguish and deep sense of failure. Though he had come to call on Mary Sue the very next day after he and Beth had talked, he had waited too long. If only he had come sooner . . .

"Yes, I do still love the Lord," she said after a moment of hesitation. "But I don't trust you anymore. I'm sorry. I don't wish to be cruel. You're Beth's husband after all, and I'm proud to call her my friend." She smiled sadly. "Perhaps I'll come to terms with my anger against you someday, maybe when I overcome my anger at Harlow. Right now, though, I can't say I feel any too kindly toward men in general."

A sense of weary resignation swamped Noah. There wasn't much hope of resolving anything today, he realized. And he could hardly blame Mary Sue for how she felt. He *had* failed her.

Noah stood. "Thank you for your honesty. I understand why you might not feel any too kindly toward me right now. Still, I had to come, offer my apologies, and ask your forgiveness."

"I appreciate that, Reverend Starr."

He turned to go, then hesitated. "For your sake, if not for mine, try and find it in your heart to forgive me someday. The Lord asks that of us all, and I've caused you enough pain. I don't wish to be the cause of further damage to your soul." Noah strode to the door, opened it, and paused. "Thank you for taking the time today to speak with me. I know it must have been hard."

Mary Sue walked up and grasped the door. "No harder than it was for you, I'm sure. Good day, Reverend Starr."

He shoved his hat back on his head and nodded. "Good day to you, Mrs. Peterson."

As he turned to leave, Mary Sue closed the door firmly behind him. Noah headed out, leaving her front yard by the gate, and made his way back down Winona Street toward the post office. He supposed he should feel something after such a fruitless visit–disappointment, hurt, or maybe even a touch of irritation at Mary Sue's refusal to remember all his efforts on her behalf in the past. But instead Noah only felt numb.

After he collected the mail, Noah walked outside and sorted through it. A letter from his mother, another from a distant cousin. Then the familiar address of the General Theological Seminary caught his eye.

Noah frowned. He had answered their last letter not long after his talk with Millie the night before the Fall Social, thanking them for their kind offer but informing them he was content to remain in Grand View. Whatever could they want now?

He glanced up. The sky was clear, the day fine, warm, and perfect for the middle of June. He settled on the wooden bench outside the post office and opened the seminary's letter.

After the usual salutations, it got right to the point. Another position had opened up–one that all agreed he was even more suited for. Though funds were tight, would he reconsider if offered a higher salary and a position as head of the sacred theology department?

A crazed mix of emotions assaulted Noah. Strange that a second and even more prestigious position should come at a time like this. Was it, perhaps, the will of God at work?

It'd be the answer to many problems–more time to spend with Beth and Emily. A job devoted to his first love–the study of God and his faith. And a respite from the frequently exhausting and frustrating job of dealing, day in and day out, with Grand View's residents. He had served them to the best of his ability for over fourteen years now. Maybe it was time to move on.

New York City . . . Noah had always loved that city. The myriad educational opportunities, the access to fine libraries, restaurants, and museums, the diversity of cultures. He'd never feel isolated again, intellectually or spiritually. The offer, with all its exciting potential, was a dream come true!

But what about Beth? Was it fair to ask her to leave her home and family? And what about her commitment to Doc Childress and her growing medical practice? She was finally building a solid reputation as an excellent diagnostician and compassionate physician.

The opportunities for her in New York City, though, would be equally as good, if not better. And how he'd love to see her situated someplace where she could find the stature and acclaim she truly deserved, and would never fully achieve in a small town. How he'd love to see her bloom and grow to her fullest capabilities!

Noah stuffed the letter back into its envelope, put it in his coat pocket, and rose. The seminary's offer was tempting, very tempting. Like every other major life decision, however, he must pray on it. And he must ask his wife for her opinion. There were two of them now, two hearts and two minds.

This time, though, there wasn't a whole lot of room for marital compromise. It was either stay or go.

Beth set the letter aside on the kitchen table and looked up at her husband. "They spoke of this being their second offer," she said. "I don't recall anything about a first one."

"I was initially approached in late October. I talked with Millie at the time, prayed over it, and decided to remain here. So I wrote, thanked them for the consideration, but politely declined."

"Oh, I see."

Unease twined about Beth's heart. Noah might have refused the first offer, but she could tell he was giving this new one some very serious consideration.

She chewed on her lower lip. "So what are you asking? Do I want to go or not?"

He didn't answer right off, but instead studied her gravely. "Well, at the very least, I'd like us to discuss the offer, then give it some thought. The head of the theology department's a very important position. I could do a lot of good there, touch many lives."

He is so excited about this, Beth thought. That letter had brought the sparkle back to his eyes, and he almost glowed with renewed energy. She hadn't seen him so animated since their wedding and honeymoon.

"You do a lot of good here, Noah. These people are important, too, you know."

He nodded, leaned forward, and took her hand. "I know that, sweetheart. But to be able to influence hundreds of future priests . . . Multiply that by all the people they'll all help and influence . . . Well, I'd touch a lot more lives, if indirectly."

"I understand that, Noah."

"But you don't want to leave here." His face fell. "You want to stay in Grand View, don't you?"

"All things being equal, yes, I do. But it's not just what I want anymore, is it? A husband and wife have to decide such things together."

Noah squeezed her hand. "Thank you for that. I don't want you to be unhappy, though. Would you at least pray on it, Beth? Give it some thought? The potential benefits to you and your medical career might be considerable. And it's not as if New York City's a totally foreign place for you."

"New York's not a place of particularly happy memories for me, either, Noah. Or have you already forgotten?"

"No, I haven't forgotten. But if we went, we'd go together, you, Emily, and me. We'd go as a family. And we'd be close to the cutting edge in medical practice, which might well be a godsend for Emily." He grinned for the first time in a week. "The more I think about it, the more the advantages seem to outweigh what few disadvantages there are."

"Maybe, Noah. Maybe."

"You'll at least think on it, won't you?"

What choice had she? He was her husband.

"Yes," Beth said with a sigh. "Of course, I'll think on it."

Noah was considerate enough not to bring up the subject for the next day or two, though Beth could tell it was nearly always on his mind. It had to be. It was nearly always on hers.

Try as she might, though, she could find no joy, no peace, and certainly no acceptance in the idea of leaving Grand View. She cherished the opportunity to get to know the people she lived with and cared for. To see the children grow, fall in love, marry, and start families of their own. To experience, along with her patients and friends, all of life's sublime mysteries and phases, from birth to death.

So much of that would be lost in the inevitable anonymity of a place like New York City. There was very little help for it, considering its size.

And how could she desert Doc like that? Little by little, the old physician was turning over his practice to her. True, they had no legal contract saying that she must stay for any set length of time. But he wasn't just her colleague. He was a cherished, longtime friend.

Still, there was Noah to consider. Though he mentioned nothing further about his fitness to remain in the priesthood, Beth knew he continued to have his doubts. She could see it in his eyes and in his subtle lack of enthusiasm for his work. Would it be in the best interests of his priestly calling for him to take this new job?

The questions whirled about endlessly in Beth's head until she could barely keep her mind focused on work. Finally, late one morning two days after Noah's surprising revelation, she decided she needed the help of more seasoned and objective minds than what she currently possessed. With Doc's permission, Beth cancelled her two afternoon appointments, rescheduling them for tomorrow. After saddling up her horse, she set out for Culdee Creek.

Could I ever tire of the sweeping panorama of this beautiful, untamed land? Beth wondered as she rode along. *The verdant, grassy hills. The cool depths of the ponderosa pine forests. The looming, timeless majesty of Pikes Peak.*

She loved the Front Range, even with its wild, unforgiving weather. She'd miss its sacred silences that nurtured the soul, opening the heart to the wonders of the universe and, inevitably, to that universe's Maker. But, most of all, how she'd miss the stalwart, brave people, especially her family.

Culdee Creek was far more than just a ranch and her girlhood home. Culdee Creek represented the hopes and dreams of her hardy Scottish and American ancestors. Ancestors who had sacrificed everything to defend all they held dear and, when the New World offered the chance of a better life, had braved countless hardships to set out for that unknown.

All because of their love of freedom and family. All because they wanted something more, something better. And all thanks to their courage.

Must she, now, also set out for the unknown of a new life because of her love for her husband? More than anything she had ever wanted, Beth wanted Noah to be happy and find renewed zeal in the service of the Lord. But was her courage—and her love—sufficient to the task?

Beth wasn't sure. Maybe, just maybe, though, she thought as she drew up before the ranch's main house, her parents might see past all the many possibilities to what really mattered. Just now, Beth desperately needed to understand and find some kind of acceptance.

Abby was the first to notice her arrival. She hurried out onto the covered front porch, the screen door closing behind her with its usual forceful bang. A dishcloth in hand, she walked over to Beth.

"My, what a pleasant surprise," her stepmother said. "Nothing's wrong, is it, for you to come visiting in the middle of the day in the middle of the week?"

Beth climbed the porch steps. "Well, as a matter of fact, I do have something to talk with you and Pa about." She glanced around. "Is he anywhere near?"

A look of concern in her eyes, Abby nodded. "As a matter of fact, he just stopped in for a quick glass of lemonade." She opened the screen door. "Come on in. Your father's in the kitchen."

Beth led the way, Abby following, and found her father sitting at the table, a glass of pink lemonade in his hand. His eyes brightened at the sight of her.

"Well, what's this? Someone sick at Culdee Creek that I don't know about?"

Beth glanced sheepishly down at her doctor's bag. "No, no one's sick that I know about. I'm just glued to this bag, I guess."

She pulled out a chair, set her bag off to one side, and took her seat. Abby poured an extra glass of lemonade. After placing it before Beth, she sat down opposite her husband.

"Beth came to visit because she has something she wants to talk with us about," Abby said. She turned to Beth. "Don't you, honey?"

Two pairs of eyes riveted on Beth. She wet her lips, paused to consider several ways to present the news, and finally discarded them all.

"Noah's been offered a position at his old seminary, and he's seriously considering taking it. In case you didn't know, the seminary's in New York City."

For a long moment, there was silence. Then Conor cleared his throat.

"How do you feel about that, girl?"

"I love Noah, and I want him to be happy." Beth toyed with her lemonade, tracing little swirls on the perspiration-coated glass. "He's so upset over Harlow's death and what he views as his part in it, that he's admitted he's considering even leaving the priesthood. But this offer, coming when it did . . . well, Noah's very excited about it. It may be what he needs to regain his heart for the ministry."

"But how do you feel about leaving your practice here, leaving Grand View, leaving us?" her father persisted. "Or doesn't anything matter to you anymore but what Noah wants?"

"That's not fair, Pa! Of course it matters that I'd have to leave everything. I love it here. I love working with Doc, love the inroads I've made with my patients. I love this place, and I'm s-so happy to be back home."

Tears filled her eyes and she had to choke back a sob. "But Noah . . . he's so unhappy, Pa. He feels like such a failure. And I fear the Petersons' tragedy, coming like it did on the heels of Alice's and Millie's deaths . . . well, it's all Noah can do right now even to hold onto his faith in God."

Conor and Abby exchanged troubled looks.

"It's gotten that bad, has it?" her father asked. "Blast Noah's stubborn streak of pride! Besides telling you, he sure hasn't let onto anyone else how despondent he's become. He's quieter of late, maybe doesn't laugh as much as he used to, but aside from that, he's hidden his pain well."

"I asked him to come talk with you, Pa," Beth said. "I told him you could help him if any man could. Has he ever come?"

"No." Conor pursed his lips and shook his head. "No, he hasn't. But I've half a mind to ride out this very afternoon, grab him up by his collar, and shake some sense into him."

Beth reached over and grasped her father's wrist. "No. Don't. I don't want him to know I've talked to you about this. It's probably not right as it is, a wife going behind her husband's back, but I just didn't know what else to do. Not only do I not want to leave here, but I don't think it's the best thing for Noah, either."

"Why not, Beth?" Abby asked. "Why don't you think it's the best thing for Noah?"

Why, indeed? Beth thought to herself. She pondered that question for several seconds.

"I don't know," she answered at last. "It's just a gut feeling. He's been so good for Grand View, and we still need him here. It's . . . it's almost as if Noah's running away from difficulties meant to help him grow. As if . . . as if he's running away from God."

"Then help him to see that." Abby leaned forward, a fierce light gleaming in her eyes. "Do what's truly best for Noah, no matter how hard it is. Don't *you* run away from the difficulties meant to help you grow, either. And don't shirk *your* responsibilities to God."

Beth met her stepmother's gaze. Something unspoken passed between them—a woman's intuition, an understanding of the depth and scope of commitment demanded in loving a man—piercing clear through to Beth's soul.

So this was how it was between her parents. This was what Abby had done for her father. And this was what she must do for Noah, in keeping her promises to him.

Beth smiled, in recognition, in gratitude, in renewed determination. Thank You, Lord. Thank You for all You have given me, in giving me such wonderful parents, in my Culdee Creek family, in my friends, and most of all, in my precious husband.

"Yes," Beth whispered. "I see, Abby. I understand at last."

21

Who hath ears to hear, let him hear.
Matthew 13:9

When it was time to leave, Beth's parents walked her out onto the front porch. She gave them both a hug and a kiss.

"I knew coming to talk with you would help," she said, glancing from one to the other. "It always has and always will. Now if I can be even half as wise when it comes to Noah . . ."

"Noah? What's this about Noah?" Ian asked, walking up from around the back of the house. "Having a marital spat already, are ye?"

Beth sighed in exasperation, shook her head at her parents, then turned to the young Scotsman. "You've an uncanny ability, you know, to turn up at the most unexpected times."

Ian grinned. "Only when it comes to ye, lass. Only when it comes to ye."

Behind Beth, her father chuckled. "Reckon we'll leave you two to your wrangling and head on back inside." He laid a hand on her shoulder. "If there's anything else you need, girl, any time, just give us a call and we'll be there for you."

She glanced over her shoulder and nodded. "I know, Pa. Thanks." Then as her parents walked inside, their departure punctuated by the snap of the screen door closing, she turned to Ian.

"I was just about to ride back to Grand View. What are you up to these days?"

He shrugged. "Not verra much. I'm thinking I'll be moving on soon. Mayhap travel farther west, to California or Washington state. Or mayhap even to Alaska."

"Really? But you haven't been here for more than a few weeks, Ian. It's not at all long enough. I haven't had a chance to spend much time with you."

"Aye," he said with a disparaging snort, "as if ye've been thinking much of me at any rate, what with yer new husband and all."

Beth climbed down the porch steps, slipped her arm through Ian's, and tugged him forward. "You're right. I've been selfish and inconsiderate. Let's take a walk and talk. It seems you've got as much to tell me as I have to tell you."

Ian arched a dark brow. "Aye, from the little I overheard as I came up, I'd say ye most certainly do. And where would we be heading on this wee walk, if ye don't mind me asking?"

"Oh, I don't know." She looked around. "How about the pines up on the hill behind Devlin and Hannah's house? We always enjoyed our times up there, talking and playing games."

"Aye, that we did, Elizabeth." Ian smiled in remembrance. "We had such verra good times together, didn't we?"

271

She laughed. "Yes, and a few times when we had *too* good a time and got everyone all riled about us." Beth squeezed his arm. "You were the first boy who ever kissed me, you know."

"Indeed?" Ian chuckled. "Well, that's something I'll always have over Noah, then, isn't it? Not that I wouldn't rather have the girl herself, mind ye, but it's a wee consolation."

"You'll always be one of my best friends, Ian. Always."

"I'm glad for that, Elizabeth. Truly, I am."

They walked for a while in silence, passing Devlin and Hannah's house, climbing the grassy hill that, the higher they went, became more and more densely inhabited with the rough, gray-barked ponderosa pines. Finally, they came upon a fallen log. After taking their seats, Beth turned to Ian.

"So, you first," she said. "I'm not really the reason you've decided to leave Culdee Creek so soon, am I?"

Ian paused to watch a sooty-headed and dark-blue-bodied Steller's jay hop overhead from branch to branch, its harsh *shack-shack-shack* call a familiar sound in the coniferous forest. Beth glanced up and grinned. As if realizing it had been discovered, the big bird quieted suddenly and glanced down at them. Then, after another round of now indignant calls, it took wing and flew away.

Ian turned to her, one corner of his mouth twisting upward in amusement. "Kind of reminds ye of me, doesn't it?" he asked. "A big, noisy bird who flies in, makes a ruckus, then flies out. It's all I know, though, Elizabeth. There's just something calling me, calling me to the next place with its promise of something better."

"Is there anything better than home and family, Ian?"

"Mayhap not, lass." He smiled sadly. "I used to think so when it was just Claire and me all those many years ago in Scotland. And I've been happy here at Culdee

Creek most times. But I don't know when I'll settle down and get this daft wanderlust out of me."

Beth laughed. "And here I was, taking your bout of jealousy over Noah so seriously."

"Aye, I did make a bit of a scene, didn't I, when ye first told me?" He took her hand, lifted it to his lips, and kissed it. "In truth, as much as I love ye, Elizabeth," Ian said, lowering her hand, "I wonder if I could've even settled down with ye. I fear . . . I fear it may not even be in me ever to make such a commitment."

"Don't sell yourself short, Ian. You're a man of high principles and capable of a deep and lasting love. All you need is to find the right woman and all your fears will be over." Beth gave his hand a quick squeeze, then disengaged her hand from his clasp. "Just have a care. Don't miss that lass when she finally comes your way. Don't get so caught up in the joy of the treasure hunt that you don't recognize the treasure when you find it."

"Aye," he said with a nod, "ye're right, of course. I'll have a care, that I will." He leaned down, picked up a bit of broken tree branch, and tossed it back down the hill where they had come. "And now that we've solved the mystery of my leaving, what about ye? What kind of wisdom were ye seeking from yer parents, when it comes to yer husband?"

Beth looked away and sighed. "Noah's thinking about taking a teaching position at his old seminary in New York City. I love him dearly, but I don't want to leave here." She turned back to him. "This is my home. This is where I belong."

"Ye belong where yer true family is, lass, and Noah's now yer family. Ye must cleave to him above all others." A look of compassion gleamed in his eyes. "Still, to be sure, it's a heart-wrenching dilemma."

"Yes, it is." Beth drew in a deep breath, then slowly expelled it. "We haven't been married a month, Ian, and then Noah goes and stuns me with this. It isn't fair. It just isn't fair!"

"And who said marriage was fair, or even a fifty-fifty split most of the time?" Ian laughed. "Why do ye think I shy away from it like I do, lass? For all its fine advantages, the cost of making a marriage work is still more than I yet care to pay."

"Well, why didn't you warn me about that beforehand?" she asked irritably. "All you said was I wasn't cut out to be a preacher's wife."

"Och, and as if ye would've listened to me at any rate!" Ian rolled his eyes. "Ye've been so head over heels in love with Noah Starr for years now. And seeing him as the perfect man that he is, leastwise in yer love-struck eyes, ye wouldn't have thought aught could ever be a problem no matter who was telling ye the opposite. So don't blame me for the fine mess ye've now gotten yerself into, lass." He shook his head vehemently. "Nay, don't blame me."

He was right. Nonetheless, Beth still hated to admit it. What she needed now was sympathy, not recriminations.

"Fine. Have it your way, Ian Sutherland," she snapped. "You always do in the end anyway. I just want to commend you, though, for your compassion and understanding." She climbed to her feet. "I think I'll be going now, thank you very much."

Before she could take two steps, Ian leaped up and grabbed her hand. "Och, lass, don't go on like that. Ye know I care. I just don't see what's to be done for yer problem, save talk with yer husband and try to convince him to stay."

"But that's just the problem, Ian." Once again, Beth sighed. "I don't know why he's suddenly so interested in a position he's turned down once already. If I knew, maybe I could—"

"Och, I think ye know, Elizabeth," Ian said. "Search yer heart, and I'd wager the answers are all there. And if they aren't, I'd wager they're just as unclear in Noah's mind, too. Ye've only then to talk with him and help him discover the truth. And once the truth's come to the fore-front, ye can both face the answer head on."

Help him discover the truth . . .

Strange, Beth mused, but Ian's advice was almost the same as Abby's had been. Was this, then, what the Lord was urging? Beth knew God often spoke through His children. He had done it so many times for Noah through Millie.

Her thoughts flitted briefly to Noah's aunt. Stand at my side, Millie, she thought, when I talk with Noah. And Lord, put the right words in my mouth. Open my own ears and heart to what Noah says. So I may truly hear him and understand. So I may be the wife and partner he needs.

Beth managed a tremulous smile. "It's time we were getting back. I need to head home."

"Aye, lass, that ye do," Ian said, releasing her hand. "Yer man needs ye."

Noah came home that night just after supper. Beth had Emily in her bathtub and was entertaining the little girl by playing patty-cake with her. Emily chortled each time the game ended, begging for more. Beth would laugh, then repeat the rhythmic hand clapping and poem. As she did, Noah noted, standing quietly in the entryway shadows, she was gradually encouraging Emily to try different things.

The realization gladdened him. Perhaps there was indeed some hope for his daughter. Perhaps the horrible events of her birth might yet find some positive resolution. Noah felt a tiny ray of hope glimmer in his heart.

And it was all because of Beth. She had never treated Emily as any less than a normal child. She seemed to see past the outward disabilities to the heart and soul beneath.

It was more than he had ever been able to do. As much as he loved his daughter, Noah knew he had always viewed her in terms of her palsied limitations. He had let his guilt and pain cloud his perceptions.

But the guilt and pain had faded, burned away by the bright radiance of Beth's presence in his life. Thanks to her, bit by bit, his perspective about many things was changing.

Love for the beautiful woman kneeling there in the kitchen rose up and overwhelmed him, drenching him with such a piercing joy he almost cried out from the sweet pain. Instead, Noah strode into the kitchen, hurrying to his wife's side.

She lifted her face for a kiss. "Your supper's in the warming oven," she said. "I'm just finishing with Emily's bath. Enjoy your meal while I take her upstairs and get her ready for bed."

"I hate to miss so much of her growing up." Noah walked to the stove, opened the warming-oven door, and retrieved his plateful of food. "I'm glad the seminary job will provide me with a much more regular schedule and hours. I'm looking forward to having more time to spend with you and Emily."

Beth shot him an enigmatic glance. "You talk as if you've made up your mind."

"Well, I have. All I'm waiting on is your agreement to send back a letter of acceptance."

"And if I don't agree?" she asked, wrapping a towel around Emily and lifting her from the tub. "What then, Noah?"

276

He frowned in puzzlement. "Well, I guess we'll need to talk about it. I've just been waiting for your decision and trying to be patient in the doing."

"Well, your patience has been rewarded. We'll talk, just as soon as I put Emily to bed."

Plate in hand, Noah watched Beth leave with his daughter, a sense of foreboding rising within him. This apparently wasn't going to be an easy discussion. If the look in his wife's eyes wasn't enough of a warning, the tone of her voice certainly was. She didn't want to leave Grand View, and she wasn't going to do so without a fight.

With a sigh, Noah collected a knife and fork from the cupboard's silverware drawer and carried his plate to the table. The pork chops, mashed potatoes and gravy, and spinach salad from the last spinach plants in the garden were good, but he found himself picking at his food. His mind was just too preoccupied with what Beth would say, and how he might convince her moving back East was God's will for them.

At long last, Beth reentered the kitchen. Noah glanced up from the cup of coffee he had just poured himself after cleaning his plate and washing it. Relief filled him. Beth's expression was pleasant, if a bit guarded.

"Would you like a cup of coffee?" he asked, standing. "I could get you—"

She motioned him back into his seat. "Sit. I'm already up and can get my own coffee."

Noah complied and watched as his wife took down a mug, walked back to the stove, and poured herself a steaming cup of coffee. Then, after adding a generous dollop of cream from the creamer in the icebox, she pulled out a chair at the kitchen table across from him.

"So," Noah began as Beth sat, pulled over the sugar bowl, and proceeded to stir a teaspoonful of sugar into her coffee, "you said you're ready to talk about the seminary position. How do you feel about it?"

Beth laid aside her teaspoon and took a tentative sip of her coffee. "I think it's a wonderful offer, Noah, and one you richly deserve," she said. "However, that said, I'm against you accepting it."

"Why, Beth?" As best he could, Noah tried to keep the frustration from his voice. "I know it'll be hard at first, you leaving here, leaving your family, leaving your practice. But there are people in New York City who stand to benefit just as much from you and your medical skills. And it's not as if we can't come home—every year or so, even—to Culdee Creek. The trains are faster and far more comfortable nowadays."

Beth looked up from her coffee cup. "Though all of those things are definitely concerns of mine, they're not the biggest reason I'm against this plan of yours. You and Emily are my family now and come first. But I'm concerned about how despondent you've been since Harlow's death and that you're even considering giving up the priesthood. More than anything, I don't want you making such a momentous decision in your current state of mind. I don't want you so quickly to decide on another job."

"A teaching position like this isn't going to stay open indefinitely, Beth."

"But might not others come available later, if you finally determine that's where God's really calling you?"

His hands clenched on the table. "And why are you so convinced God isn't calling me to it now? *I* feel He is."

"Why, Noah? Why do you feel the Lord's calling you to leave Grand View? And why now?"

He frowned, struggling to contain his growing anger. How dare she question him when it came to his relationship with the Lord? But then, hadn't that been exactly what he had been doing for a while now?

"So you don't see this offer as a call from God?" Noah asked tersely, "Is that it, Beth? I think I know a call from God when I hear one."

"Oh, I'm not denying God's calling you, Noah Starr." Beth leaned forward. "I'm just wondering if you truly understand what He's asking of you."

Whatever in the world was she getting at now? Noah's rapidly thinning patience finally frayed and snapped.

"Stop playing games with me, Beth. Just spit it out, will you? Spit it out, this grand revelation of yours about God's will for me."

She settled back in her chair. "Fine. I will. Be forewarned, though. You may not like what I'm going to say."

He gave a harsh bark of laughter. "And when has that ever stopped you?"

"You needn't get cross, you know." Beth's mouth tightened, and she eyed him narrowly. "You wanted to know, and you said I had a say in this decision. And I'm only telling you this because I believe it with all my heart."

Remorse filled him. "I'm sorry, Beth." Noah reached across the table and took her hand. "I've just been under such a strain lately, trying to sort through all my feelings about the Petersons, plus thinking so much about this position. . . . Well, I guess it's all starting to wear me down."

She smiled in gentle understanding. "I realize that, Noah. But I also think you're missing what the Lord is trying to teach you in all this. Things like self-forgiveness. Things like taking a closer look at the pride that drives you to imagine you must always be perfect, just because you aspire to imitate a perfect God.

"And then there are the fears. The fear of failing, of not knowing which way to turn because life has become difficult here. But you know what, Noah? It doesn't necessarily mean the Lord wishes you to move on, just because the times have gotten bad. Just because you now doubt God's plan for you here in Grand View, doesn't mean it still isn't His plan."

"It's not prideful," he said through gritted teeth, "to aspire to spiritual perfection. It's because I love God that I wish to imitate Him. It's because I love Him that it hurts so much when I fail His children."

"But it *is* prideful to berate and punish yourself when you fall short. Sooner or later, that pride can lead to an inability to forgive yourself. It can even lead to the greatest faith killer of all—despair."

Despair.

Noah's heart twisted in his breast. He *had* come very close to despair. He *had* contemplated turning from his Lord and Savior in his sense of utter failure and unworthiness. What a fool he had been to allow anything, most especially his pride, to separate him from the Lord.

"It's very insidious, you know." Noah looked down at his hands, clenching and unclenching them on the table. "Pride, I mean. It leads you where you never intended to go. And once it gets you there, it tries to destroy you. Destroy what you hold most dear." He lifted his gaze. "I thought I'd mastered my pride. I'd thought I'd eliminated it from my life. But, indeed, I realize now I even took pride in my humility."

His mouth quirked sadly. "Yet it was my pride in what I considered my ministerial skills that ultimately led to my problem with the Petersons. I thought I knew what was best for them and so didn't truly listen to what they were really trying to tell me."

Beth sighed. "You're right. Pride is insidious. But that doesn't make you a failure as a priest. It's an honest human weakness we must all fight each and every day of our lives. And it's no reason to give up and leave Grand View."

"No, it's not," Noah admitted. "But it's also no reason *not* to accept that teaching position, either."

"True enough. Still, there's a lot to be said for stability, and patience in that stability. How else can you give God the time He needs to temper your soul, to prune you so you bear more fruit, to teach you what you need most to learn? Did you ever think that perhaps that's the reason it has all become so hard? Because the Lord's allowing life to test you, hoping you'll grow from it and come to abide even more closely with Him?"

Noah gazed at her, not certain if he should be angry at her presumption in trying to teach him truths she, in her spiritual immaturity, had no reason to know, or fall down on his knees in awe and gratitude for the Lord's mercy in speaking to him through his wife. Frustration filled him. These days, it was getting so he didn't know what to do anymore or what to believe.

"Don't you think if I really imagined God was but tempering me," he cried in anguish, "in spite of it all, in spite of anything else He might see fit to put in my way, I'd stay no matter how hard it was? But I don't know that, Beth. All I see are my own mistakes, mistakes that are hurting others and causing all my problems. And the Lord seems so far away right now. I can't hear or see Him anymore."

"And what would it take to open your eyes and ears, Noah? What would you want God to do to help you?"

For a long moment, Noah didn't know what to say. Was there anything the Lord could do for him while he groped about in such a state? Indeed, who was he even to expect anything?

Then the answer came, though his shame at such a thought almost kept him from uttering the words. "A sign," Noah finally choked out. "I need some sign the Lord wants me to stay here. More than anything I've ever needed, I need it now."

Understanding sparkled in Beth's warm brown eyes. "Then let's wait a time longer in patience," she said, her voice little more than a whisper. "Let's wait and hold unswervingly to the hope we profess. God is faithful. He won't forsake us. And as we do His will, we will surely receive His promises."

Noah nodded his acquiescence. "Yes. Let's wait a time longer." He shoved back his chair and stood.

Beth looked up, a slender brow arching in inquiry. "Where are you going?"

"Where else? I'm going to the church. I need to do a heap more praying."

"And listening, too," she called after him as he turned to go.

A sense of peace like he had never felt before flooded him. He smiled.

"Oh, yes indeed. And a heap of listening, too."

22

Let us hold unswervingly to the hope we profess, for he
who promised is faithful.

Hebrews 10:23

The day before Mary Sue's trial, Beth arranged to meet her late that afternoon in Bledsoe's Quality Baked Goods and Café. After taking care to find the most private table at the rear of the little dining area, she ordered a cup of tea and a blueberry scone, then sat back to await her friend's arrival.

It was a balmy day for the end of June, barely two weeks since she and Noah had their talk in the kitchen. Two weeks waiting on a sign from God, and none had come. She knew Noah was becoming concerned. His prayers had failed to garner any answer so far, and he couldn't keep his seminary waiting much longer.

Was no sign from the Lord a sign? If so, what did it mean? Sometimes—well, most times, Beth admitted on second thought—she wished God's mysterious ways weren't always so mysterious. Surely He understood the seriousness of this decision and the time constraints. Why couldn't He work just a bit faster?

Mary Sue entered the café just then, effectively calling to a halt Beth's frustrating thoughts. At sight of Beth, Mary Sue smiled and hurried over.

"Thank you ever so much for asking me out for tea and sweets." Mary Sue laid her purse on the table and paused to remove her fine cotton gloves before sitting down. "I've been moping about the past few days, worrying myself sick over the trial. Your thoughtfulness was a real blessing."

Beth smiled. "I didn't want you thinking you'd been deserted by your friends. You've been in all our thoughts of late—Noah's, Doc's, Helen's, and all the MacKays at Culdee Creek. In fact"—she paused to draw out a small, wrapped parcel—"this is from Hannah."

As Beth offered the gift, she saw hesitation spring into the other woman's eyes. She wasn't surprised. Mary Sue had never cared much for Devlin's beautiful wife.

"Please accept it, Mary Sue," Beth urged. "Hannah made it and meant it for you with deepest sympathy and love."

"Yes, I suppose she did." Mary Sue took the package. "Whenever we've crossed paths over the years, Hannah's never been anything but kind to me. I've been the one who has shunned and maligned her." She sighed. "Despite her sordid beginnings, she has managed to make a greater success out of her life than I ever could. Maybe I've hated her most because of that."

"It's never too late to begin fresh." Beth watched as Mary Sue unwrapped the parcel. "After tomorrow's trial, you'll be completely free to start anew and find the better, happier life you've always sought."

"If I truly am free. If I don't end up sentenced to the penitentiary for Harlow's murder."

Mary Sue pulled a padded book from the wrappings. It was covered in what Beth could only call a miniature quilt composed of tiny bits of blue, pink, and green calico and gingham, trimmed with lace and colored rickrack. Ever so carefully, Mary Sue thumbed through the pages.

"She picked topics, such as New Life, Love of God, Fortitude, Hope, and Forgiveness, then penned in special Bible verses pertaining to each topic," Mary Sue explained. "The first page is on forgiveness. . . ."

Her voice softened as she began to read aloud. "Hatred stirreth up strifes; but love coverth all sins. . . . Forgive, and ye shall be forgiven. . . . Though your sins be as scarlet, they shall be as white as snow. . . ."

Mary Sue glanced up and met Beth's gaze. Her eyes were filled with tears. Impulsively, Beth reached over and took her free hand.

"H-how could H-Hannah know what thoughts and fears have been running through my head these past weeks?" Mary Sue asked, her voice wobbling. "That I imagined I'd done the unpardonable and would never be absolved? That I didn't know what to do next, or where to turn? But she . . . she who I always treated as some pariah . . . she kn-knew!"

"And why wouldn't Hannah, of all women, know how it felt to be scorned and shunned?" Beth asked softly. "Don't you think she, time and again, also found answers for her own life in the Book she came to love above all others?"

"I . . . I've all but stopped reading the Bible of late," Mary Sue said. "Just as I stopped attending services because I couldn't bear to see Noah at the altar and in the pulpit."

Beth gave Mary Sue's hand a reassuring squeeze. "It's been hard for you, I know. Noah told me of your meeting that day he finally gathered the courage to come and ask your forgiveness."

"And d-did he tell you I refused to forgive him? That I didn't tr-trust him anymore? Is that how you kn-knew?"

"No. He didn't tell me that. That's between you and him. I sense, though, that he continues to grieve over what has happened." Beth smiled sadly. "And I noticed your absence from Sunday services. It wasn't hard to guess what had transpired between you."

"It hurt him, my refusal to forgive him," Mary Sue said. "I could tell, and I must confess it made me glad. But now . . . now I think more and more on what he said that day. About me forgiving him for my sake, if not for his. About him having caused me enough pain and not wishing to cause further damage to my soul."

"He meant that from the bottom of his heart, Mary Sue."

"Perhaps he did. And I want to forgive him, Beth. I need to. How can I ever find peace with the Lord for what I did to Harlow if I can't forgive in turn? But I can't. Something . . . something's still stopping me."

"What, Mary Sue?" Beth leaned closer, almost as if closing the physical distance between them would dispel all barriers and she'd see into Mary Sue's mind. "What's still stopping you?"

"I don't know." Mary Sue shook her head. "I still feel like he has his limits. Like if it came down to it, he wouldn't risk himself for my sake." She smiled apologetically. "Forgive me for saying this, but I no longer see him as a man of God, willing to lay down his life for a friend."

It was hard for Beth to hear such words spoken about her husband, especially knowing him for the man he truly was and what the Peterson tragedy had done to him. It was equally hard not to point out that true forgiveness meant putting the hurt and anger aside and pardoning because Christ asked it of her, not because she had found some saving grace in the other to justify the forgiveness. Or, Beth amended, leastwise no saving grace other than the fact the person was as much a child of God as was Mary Sue.

But Beth sensed Mary Sue wasn't ready to hear or absorb a sermon on forgiveness today, and the rest was for Noah to say, if he ever wished to. "You must come to forgiveness in your own time," she replied at last. "The Lord knows that and is patient. Noah understands that, too. Just know that he loves you and suffers still over what happened."

Mary Sue gave a shaky laugh and held up Hannah's book. "Did you know I'd been praying for some answers, for a light to guide my way? I'd prayed and prayed and received no reply. But you know something, Beth? I believe God has finally given me my answers in this little book. And He used Hannah as His messenger."

A messenger . . . Would Noah's sign from God also be carried by a messenger? And would Noah have the clarity of heart to recognize it when it came? Please, Lord, make it so!

"Yes, He may well have done just that." Beth smiled and shook her head. "Funny, isn't it, how we expect one thing of the Lord and risk missing the gift He eventually sends us in another way. Yet He never, ever gives us stones for bread, does He?"

"No, He doesn't." Mary Sue clasped the book to her breast, her eyes shining with a fierce joy. "What Father would?"

The trial commenced the next morning as any other would: The judge instructed the jury, the two lawyers made their opening statements, then called witnesses to the stand. The defense soon completed questioning Doc and Beth on the repeated injuries they had noted on Mary Sue's person. Neighbors admitted that for the past several years they had periodically heard shouting and screaming coming from the Petersons' house.

And then Noah took the stand.

The defense lawyer, Mr. Sweeney, asked him only two questions: Had the Petersons sought him out for pastoral counseling? and, Why hadn't they continued to come for talks? Noah admitted that Harlow had stormed off after the first visit, claiming Mary Sue was the cause of all their marital problems.

Mr. Henderson, the prosecuting attorney, immediately took a different tack and kept Noah on the stand. "You said you were Mr. Peterson's pastor, Reverend Starr?" he asked, hands clasped and fingers steepled beneath his chin, pacing back and forth before the witness stand. "And exactly what are your duties? As a pastor, I mean?"

Noah frowned in puzzlement. "Well, pretty much what you see most pastors do, Mr. Henderson. Oversee the church proper, conduct services, preach, visit the sick, pray over the dying, and bury the dead."

"And you also offer counsel and consolation?"

"Yes, I think that was made clear in my earlier testimony for Mr. Sweeney."

"How exactly do you see your role as a pastoral counselor? Could you describe the elements of the job?"

For a long moment, Noah gathered his thoughts. "Like the Lord Jesus, a pastor is a good shepherd. The congregation is his flock," he began at last. "He's a shepherd of souls and offers direction in the spiritual life. He's also a physician of souls and offers God's healing. And he should be"–Noah's glance turned to Mary Sue, sitting only yards away–"a living example of how to live a holy life, as well as a teacher, a protector, a friend, and a guide."

Mr. Henderson drew up before him. "An impressive list of duties, to be sure. And were you all that to the Petersons, Reverend Starr?"

"I tried to be," Noah replied, never breaking gazes with Mary Sue. "I tried, but it wasn't enough. I wasn't—"

"Sometimes, no matter how hard one tries, people refuse to be helped, don't they, Reverend Starr? And miracles are in short supply these days, leastwise in regards to making folk take a second look at themselves and the destruction they're headed for."

"Some would say miracles are a daily occurrence, if one only has a heart open and willing to see them."

The lawyer nodded and began his pacing again. "Yes, some *would* say that, especially if they're of a spiritual persuasion." He paused to draw in a breath, and Noah was struck by the realization that Mr. Henderson was preparing to drive home his point.

"Now," the prosecutor said, "that night Harlow was killed." He looked up at Noah. "Didn't you think it strange that, after having claimed she had received yet another beating, Mrs. Peterson seemed most eager to return home with her husband? Your wife, Dr. MacKay, testified earlier she had repeatedly warned, then begged, Mrs. Peterson on the night of June 11 not to go home with her husband. But she did anyway. Why do you think that was so?"

"I believe Mrs. Peterson decided to return home with her husband that night," Noah replied, wondering where these questions were leading, "because she loved him in spite of his brutality, and because I, as her pastor, advised her to do so, and she trusted me."

Henderson gave a disbelieving snort. "Well, perhaps. But then, perhaps not. I submit"—he wheeled about to face the assembled jurors—"that perhaps Mrs. Peterson had an altogether different plan in mind. Perhaps Mrs. Peterson had decided the time was right to do away with her husband and put into play a plan she'd been formulating for a long while. After months of infuriating and tormenting Mr. Peterson past the point of human tolerance, interspersed with self-inflicted injuries meant to appear as if he had beaten her, she knew it was time to kill him. Cold-bloodedly and with the greatest premeditation, Mrs. Peterson then set out to murder her husband."

"Objection, your honor! Objection!" Mr. Sweeney cried. "That's—"

"No! No!" Her face waxen, Mary Sue leaped to her feet. "I didn't want Harlow dead. I loved him. But he kept on coming and coming, and I was so afraid and so tired of the pain! But I never planned to kill him. Never!"

Behind her, the courtroom erupted in an explosion of noise. People stood, milled about, and babbled excitedly to their neighbors. The judge tolerated the uproar for about ten seconds, then slammed his gavel down several times on his desk.

"Order! Order in the court! I'll have order now, or I'll have this courtroom emptied of all onlookers."

Mr. Henderson, a calculated gleam in his eyes, waited calmly for the courtroom to settle. Then he glanced up at the judge. "Thank you, your honor." Not missing a step, he turned back to Noah. "Reverend Starr. Did you ever, even for a moment, doubt Mrs. Peterson's claims that Mr. Peterson was beating her? Did you?"

Noah hesitated. He *had* found Mary Sue's claims hard to believe, especially in those early days after he had accepted there was something amiss in the Peterson household. In all the years he had known Mary Sue, especially when she was a young woman, her temper had been as infamous as her self-serving and frequently manipulative behavior. Harlow, on the other hand, had always been the soul of self-control and decorum—the quintessential bank president.

To her credit, however, Mary Sue had gradually changed over the years. She wasn't the same woman she had once been. How, though, to make that point?

"I remind you, Reverend Starr, that you're under oath," the attorney said.

"Yes," Noah admitted, "I had some initial doubts. But they were dispelled when I remembered Mrs. Peterson's charitable work for the church, her faithful Sunday attendance, and the evident love she had for her husband."

"If that love wasn't all for show," Mr. Henderson shot back, pacing again. He stopped and turned to Noah.

"I can't help but wonder why you advised her to return home with her husband that night, if you didn't think it was safe. And you *did* think it was safe, didn't you, Reverend Starr?"

"Yes, I did. I was wrong, though. Very wrong."

"Well, perhaps in retrospect, but at the time—"

"No, at the time, too, Mr. Henderson," Noah said, hunching forward and impaling the attorney with a steely gaze. "I chose to make a decision my wife warned me against and my instincts told me was wrong. I thought I knew more than my wife and Mrs. Peterson that night because I felt empowered by God. I felt it was my duty to save that marriage at all costs. But I was so puffed up with pride that it blinded me to the truth."

He gave a disparaging laugh. "Even if I'd seen the truth, I think I would've forced the reconciliation anyway. It was my duty, after all, to keep the marriage together. And I was so very, very good at what I did."

"Now, Reverend Starr," Henderson began, his gaze narrowing, "be that as it may, that doesn't mean Mrs. Peterson didn't manipulate you. It doesn't mean—"

"No, you don't understand, Mr. Henderson." Noah's voice rose, all but commanding the man to silence. "I manipulated her *and* her husband, for that matter, to do what I thought was best. But I didn't do it out of Christian love or compassion. I did it because I had become complacent in my ministry. I did it out of some misguided sense of power, because I felt it was the right thing to do. And, in all fairness, if you insist on putting Mary Sue on trial for the death of Harlow Peterson, then you should put me on trial for his death, too. I had the power to prevent what happened that night, just as Harlow did. But Harlow was a sick, tormented man, and in part can be excused. But I, Mr. Henderson, deserve no excuse."

Noah's eyes filled with tears. His throat tightened, but he forced himself to go on, to say all that was in his heart, so all of Grand View would finally hear and know.

"For am I not my brother's keeper? And if I see one of my brothers or sisters in need and turn my back on their pleas for help, am I not a worse sinner than they? Because, Mr. Henderson, that's exactly what I did. And that's exactly why I don't deserve to call myself anyone's pastor anymore."

As the lawyer standing before him stared in utter amazement, the courtroom burst into bedlam once more. The judge roared out for order; he pounded his gavel until the chamber reverberated with the earsplitting staccato beat, and still the people shouted and cried out to each other.

The chaos in the room, however, blurred and faded into background noise as shame and remorse rose once more to engulf Noah. He lowered his face into his hands and wept.

ॐ

Two days later, Noah rose early to prepare for Sunday services. He had sketched out his sermon yesterday afternoon but always liked, after saying his morning prayers and meditating on his scriptural readings for the day, to go over his ideas once more in his head.

He had chosen a passage from the twenty-first chapter of John, where Jesus instructed Simon Peter to feed His lambs, feed His sheep. It was a divine commission, Noah well knew, given not only to those first disciples but one that echoed down the centuries to men like himself, too. Of late, however, he had felt like he had failed miserably in caring for the flock the Lord had put in his care.

But Simon Peter had failed—and failed miserably—for a time, too, and still the Lord loved him and called him repeatedly to feed His sheep. Could his own transgressions, his own failings be any worse? And was his love any more weak and uncertain than Peter's had been in those years of Jesus' earthly ministry?

In the end, it didn't matter. His call to the priesthood had never been an issue of worthiness, just as it had never been with the apostles. What mattered was answering the call and striving each and every day to follow. Promises had been made and exchanged—he to serve the Lord all the days of his life, and God never to forsake him. No matter the obstacles, no matter the mistakes, no matter the doubts and fears, Noah knew he must remain the priest he had vowed to be.

The admission filled him with a warm rush of peace and certainty. And though no sign had yet been forthcoming as to whether he should accept the seminary position, Noah realized too that was no longer of such pressing importance.

What mattered most wasn't his pride, wasn't the shame that the entire town knew his failings, wasn't the pain he'd feel every time he met Mary Sue Peterson. What mattered most was loving God and feeding His sheep. Until the Lord told him otherwise, Noah would remain in Grand View.

He glanced out the window across from his desk. In the distance, the sun rose in all its gentle glory. Its rays spilled over the land, drenching it in warm, red-gold light.

Gladness swelled in Noah's breast. What a glorious day, a day ripe with promise. The Lord's day.

A few more notes in the margins of his sermon, and he was finished. Noah rose, folded his homily, and tucked it into his Bible. He could smell the mouthwatering scent of frying meat, so he headed for the kitchen.

Beth was already up and dressed, busily scrambling eggs in one pan while sausage fried in another. Emily, also garbed in her Sunday finest, sat in her wheelchair at the table, banging her bowl with a spoon. Her grip on the utensil was awkward, as were her movements with it, but she managed to hold onto the spoon and make quite a bit of noise in the process.

Surprisingly, even over the din, his wife noted his arrival. She looked up. "All set for today's services, are you?"

Noah smiled. "As ready as I ever am."

"Well, then we're all in for another inspiring and riveting service." She grinned and motioned toward the table. "Sit. I just poured you a cup of coffee, and the toast needs buttering. The rest of this will be ready in another minute or two."

He pulled out a chair beside Emily and took a seat. Emily chortled in greeting but never paused in her energetic banging. Noah tolerated the noise while he buttered the toast, but eventually confiscated the spoon from his daughter. For a moment, the little girl's lower lip quivered, and he feared a temper tantrum. Then Emily laughed and, reaching over, began to tug on his shirtsleeve.

"Dadadada!" she said. "Wuv dada."

Noah stared in surprise, then turned to Beth. "When did she learn that?"

"I've been working with her on it for a while. I wanted to surprise you." She walked over and set the platter of sausages and scrambled eggs on the table, then sat down across from Noah. "She also knows how to count to five. Emily's quite bright, you know."

"Guess I've a lot to learn about my daughter."

He picked up the platter, scooped a generous serving of eggs and sausages onto his plate, then passed the platter to Beth. After cutting a sausage into bite-sized pieces, Noah added the meat to Emily's bowl, along with some eggs and a half slice of toast.

As they ate, Noah periodically turned from Beth to Emily, savoring the warm, comforting sense of family he felt. He was so blessed. So very, very blessed.

After finishing breakfast and putting the dishes and pans to soak, they headed out for the church. Hardly anyone was about yet, but plenty of buggies and buckboards would begin arriving within the next half hour. Just enough time, with Beth's help, to dress the altar, light the candles, and don his vestments.

Helen Yates was already inside, warming up at the old Grand Chapel reed organ. Noah had long dreamt of a bigger, finer pipe organ—a state-of-the-art Hook and Hastings whose music would resound off the rafters and make the heavens vibrate with deep, rich tones. But what with the church renovations still needed and the necessity of a substantial downpayment before work could even begin on an instrument that took years to build, such an organ would be a long time in coming.

Still, Helen was an excellent organist and always coaxed the fullest performance from the little organ they did have.

Their choir, though small as well, was excellent. Noah missed Mary Sue Peterson's stunning voice, however. But then, she had been an asset to the church in so many ways.

Noah was profoundly grateful the jury had found Mary Sue innocent of premeditated murder, choosing to accept her claim of justifiable self-defense. Thank the Lord two lives hadn't been ruined on the night of Harlow Peterson's death.

The communion service went smoothly, and Noah's sermon evoked a favorable response, if the lack of coughing, snoring, and nodding heads was any indication. However, as Noah turned to the congregation to deliver the final blessing, Conor MacKay stood, walked up the aisle, and climbed the altar steps to stand beside Noah.

A quizzical look on his face, Noah turned to Conor. "Is there something you wish to say to us before I conclude the service?"

Culdee Creek's owner nodded. "Most certainly, Father Starr." He turned to face the congregation.

"Sometimes," Conor began, his deep voice reaching to the back of the church, "we take for granted people we cherish the most, imagining they'll always be there for us and that, because of their great strength and holiness of life, they don't need or want our meager approbation or thanks. All of us, however, are human. All of us have times when life seems to be handing out one misfortune after another, when it almost seems as if the Lord has forgotten us or turned His back on us.

"But that's when the Lord comes in disguise, in the form of his beloved creatures, to bolster that person up, to comfort, reassure, and bless. That's when the Lord

296

looks to His people to take a turn at being Christ to each other."

Conor laid a hand on Noah's shoulders. "I think that time is long past due for our brother here, don't you? He's weighed down mightily just now with pain and loss. And any of you who were present at Mary Sue Peterson's trial two days ago must have surely seen his torment and heard him speak of his grief at how he had failed as a pastor. But I'm here to say that I've known Father Starr for over fourteen years now, and I find no better man among us. He has helped me and my family through countless crises, comforted us in our pain, and shared in our joys. Indeed, I wouldn't be the man I am in Christ today without his guidance, and that of my wife."

Conor paused to look around. "So what I'm asking is for anyone who feels called to do so, to stand up and share what this man has meant to him or her. As he has always bolstered us in our times of need, let us do the same for him now."

The heat rising in his face, Noah turned to his friend. "Really, Conor, this isn't necessary. I don't—"

Hannah MacKay stood. "He welcomed me into the church when most people shunned me," she said, speaking up in a strong, clear voice. "He taught me of grace, of the countless second chances to be found in the Lord's open, loving arms. I don't know what I would've done or if I'd ever have had the courage to walk with the Lord, if it hadn't been for Noah Starr."

Noah smiled at Hannah in gratitude. She smiled and nodded in turn, then took her seat. As she did, Claire MacKay stood, tugging her husband to his feet beside her.

"Ye taught us both, my Evan and me, of the great treasure to be found in a loving, generous heart and of the

297

blessings of family. Ye saved our marriage, too, didn't he, Evan?"

Evan grinned sheepishly. "Yes, you did, Noah. And if not in words but only in my heart, I thank you for that every day."

Before the couple could even sit back in their pew, three or four others climbed to their feet. Each took their turn sharing their experiences of Noah's contributions in their lives. And as Noah gazed back at the beloved people he had known and served all these years, each one spoke up until the entire church had had their say.

Each and every one, until there was only one person left, a slender woman in a dark hat and veil that covered her face, standing in the back of the church. When no one else remained standing but her, she lifted her veil and stared straight into Noah's eyes.

"I forgive you," she said. "Can you forgive me?"

Until this moment, Noah had managed to maintain a strict control over his emotions. Seeing Mary Sue Peterson standing there, however, was the final blow to his already wavering resolve not to break down.

The tears came even as he said, "Yes, of course I forgive you. Of course."

Conor's hand tightened on Noah's shoulder. "Do you see now how we feel about you?" he asked. "Do you still doubt for a moment the profound effect you've had on our lives? Do you?"

"No," Noah replied hoarsely, fiercely blinking back the tears. "No, I don't."

His friend smiled. "Then all that's left is the final blessing. Only this time, permit us to bless you."

He raised his hand over Noah's head. As he did, the rest of the congregation joined him in lifting theirs.

"The Lord bless thee, and keep thee," Conor said, intoning the blessing from Numbers that the Lord had spoken to Moses. "The Lord make his face shine upon thee, and be gracious unto thee: The Lord lift up his countenance upon thee, and give thee peace."

As the words flowed over him like a healing balm, Noah looked up and found his wife in the first pew. Their gazes locked, their love arcing across the small distance separating them to meet and meld in gentle, joyous union.

In that moment, a sudden realization filled Noah. The sign. The sign he had prayed for and waited on had come.

The Lord had answered him in the most perfect of ways. He had kept His promise. He had never deserted him. He had always been there in the hearts of these, His beloved people.

And He had always been there in the heart of a woman who had long, and faithfully, loved him.

Discussion Questions for Child of Promise

1. The meaning of the name Elizabeth, the heroine of *Child of Promise*, is "God's promise." God has promised so much to all of us, if only we are patient and strive to do His will. We have a tendency, however, toward blindness and ingratitude when it comes to all the Lord has given us. Many times we fail to fully value and use our unique, God-given gifts. What more can you do to accept and draw on the talents—and special people in your life—that are gifts from God? What more would it take to see them as the exquisite blessings they truly are?

2. Noah battles mightily with a growing sense of disillusionment over his ministry. As a pastor beset with many trials, he increasingly finds himself feeling alone and weighed down with doubts and fears of failure. Sound familiar? In such times, what has most helped you overcome your doubts and fears and regain your lost sense of purpose and worth? Can you recall any times when you've helped others with similar experiences? When you've been Christlike to others?

3. Beth carries deep wounds, some from her childhood and some that were inflicted on her when

301

she went away to obtain her medical degree. She returns home embittered and wary, determined to keep her distance from everyone—including God. Have you ever experienced such emotional pain that you chose to avoid others rather than risk further hurt? What did it take to open your heart again to forgiveness and love?

4. Noah is plagued with guilt over what he feels is his failure to be there for the people he loved when they needed him. How does this tragedy affect his budding relationship with Beth? Have you ever regretted some action that, at the time, you felt completely justified in doing but later regretted? How did you come to a resolution of that inner conflict?

5. In his torment and confusion, Noah finally turns to Conor MacKay, Beth's father, for advice. Conor counsels Noah to trust in the Lord and listen to His call. Conor also encourages Noah to do his best. We all needs friends whose opinions we respect and whom we trust enough to bare our hearts and souls to. Who are some of your special friends? In what ways has their presence in your life been a blessing to you?

6. Were there any characters that touched or inspired you in *Child of Promise*? If so, which ones and in what ways?

7. What story themes did you discover while reading this book? Was there one in particular that struck home more forcibly? Why?

8. If you could ask the author any question, what would it be?

Dear Readers,

I can't believe that, with the completion of *Child of Promise*, I've come to the end of the Brides of Culdee Creek series. Though these books were a challenge to write, they were also books that, in the writing, taught me so much about God, myself, and life. Their creation enriched me personally, professionally, and spiritually, as I hope they also enriched you.

It's time, however, to move on to new literary challenges, new settings, and new characters. But that doesn't mean I've turned my back forever on the Mac-Kays. On the contrary. There are now two Culdee Creek spin-off, stand-alone, hardcover Christmas novellas available—*All Good Gifts* and *The Christkindl's Gift*—as well as a third novella in progress that will be released in fall 2008. And, in time, I may begin a new series based on the MacKay ancestors and take you back to wild, glorious Scotland, in the times when real men wore kilts, claymores flashed in defense of clan and honor, and bagpipes skirled their plaintive, poignant songs.

Meanwhile, my next book will be released in September 2007 and will be the third book in my Scottish series, These Highland Hills. It's titled *A Fire Within* and will be the story of Caitlin Campbell. In case you have yet to discover the first two books in that series—*Child of the Mist* and *Wings of Morning*—both are still available. Just ask your local bookseller to order them for you. Nothing beats having a complete series to read one after another, especially when the weather turns cold and all you want to do is snuggle up in a comfy chair with a warm throw and a steaming mug of tea or cocoa.

Blessings,

Kathleen Morgan

P.S. I'm always happy to hear from readers. To be included on a mailing list, just look up my website and sign up for "Kathleen's Korner," my newsletter. You'll also find excerpts of all my books there, as well as other fun information and a way to contact me via email if you so desire.

Kathleen Morgan has authored numerous novels for the general market and now focuses her writing on inspirational books. She has won many awards for her romance writing, including the 2002 Rose Award for Best Inspirational Romance. If you wish you contact Kathleen, look her up online or write to her at P.O. Box 62365, Colorado Springs, CO 80962.